Universal Raves For GREG BEAR

"Bear is one of the few SF writers capable of traveling beyond the limits of mere human ambition and geological time. . . . Whether he's tinkering with human genetic material or prying apart planets, Bear goes about the task with intelligence and a powerful imagination."

—*Locus*

➤

"His wonders are state-of-the-art."

—*New York Newsday*

➤

"A superior work . . . will certainly enhance Bear's deservedly high reputation."

—*Booklist* on *Queen of Angels*

➤

"Both big and good . . . excellent."

—*Chicago Sun-Times* on *Queen of Angels*

➤

"A cohesive and original vision of the future . . . Bear has combined a lively set of characters, colorful writing, and gripping psychological-technological fabrications into a very seductive read."

—*People* on *Queen of Angels*

ALSO BY GREG BEAR

ETERNITY
QUEEN OF ANGELS
TANGENTS
THE WIND FROM A BURNING WOMAN

A Time Warner Company

"Mandala" appeared in substantially different form in *New Dimensions Eight*, copyright © 1978 by Robert Silverberg.

"Resurrection" appeared in *Rigel* under the title "Strength of Stones, Flesh of Brass," copyright © 1981 by Greg Bear.

WARNER BOOKS EDITION

This Warner Books Edition is published by arrangement with the author.

Cover design by Don Puckey
Cover illustration by Bob Eggleton

Warner Books, Inc.
666 Fifth Avenue
New York, NY 10103

A Time Warner Company

Printed in the United States of America

First Warner Books Printing: November, 1991

10 9 8 7 6 5 4 3 2 1

For my grandmother, Florence M. Bear,
provider of a home
for wandering adventurers.

11 "What is my strength, that I should
wait?
And what is mine end, that I
should be patient?

12 Is my strength the strength of stones?
Or is my flesh of brass?

13 Is it that I have no help in me,
And that sound wisdom is driven
quite from me?"

JOB 6, the Masoretic Text

The final decade of Earth's twentieth century was cataclysmic. Moslem states fought horrible wars in 1995, 1996, and 1998, devastating much of Africa and the Middle East. In less than five years, the steady growth of Islam during the latter half of the century became a rout of terror and apostasy, one of the worst religious convulsions in human history.

Christian splinter cults around the world engaged in every imaginable form of social disobedience to hasten the long-overdue Millennium, but there was no Second Coming. Their indiscretions rubbed off on all Christians.

As for the Jews—the world had never needed any reason to hate Jews.

The far-flung children of Abraham had their decade of unbridled fervor, and they paid for it. Marginally united by a world turning to other religions and against them, Jews, Christians and Moslems ratified the Pact of God in 2020. They desperately harked back to ages past to find common ground. Having spoiled their holy lands, there was no place where they could unite geographically.

In the last years of the twenty-first century, they looked outward. The Heaven Migration began in 2113. After decades more of persecution and ridicule, they pooled their resources to buy a world of their own. That world was renamed God-Does-Battle, tamed by the wealth of the heirs of Christ, Rome, Abraham and OPEC.

They hired the greatest human architect to build their new cities for them. He tried to mediate between what they demanded, and what would work best for them.

He failed.

BOOK ONE
3451 A.D.

Mandala

THE city that had occupied Mesa Canaan was now marching across the plain. Jeshua watched with binoculars from the cover of the jungle. It had disassembled just before dawn, walking on elephantine legs, tractor treads and wheels, with living bulkheads upright, dismantled buttresses given new instructions to crawl instead of support; floors and ceilings, transports and smaller city parts, factories and resource centers, all unrecognizable now, like a slime mold soon to gather itself in its new country.

The city carried its plan deep within the living plasm of its fragmented body. Every piece knew its place, and within that scheme there was no room for Jeshua, or for any man.

The living cities had cast them out a thousand years before.

He lay with his back against a tree, binoculars in one hand and an orange in the other, sucking thoughtfully on a bitter piece of rind. No matter how far back he probed, the first thing he remembered was watching a city break into a tide of parts, migrating. He had been three years old, two by the seasons of God-Does-Battle, sitting on his father's shoulders as they came to the village of Bethel-Japhet to live. Jeshua—ironically named, for he would always be chaste—remembered nothing of importance before coming to Bethel-Japhet. Perhaps it had all been erased by the shock of falling into the campfire a month before reaching the village. His body still carried the marks: a circle of scars on his chest, black with the tiny remnants of cinders.

Jeshua was huge, seven feet tall flat on his feet. His arms were as thick as an ordinary man's legs, and when he inhaled, his chest swelled as big as a barrel. He was a smith in the village, a worker of iron and caster of bronze and silver. But his strong hands had also acquired delicate skills to craft ritual and family jewelry. For his trade he had been given the surname Tubal—Jeshua Tubal Iben Daod, craftsman of all metals.

The city on the plain was marching toward the Arat range. It moved with faultless deliberation. Cities seldom migrated more than a hundred miles at a time or more than once in a hundred years, so the legends went; but they seemed more restless now.

He scratched his back against the trunk, then put his binoculars in a pants pocket. His feet slipped into the sandals he'd dropped on the mossy jungle floor, and he stood, stretching. He sensed someone behind him but did not turn to look, though his neck muscles knotted tight.

"Jeshua." It was the chief of the guard and the council of laws, Sam Daniel the Catholic. His father and Sam Daniel had been friends before his father disappeared. "Time for the Synedrium to convene."

Jeshua tightened the straps on his sandals and followed.

Bethel-Japhet was a village of moderate size, with about two thousand people. Its houses and buildings laced through the jungle until no distinct borders remained. The stone roadway to the Synedrium Hall seemed too short to Jershua, and the crowd within the hearing chamber was far too large. His betrothed, Kisa, daughter of Jake, was not there, but his challenger, Renold Mosha Iben Yitshok, was.

The representative of the seventy judges, the Septuagint, called the gathering to order and asked that the details of the case be presented.

"Son of David," Renold said, "I have come to contest your betrothal to Kisa, daughter of Jake."

"I hear," Jeshua said, taking his seat in the defendant's docket.

"I have reasons for my challenge. Will you hear them?"

Jeshua didn't answer.

"Pardon my persistence. It is the law. I don't dislike you—I remember our childhood, when we played together—but now we are mature, and the time has come."

"Then speak." Jeshua fingered his thick dark beard. His flushed skin was the color of the fine sandy dirt on the riverbanks of the Hebron. He towered a good foot above Renold, who was slight and graceful.

"Jeshua Tubal Iben Daod, you were born like other men but did not grow as we have. You now look like a man, but the Synedrium has records of your development. You cannot consummate a marriage. You cannot give a child to Kisa. This annuls your childhood betrothal. By law and by my wish I am bound to replace you, to fulfil your obligation to her."

Kisa would never know. No one here would tell her. She would come in time to accept and love Renold, and to think of Jeshua as only another man in the Expolis Ibreem and its twelve villages, a man who stayed alone and unmarried. Her slender warm body with skin smooth as the finest cotton would soon dance beneath the man he saw before him. She would clutch Renold's back and dream of the time when humans would again be welcomed into the cities, when the skies would again be filled with ships and God-Does-Battle would be redeemed—

"I cannot answer, Renold Mosha Iben Yitshok."

"Then you will sign this." Renold held out a piece of paper and advanced.

"There was no need for a public witnessing," Jeshua said. "Why did the Synedrium decide my shame was to be public?" He looked around with tears in his eyes. Never before, even in the greatest physical pain, had he cried; not even, so his father said, when he had fallen into the fire.

He moaned. Renold stepped back and looked up in anguish. "I'm sorry, Jeshua. Please sign. If you love either Kisa or myself, or the expolis, sign."

Jeshua's huge chest forced out a scream. Renold turned and ran. Jeshua slammed his fist onto the railing, struck himself on the forehead and tore out the seams of his shirt. He had had too much. For nine years he had known of his inability to be a whole man, but he had hoped that would change, that his genitals would develop like some tardy flower just beyond normal season, and they had. But not enough. His testicles were fully developed, enough to give him a hairy body, broad shoulders, flat stomach, narrow hips, and all the desires of any young man—but his penis was the small pink dangle of a child.

Now he exploded. He ran after Renold, out of the hall, bellowing incoherently and swinging his binoculars at the end of their leather strap. Renold ran into the village square and screeched a warning. Children and fowl scattered. Women grabbed their skirts and fled for the wood and brick homes.

Jeshua stopped. He flung his binoculars as high as he could above his head. They cleared the top of the tallest tree in the area and fell a hundred feet beyond. Still bellowing, he charged a house and put his hands against the wall. He braced his feet and heaved. He slammed his shoulder against it. It would not move. More furious still, he turned to a trough of fresh water, picked it up, and dumped it over his head. The cold did not slow him. He threw the trough against the wall and splintered it.

"Enough!" cried the chief of the guard. Jeshua stopped and blinked at Sam Daniel the Catholic. He wobbled, weak with exertion. Something in his stomach hurt.

"Enough, Jeshua," Sam Daniel said softly.

"The law is taking away my birthright. Is that just?"

"Your right as a citizen, perhaps, but not your birthright.

You weren't born here, Jeshua. But it is still no fault of yours. There is no telling why nature makes mistakes.''

"No!" He ran around the house and took a side street into the market triangle. The stalls were busy with customers picking them over and carrying away baskets filled with purchases. He leaped into the triangle and began to scatter people and shops every which way. Sam Daniel and his men followed.

"He's gone berserk!" Renold shouted from the rear. "He tried to kill me!"

"I've always said he was too big to be safe," growled one of the guard. "Now look what he's doing."

"He'll face the council for it," Sam Daniel said.

"Nay, the Septuagint he'll face, as a criminal, if the damage gets any heavier!"

They followed him through the market.

Jeshua stopped at the base of a hill, near an old gate leading from the village proper. He gasped painfully, and his face was wine-red. Sweat gnarled his hair. In the thicket of his mind he searched for a way out, the only way out. His father had told him about it when he was thirteen or fourteen. "The cities were like doctors," his father had said. "They could alter, replace, or repair anything in the human body. That's what was lost when the cities grew disgusted and cast the people out."

No city would let any real man or woman enter. But Jeshua was different. Real people could sin. He could be a sinner not in fact, but only in thought. In his confusion the distinction seemed important.

Sam Daniel and his men found him at the outskirts of the jungle, walking away from Bethel-Japhet.

"Stop!" the chief of the guard ordered.

"I'm leaving," Jeshua said without turning.

"You can't go without a ruling!"

"I am."

"We'll hunt you!"

"Then I'll hide, damn you!"

There was only one place to hide on the plain, and that was underground, in the places older than the living cities and known collectively as Sheol. Jeshua ran. He soon outdistanced them all.

Five miles ahead he saw the city that had left Mesa Canaan. It had reassembled itself below the mountains of Arat. It gleamed in the sun, as beautiful as anything ever denied mankind. The walls began to glow as the sky darkened, and in the evening silence the air hummed with the internal noises of the city's life. Jeshua slept in a gully, hidden by a lean-to woven out of reeds.

In the soft yellow light of dawn, he looked at the city more closely, lifting his head above the gully's muddy rim. The city began with a ring of rounded outward-leaning towers, like the petals of a monumental lotus. Inward was another ring, slightly taller, and another, rising to support a radiance of buttresses. The buttresses carried a platform with columns atop it, segmented and studded like the branches of a diatom. At the city's summit, a dome like the magnified eye of a fly gave off a corona of diffracted colors. Opal glints of blue and green sparkled in the outside walls.

With the help of the finest architect humanity had ever produced, Robert Kahn, Jeshua's ancestors had built the cities and made them as comfortable as possible. Huge laboratories had labored for decades to produce the right combination of animal, plant, and machine, and to fit them within the proper designs. It had been a proud day when the first cities were opened. The Christians, Jews, and Moslems of God-Does-Battle could boast of cities more spectacular than any that Kahn had built elsewhere, and the builder's works could be found on a hundred worlds.

Jeshua stopped a hundred yards from the glassy steps beneath the outer petals of the city. Broad, sharp spikes rose from the pavement and smooth garden walls. The plants within the garden shrank away at his approach. The entire circuit of paving around the city shattered into silicate thorns and bristled. There was no way to enter. Still, he walked closer.

He faced the tangle of sharp spines and reached to stroke one with a hand. It shuddered at his touch.

"I haven't sinned," he told it. "I've hurt no one, coveted only that which was mine by law." The nested spikes said nothing but grew taller as he watched, until they extended a hundred yards above his head.

He sat on a hummock of grass outside the perimeter and clasped his stomach with his hands to ease the hunger and pressure of his sadness. He looked up at the city's peak. A thin silvery tower rose from the midst of the columns and culminated in a multifaceted sphere. The sunlit side of the sphere formed a crescent of yellow brilliance. A cold wind rushed through his clothes and made him shiver. He stood and began to walk around the city, picking up speed when the wind carried sounds of people from the expolis.

Jeshua knew from long hikes in his adolescence that a large entrance to Sheol yawned two miles farther west. By noon he stood in the cavernous entrance.

The underground passages that made up Sheol had once been service ways for the inorganic cities of twelve centuries ago. All of those had been leveled and their raw material recycled with the completion of the living cities. But the underground causeways would have been almost impossible to destroy, so they had been blocked off and abandoned. Some had filled with groundwater, and some had collapsed. Still others, drawing power from geothermal sources, maintained themselves and acted as if they yet had a purpose. A few became the homes of disgruntled expolitans, not unlike Jeshua.

Many had become dangerous. Some of the living cities, just finished and not completely inspected, had thrown out their human builders during the Exiling, then broken down. Various disembodied parts—servant vehicles, maintenance robots, transports—had left the shambles and crept into the passages of Sheol, ill and incomplete, to avoid the natural cycle of God-Does-Battle's wilderness and the wrath of the exiles. Most had died and disintegrated, but a few had found ways to survive, and rumors about those made Jeshua nervous.

He looked around and found a gnarled sun-blackened vine hard as wood, with a heavy bole. He hefted it, broke off its weak tapering end, and stuck it into his belt where it wouldn't tangle his legs.

Before he scrambled down the debris-covered slope, he looked back. The expolitans from Ibreem were only a few hundred yards away.

He lurched and ran. Sand, rocks, and bits of dead plants had spilled into the wide tunnel. Water dripped off chipped white ceramic walls, plinking into small ponds. Moss and tiered fungus imparted a shaggy veneer to the walls and supports.

The villagers appeared at the lip of the depression and shouted his name. He hid in the shadows for a while until he saw that they weren't following.

A mile into the tunnel, he saw lights. The floor was ankle-deep with muddy water. He had already seen several of God-Does-Battle's native arthropods and contemplated catching one for food, but he had no way to light a fire. He'd left all his matches in Bethel-Japhet, since it was against the law to go into the jungles carrying them unless on an authorized hunt or expedition. He couldn't stand the thought of raw creeper flesh, no matter how hungry he was.

The floor ahead had been lifted up and dropped. A lake had formed within the rimmed depression. Ripples shivered with oily slowness from side to side. Jeshua skirted the water on jagged slabs of concrete. He saw something long and white in the lake, waiting in the shallows, with feelers like the soft feathers of a mulcet branch. It had large grey eyes and a blunt rounded head, with a pocketknife assortment of clippers, grabbers, and cutters branching from arms on each side. Jeshua had never seen anything like it.

God-Does-Battle was seldom so bizarre. It had been a straightforward, slightly dry Earth-like world, which was why humans had colonized in such large numbers thirteen centuries ago, turning the sluggish planet into a grand imitation of the best parts of ten planets. Some of the terraforming had slipped since then, but not drastically.

Water splashed as he stepped on the solid floor of the opposite shore. The undulating feathery nightmare glided swiftly into the depths.

The lights ahead blazed in discrete globes, not the gentle glows of the walls of the living cities. Wiring hissed and crackled around a black metal box. Tracks began at a buffer and ran off around the distant curve. Black strips, faded and scuffed, marked a walkway. Signs in Old English and something akin to the Hebraic hodgepodge spoken in Ibreem warned against deviating from the outlined path. He could read the English more easily than the Hebrew, for Hebraic script had been used. In Ibreem, all writing was in Roman script.

Jeshua stayed within the lines and walked around the curve. Half of the tunnel ahead was blocked by a hulk. It was thirty feet wide and some fifty long, rusting and frozen in its decay. It had been man-operated, not automatic—a seat bucket still rose above a nest of levers, pedals, and a small arched instrument panel. As a smith and designer of tools and motor-driven vehicles, Jeshua thought there were parts of the rail-rider that didn't seem integral. He examined them more closely and saw they hadn't come with the original machine. They were odds and ends of mobile machinery from one of the cities. Part machine, part organism, built with treads and grips, they had joined with the tar-baby rail-rider, trying to find a place on the bigger, more powerful machine. They had found only silence. They were dead now, and what could not rot had long since dusted away. The rest was glazed with rust and decay.

In the tunnel beyond, stalactites of concrete and rusted steel bristled from the ceiling. Fragments of pipes and wiring hung from them on brackets. At one time the entire tunnel must have been filled with them, with room only for railriders and maintenance crews walking the same path he was taking. Most of the metal and plastic had been stripped away by scavengers.

Jeshua walked beneath the jagged end of an air duct and heard a susurrus. He cocked his head and listened more closely. Nothing. Then again, almost too faint to make out. The plastic of the air duct was brittle and added a timbre of falling dust to the voices. He found a metal can and stood on it, bringing his ear closer.

"Moobed . . ." the duct echoed.

". . . not 'ere dis me was . . ."

"Bloody poppy-breast!"

"Not'ing . . . do . . ."

The voices stopped. The can crumpled and dropped him to the hard floor, making him yelp like a boy. He stood on wobbly legs and walked farthcr into the tunnel.

The lighting was dimmer. He walked carefully over the shadow-pocked floor, avoiding bits of tile and concrete, fallen piping, snake wires and loose strapping bands. Fewer people had been this way. Vaguely seen things moved off at his approach: insects, creepers, rodents, some native, some feral. What looked like an overturned drum became, as he bent closer, a snail wide as two handspans, coursing on a shiny foot as long as his calf. The white-tipped eyes glanced up, cat-slits dark with hidden fluids and secret thoughts, and a warm, sickening odor wafted from it. Stuck fast to one side was the rotting body of a large beetle.

A hundred yards on, the floor buckled again. The rutted underground landscape of pools, concrete, and mud smelled foul and felt more foul to his sandaled feet. He stayed away from the bigger pools, which were surrounded by empty larvae casings and filled with snorkeling insect young.

He regretted his decision. He wondered how he could return to the village and face his punishment. To live within sight of Kisa and Renold. To repair the water trough and do labor penance for the stall owners.

He stopped to listen. Water fell in a cascade ahead. The sound drowned out anything more subtle, but sounds of a squabble rose above. Men were arguing and coming closer.

Jeshua moved back from the middle of the tunnel and hid behind a fallen pipe.

Someone ran from block to block, dancing agilely in the tunnel, arms held out in balance and hands gesturing like wing tips. Four others followed, knife blades gleaming in the half-light. The fleeing man ran past, saw Jeshua in the shadows, and stumbled off into black mud. Jeshua pushed against the pipe as he stood and turned to run. He felt a tremor through his hand on the wall. A massive presence of falling rock and dirt knocked him over and tossed debris around him. Four shouts were severed. He choked on the dust, waving his arms and crawling.

The lights were out. Only a putrid blue-green swamp glow remained. A shadow crossed the ghost of a pond. Jeshua stiffened and waited for the attacking blow.

"Who?" the shadow said. "Go, spek. Shan hurt."

The voice sounded like it might come from an older boy, perhaps eighteen or nineteen. He spoke a sort of English. It wasn't the tongue Jeshua had learned while visiting Expolis Winston, but he could understand some of it. He thought it might be Chaser English, but there weren't supposed to be chasers in Expolis Ibreem. They must have followed the city . . .

"I'm running, like you," Jeshua said in Winston dialect.

"Dis me," said the shadow. "Sabed my ass, you did. Quartie ob toms, lie dey t'ought I spek. Who appel?"

"What?"

"Who name? You."

"Jeshua," he said.

"Jeshoo-a Iberhim."

"Yes, Expolis Ibreem."

"No' far dis em. Stan' an' clean. Takee back."

"No, I'm not lost. I'm running."

"No' good t'stay. Bugga bites mucky, bugga bites you more dan dey bites dis me."

Jeshua slowly wiped mud from his pants with broad hands. Dirt and pebbles scuttled down the hill where the four lay tombed.

"Slow," the boy said. "Slow, no? Brainsick?" The boy advanced. "Dat's it. Slow you."

"No, tired," Jeshua said. "How do we get out of here?"

"Dat, dere an' dere. See?"

"Can't see," Jeshua said. "Not very well."

The boy advanced again and laid a cool, damp hand on his forearm. "Big, you. Skeez, maybe tight." The hand gripped and tested. Then the shadow backed off. Jeshua's eyes were adjusting, and he could see the boy's thinness.

"What's your name?" he asked.

"No' matta. Go 'long wi' dis me now."

The boy led him to the hill of debris and poked around in the pitchy black to see if they could pass. "Allry. Dis way." Jeshua climbed up the rubble and pushed through the hole at the top with his back scraping the ceramic roof. The other side of the tunnel was dark. The boy cursed under his breath. "Whole tube," he said. "Ginger walk, now."

The pools beyond were luminous with the upright glows of insect larvae. Some were a foot long and solitary; others were smaller and grouped in hazes in meager light. Always there was a soft sucking sound and thrash of feelers, claws, legs. Jeshua's skin crawled, and he shivered in disgust.

"Sh," the boy warned. "Skyling here, sout' go, tro sound."

Jeshua caught none of the explanation but stepped more lightly. Dirt and tiles dropped in the water, and a chitinous chorus complained.

"Got dur here," the boy said, taking Jeshua's hand and putting it against a metal hatch. "Ope', den go. Compree?"

The hatch slid open with a drawn-out squeal, and blinding

glare filled the tunnel. Things behind hurried for shadows. Jeshua and the boy stepped from the tunnel into a collapsed anteroom open to the last light of day. Vegetation had swarmed into the wet depression, decorating hulks of pipe valves and electric boxes. As the boy closed the hatch, Jeshua scraped at a metal cube with one hand and drew off a layered clump of moss. Four numbers were engraved beneath: "2278".

"Don' finga," the boy warned. He had wide grey eyes and a pinched, pale face. A grin spread between narcissus-white cheeks. He was tight-sewn, tense, with wide knees and elbows and little flesh to cover his long limbs. His hair was rusty orange and hung in strips across his forehead and ears. Beneath a ragged vest, his chest bore a tattoo. The boy rubbed his hand across it, seeing Jeshua's interest, and left a smear of mud behind.

"My bran'," the boy said. The 'brand' was a radiant circle in orange and black, with a central square divided by diagonals. Triangles diminished to points in each division, creating a vibrant skewedness. "Dat put dere, long 'go, by Mandala."

"What's that?"

"De gees run me, you drop skyling on, woodna dey lissen wen I say, say dis me, dat de polis, a dur go up inna." He laughed. "Dey say, 'Nobod eba go in polis, no mo' eba.' "

"Mandala's a city, a polis?"

"Ten, fi'teen lees fr' 'ere."

"Lees?"

"Kileemet'. Lee."

"You speak anything else?" Jeshua asked, his face screwed up with the strain of turning instant linguist.

"You, 'Ebra spek, bet. But no good dere. I got better Englise, tone up a bit?"

"Hm?"

"I can . . . try . . . this, if it betta." He shook his head. "Blow me ou' to keep up long, do."

"Maybe silence is best," Jeshua said. "Or you just nod

yes or no if you understand. You've found a way to get into a polis?''

Nod.

"Named Mandala. Can you get back there, take me with you?''

Shake, no. Smile.

"Secret?''

"No secret. Dey big machee . . . machine dat tell dis me neba retourn. Put dis on my bod.'' He touched his chest. "Tro me out.''

"How did you find your way in?''

"Dur? Dis big polis, it creep afta exhaus'—sorry, moob afta run outta soil das good to lib on, many lee fro' 'ere, an' squat on top ob place where tube ope' ri' middle ob undaside. I know dat way, so dis me go in, an' out soon afta . . . after. On my—'' He slapped his butt. "Coupla bounce, too.''

The collapsed ceiling—or styling, as the boy called it—of the anteroom formed a convenient staircase from the far wall to the surface. They climbed and stood on the edge, looking each other over uncertainly. Jeshua was covered with dark green mud. He picked at the caked rings with his hands, but the mud clung to his skin fiercely.

"Maybe, come fine a bod ob wet to slosh in.''

A branch of the Hebron River, flowing out of the Arat range, showed itself by a clump of green reeds a half mile from the tunnel exit. Jeshua drew its muddy water up in handfuls and poured it over his head. The boy dipped and wallowed and spumed it from puffed cheeks, then grinned like a terrier at the Ibreemite, mud streaming down his face.

"Comes off slow,'' Jeshua said, scraping at his skin with clumped silkreeds.

"Why you interest' in place no man come?''

Jeshua shook his head and didn't answer. He finished with his torso and kneeled to let his legs soak. The bottom of the stream was rocky and sandy and cool. He looked up and let his eyes follow the spine of a peak in Arat, outlined in sunset glow. "Where is Mandala?''

"No," the boy said. "My polis."

"It kicked you out," Jeshua said. "Why not let somebody else try?"

"Somebod alread' tried," the boy informed him with a narrowed glance. "Dat dey tried, and got in, but dey didna t'rough my dur go. Dey—shee—one gol, dat's all—got in widout de troub' we aw ekspek. Mandala didna sto' 'er."

"I'd like to try that."

"Dat gol, she special, she up an' down legen' now. Was a year ago she went and permissed to pass was. You t'ink special you might be?"

"No," Jeshua admitted. "Mesa Canaan's city wouldn't let me in."

"One it wander has, just early yes'day?"

"Hm?"

"Wander, moob. Dis Mase Cain' you mumbur 'bout."

"I know."

"So't don' let dis you in, why Mandala an' differs?"

Jeshua climbed from the river, frowning. "Appel?" he asked.

"Me, m'appel, not true appel or you got like hair by demon grab, m'appel for you is Thinner."

"Thinner, where do you come from?"

"Same as de gol, we follow de polis."

"City chasers?" By Ibreem's estimation, that made Thinner a ruthless savage. "Thinner, you don't want to go back to Mandala, do you? You're afraid."

"Cumsay, afraid? Like terrafy?"

"Like tremble in your bare feet in the dirtafy."

"No' possible for Thinner. Lead'er like, snake-skin, poke an' I bounce, no' go t'rough."

"Thinner, you're a faker." Jeshua reached out and lifted him from the water. "Now stop with the nonsense and give me straight English. You speak it—out!"

"No!" the boy protested.

"Then why do you drop all 'thu's' but in your name and

change the word order every other sentence? I'm no fool. You're a fake."

"If Thinner lie, feet may curl up an' blow! Born to spek dis odd inflek, an' I spek differs by your ask! Dis me, no fake! Drop!" Thinner kicked Jeshua on the shin but only bent his toe. He squalled, and Jeshua threw him back like a fingerling. Then he turned to pick up his clothes and lumbered up the bank to leave.

"Nobod dey neba treat Thinner dis way!" the boy howled.

"You're lying to me," Jeshua said.

"No! Stop." Thinner stood in the river and held up his hands. "You're right."

"I know I am."

"But not completely. I'm from Winston, and I'm speaking like a city chaser for a reason. And speaking accurately, mind you."

Jeshua frowned. The boy no longer seemed a boy. "Why fool me, or try to?" he asked.

"I'm a free-lance tracker. I'm trying to keep tabs on the chasers. They've been making raids on the farmlands outside of Winston. I was almost caught by a few of them, and I was trying to convince them I was part of a clan. When they were buried, I thought you might have been another, and after speaking to you like that—well, I have an instinct to keep a cover in a tight spot."

"No Winstoner has a tattoo like yours."

"That part's the truth, too. I did find a way into the city, and it did kick me out."

"Do you still object to taking me there?"

Thinner sighed and crawled out of the stream. "It's not part of my trip. I'm heading back for Winston."

Jeshua watched him cautiously as he dried himself. "You don't think it's odd that you even got into a city at all?"

"No. I did it by trick."

"Men smarter than you or I tried for centuries before they all gave up. Now you've succeeded, and you don't even feel special?"

Thinner put on his scrappy clothes. "Why do you want to go?"

"I've got reasons."

"Are you a criminal in Ibreem?"

Jeshua shook his head. "I'm sick," he said. "Nothing contagious. But I was told a city might cure me, if I could find a way in."

"I've met your kind before," Thinner said. "But they've never made it. A few years ago Winston sent a whole pilgrimage of sick and wounded to a city. Bristled its barbs like a fighting cat. No mercy there, you can believe."

"But you have a way, now."

"Okay," Thinner said. "We can go back. It's on the other side of Arat. You've got me a little curious now. And besides, I think I might like you. You look like you should be dumb as a creeper, but you're smart. Sharp. And besides, you've still got that club. Are you desperate enough to kill?"

Jeshua thought about that for a moment, then shook his head.

"It's almost dark," Thinner said. "Let's camp and start in the morning."

In the far valley at the middle of Arat, the Mesa Canaan city—now probably to be called the Arat city—was warm and sunset-pretty, like a diadem. Jeshua made a bed from the reeds and watched Thinner as he hollowed out the ground and made his own nest. Jeshua slept lightly that evening and came awake with dawn. He opened his eyes to a small insect on his chest, inquiring its way with finger-long antennae. He flicked it off and cleared his throat.

Thinner jack-in-the-boxed from his nest, rubbed his eyes and stood.

"I'm amazed," he said. "You didn't cut my throat."

"Wouldn't do me any good."

"Work like this rubs down a man's trust."

Jeshua returned to the river and soaked himself again, pouring the chill water on his face and back in double handloads. The pressure in his groin was lighter this morning than most, but it still made him grit his teeth. He wanted to roll in the reeds and groan, rut the earth, but it would do him no good. Only the impulse existed.

They agreed on which pass to take through the Arat peaks and set out.

Jeshua had spent most of his life within sight of the villages of the Expolis Ibreem and found himself increasingly nervous the farther he hiked. They crawled up the slope, and Thinner's statement about having tough soles proved itself. He walked barefoot over all manner of jagged rocks without complaining.

At the crest of a ridge, Jeshua looked back and saw the plain of reeds and the jungle beyond. With some squinting and hand-shading, he could make out the major clusters of huts in two villages and the Temple Josiah on Mount Miriam. All else was hidden.

In two days they crossed Arat and a rilled terrain of foothills beyond. They walked through fields of wild oats. "This used to be called Agripolis," Thinner said. "If you dig deep enough here, you'll come across irrigation systems, automatic fertilizing machines, harvesters, storage bins—the whole works. It's all useless now. For nine hundred years it wouldn't let any human cross these fields. It finally broke down, and those parts that could move, did. Most died."

Jeshua knew a little concerning the history of the cities around Arat and told Thinner about the complex known as Tripolis. Three cities had been grouped on one side of Arat, about twenty miles north of where they were standing. After the Exiling, one had fragmented and died. Another had moved successfully and had left the area. The third had tried to cross the Arat range and failed. The major bulk of its wreckage lay in a disorganized mute clump not far from them.

They found scattered pieces of it on the plain of Agripolis. As they walked, they saw bulkheads and buttresses, most hardy of a city's large members, still supported by desiccated legs. Some were fifty to sixty yards long and twenty feet across, mounted on organic wheel movements. Their metal parts had corroded badly. The organic parts had disappeared, except for an occasional span of silicate wall or internal skeleton of colloid.

"They're not all dead, though," Thinner said. "I've been across here before. Some made the walk a little difficult."

In the glare of afternoon they hid from a wheeled beast armored like a great translucent tank. "That's something from deep inside a city—a mover or loader," Thinner said. "I don't know anything about the temper of a feral city part, but I'm not going to aggravate it."

When the tank thing passed, they continued. There were creatures less threatening, more shy, which they ignored. Most of them Jeshua couldn't fit into a picture of ancient city functions. They were queer, dreamy creatures: spinning tops, many-legged browsers, things with bushes on their backs, bowls built like dogs but carrying water—insane, confusing fragments.

By day's end they stood on the outskirts of Mandala. Jeshua sat on a stone to look at the city. "It's different," he said. "It isn't as pretty." Mandala was more square, less free and fluid. It had an ungainly ziggurat-like pear shape. The colors that were scattered along its walls and light-banners—black and orange—didn't match well with the delicate blues and greens of the city substance.

"It's older," Thinner said. "One of the first, I think. It's an old tree, a bit scabrous, not like a young sprout."

Jeshua looped his belt more tightly about his club and shaded his eyes against the sun. The young of Ibreem had been taught enough about cities to identify their parts and functions. The sunlight-absorbing banners that rippled near Mandala's peak were like the leaves of a tree and also like flags. Designs on their surfaces formed a language conveying the city's purpose and attitude. Silvery reflectors cast shadows below the banners. By squinting, he could see the gardens and fountains and crystalline recreation buildings of the uppermost promenade, a mile above them. Sunlight illuminated the green walls and showed their mottled innards, pierced the dragonfly buttresses whose wings with slow in-out beats kept air moving, and crept back and forth through the halls, light wells, and living quarters, giving all of Mandala an interior luminosity. Despite the orange and black of the colored surfaces, the city had an innate glory that made Jeshua's chest ache with desire.

"How do we get in?" he asked.

"Through a tunnel, about a mile from here."

"You mentioned a girl. Was that part of the cover?"

"No. She's here. I met her. She has the liberty of the city. I don't think she has to worry about anything, except loneliness." He looked at Jeshua with an uncharacteristic wry grin. "At least she doesn't have to worry about where the next meal comes from."

"How did she get in? Why does the city let her stay?"

"Who can judge the ways of a city?"

Jeshua nodded thoughtfully. "Let's go."

Thinner's grin froze and he stiffened, staring over Jeshua's shoulder. Jeshua looked around and surreptitiously loosened his club in his belt. "Who are they?" he asked.

"The city chasers. They usually stay in the shadow. Something must be upsetting them today."

At a run through the grass, twenty men dressed in rough orange-and-black rags advanced on them. Jeshua saw another group coming from the other side of the city perimeter. "We'll have to take a stand," he said. "We can't outrun them."

Thinner looked distressed. "Friend," he said. "It's time I dropped another ruse. We can get into the city here, but they can't."

Jeshua ignored the non sequitur. "Stand to my rear," he said. Jeshua swung his club up and took a stance, baring his teeth and hunkering low as his father had taught him to do when facing wild beasts. The bluff was the thing, especially when backed by his bulk. Thinner pranced on his bandy legs, panic tightening his face. "Follow me, or they'll kill us," he said.

He broke for the glassy gardens within the perimeter. Jeshua turned and saw the polis chasers were forming a circle, concentrating on him, aiming spears for a throw. He ducked and lay flat as the metal-tipped shafts flew over into the grass. He rose, and a second flight shot by, one grazing him painfully on the shoulder. He heard Thinner rasp and curse. A chaser held him at arm's length, repeatedly slashing his chest with a knife. Jeshua stood tall and ran for the circle, club held out before him. Swords came up, dull grey steel spotted with blood-rust. He blocked a thrust and cut it aside with the club, then killed the man with a downward swing.

"Stop it, you goddamn idiots!" someone shouted. One of the chasers shrieked, and the others backed away from Jeshua. Thinner's attacker held a head, severed from the boy's body. It trailed green. Though decapitated, Thinner shouted invective in several languages, including Hebrew and Chaser English. The attackers abandoned their weapons before the oracular monster and ran pale and stumbling. The petrified man who held the head dropped it and fell over.

Jeshua stood his ground, bloody club trembling in his loosening hand.

"Hey," said the muffled voice in the grass. "Come here and help!"

Jeshua spotted six points on his forehead and drew two meshed triangles between. He walked slowly through the grass.

"El and hell," Thinner's head cried out. "I'm chewing grass. Pick me up."

He found the boy's body first. He bent over and saw the red, bleeding skin on the chest, pulpy green below that, and the pale colloid ribs that supported. Deeper still, glassy machinery and pale blue fluids in filigree tubes surrounded glints of organic circuit and metal. The chaser nearby had fainted from shock.

He found Thinner's head facedown, jaw working and hair standing on end. "Lift me out," the head said. "By the hair, if you're squeamish, but lift me out."

Jeshua reached down and picked the head up by the hair. Thinner stared at him above green-leaking nose and frothing mouth. The eyes blinked. "Wipe my mouth with something." Jeshua picked up a clump of grass and did so, leaving bits of dirt behind, but getting most of the face clean. His stomach squirmed, but Thinner was obviously no mammal, nor a natural beast of any form, so he kept his reactions in check.

"I wish you'd listen to me," the head said.

"You're from the city," Jeshua said, twisting it this way and that.

"Stop that—I'm getting dizzy. Take me inside Mandala."

"Will it let me in?"

"Yes, dammit, I'll be your passkey."

"If you're from the city, why would you want me or anyone else to go inside?"

"Take me in, and you'll discover."

Jeshua held the head at arm's length and inspected it with half-closed eyes. Then, slowly, he lowered it, looked at the tiled gardens within the perimeter, and took his first step. He stopped, shaking.

"Hurry," the head said. "I'm dripping."

At any moment Jeshua expected the outskirts to splinter and bristle, but no such thing happened. "Will I meet the girl?" he asked.

"Walk, no questions."

Eyes wide and stomach tense as rock, Jeshua entered the city of Mandala.

"There, that was easier than you expected, wasn't it?" the head asked.

Jeshua stood in a cyclopean green mall, light bright but filtered, like the bottom of a shallow sea, surrounded by the green of thick glass and botanic fluids. Tetrahedral pylons and slender arches rose all around and met high above in a circular design of orange and black, similar to the markings on Thinner's chest. The pylons supported four floors opening onto the court. The galleries were empty.

"You can put me down here," Thinner said. "I'm broken. Something will come along to fix me. Wander for a while if you want. Nothing will hurt you. Perhaps you'll meet the girl."

Jeshua looked around apprehensively. "Would do neither of us any good," he said. "I'm afraid."

"Why, because you're not a whole man?"

Jeshua dropped the head roughly on the hard floor, and it bounced, screeching.

"How did you know?" he asked loudly, desperately.

"Now you've made me confused," the head said. "What did I say?" It stopped talking, and its eyes closed. Jeshua touched it tentatively with his boot. It did nothing. He straightened up and looked for a place to run. The best way would be out. He was a sinner now, a sinner by anger and shame. The city would throw him out violently. Perhaps it would brand him, as Thinner had hinted earlier. Jeshua wanted the familiarity of the grasslands and tangible enemies like the city chasers.

The sunlight through the entrance arch guided him. He ran for the glassy walkway and found it rising to keep him in. Furious with panic, he raised his club and struck at the spines. They sang with the blows but did not break.

"Please," he begged. "Let me out, let me out!"

He heard a noise behind him and turned. A small wheeled cart gripped Thinner's head with gentle mandibles and lifted its segmented arms to send the oracle down a chute into its back. It rolled from the mall into a corridor.

Jeshua lifted his slumped shoulders and expanded his chest. "I'm afraid!" he shouted at the city. "I'm a sinner! You don't want me, so let me go!"

He squatted on the pavement with club in hand, trembling. The hatred of the cities for man had been deeply impressed in him. His breathing slowed until he could think again, and the fear subsided. Why had the city let him in, even with Thinner? He stood and slung the club in his belt. There was an answer someplace. He had little to lose—at most, a life he wasn't particularly enjoying.

And in a city, there was the possibility of healing arts now lost to the expolitans.

"Okay," he said. "I'm staying. Prepare for the worst."

He walked across the mall and took a corridor beyond. Empty rooms with hexagonal doors waited silent on either side. He found a fountain of refreshing water in a broad cathedral-nave room and drank from it. Then he spent some time studying the jointing of the arches that supported the vault above, running his fingers over the grooves.

A small anteroom had a soft couchlike protrusion, and he rested there, staring blankly at the ceiling. For a short while he slept. When he awoke, both he and his clothes were clean. A new pair had been laid out for him—standard Ibreem khaki shirt and short pants and a twine belt, more delicately knitted than the one he was wearing. His club hadn't been removed. He lifted it. It had been tampered with—and improved. It fitted his grip better now and was weighted for balance. A table was set with dishes of fruit and what looked like bread-gruel. He had been accommodated in all ways, more than he deserved from any city. It almost gave him the courage to be bold. He took off his ragged clothes and tried on the new set. They fit admirably, and he felt less disreputable. His sandals had been stitched up but not replaced. They were comfortable, as always, but sturdier.

"How can I fix myself here?" he asked the walls. No answer came. He drank water from the fountain again and went to explore further.

The ground plan of Mandala's lowest level was relatively simple. It consisted mostly of trade and commerce facilities, with spacious corridors for vehicle traffic, large warehouse areas, and dozens of conference rooms. Computing facilities were also provided. He knew a little about computers—the trade office in Bethel-Japhet still had an ancient pocket model taken from a city during the Exiling. The access terminals in Mandala were larger and clumsier, but recognizable. He came across a room filled with them. Centuries of neglect had made them irregular in shape, their plastic and thin metal parts warping. He wondered what portions of them, if any, were alive.

Most of the rooms on the lowest level maintained the sea-floor green motif. The uniformity added to Jeshua's confusion, but after several hours of wandering, he found the clue that provided guidance. Though nothing existed in the way of written directions or graphic signs or maps, by keeping to the left he found he tended to the center; and to the right, the exterior. A Mandalan of ten centuries ago would have known the organization of each floor by education, and perhaps by portable guidebooks or signalers. Somewhere, he knew, there had to be a central elevator system.

He followed all left-turning hallways. Avoiding obvious dead ends, he soon reached the base of a hollow shaft. The floor was tiled with a changing design of greens and blues, advancing and flowing beneath his feet like a cryptic chronometer. He craned his neck back and looked up through the center of Mandala. High above he saw a bluish circle, the waning daytime sky. Wind whistled down the shaft.

Jeshua heard a faint hum from above. A speck blocked out part of the skylight and grew as it fell, spiraling like a dropped leaf. It had wings, a thick body for passengers, and an insect head, like the dragonfly buttresses that provided ventilation on Mandala's exterior. Slowing its descent, it lifted its nose and came to a stop in front of him, still several feet above the floor. The bottoms of its unmoving transparent wings reflected the changing design of the floor.

Then he saw that the floor was coming to a conclusion, like an assembled puzzle. It formed a mosaic triskelion, a three-winged symbol outlined in red.

The glider waited for him. In its back there was room for at least five people. He chose the front seat. The glider trembled and moved forward. The insect-head tilted back, cocked sideways, and inspected its ascent. Metallic antennae emerged from the front of the body. A tingling filled the air. And he began to fly.

The glider slowed some distance above the floor and came to a stop at a gallery landing. Jeshua felt his heartbeat race as he looked over the black railing, down the thousand feet or so to the bottom of the shaft.

"This way, please."

He turned, expecting to see Thinner again. Instead there waited a device like a walking coat-tree, with a simple vibration speaker mounted on its thin neck, a rod for a body, and three appendages jointed like a mantis's front legs. He followed it.

Transparent pipes overhead pumped bubbling fluids like exposed arteries. He wondered whether dissenting citizens in the past could have severed a city's lifelines by cutting such pipes—or were these mere ornaments, symbolic of deeper activities? The coat-tree clicked along in front of him, then stopped at a closed hexagonal door and tapped its round head on a metal plate. The door opened. "In here."

Jeshua entered. Arranged in racks and rows in endless aisles throughout the huge room were thousands of constructions like Thinner. Some were incomplete, with their machinery and sealed-off organic connections hanging loose from trunks, handless arms, headless necks. Some had gaping slashes, broken limbs, squashed torsos. The coat-tree hurried off before he could speak, and the door closed behind.

He was beyond anything but the most rudimentary anxiety now. He walked down the central aisle, unable to decide whether this was a workshop or a charnel house. If Thinner was here, it might take hours to find him.

He stared straight ahead and stopped. There was someone not on the racks. At the far end of the room, it stood alone, too distant to be discerned in detail. Jeshua waited, but the figure did not move. It was a stalemate.

He made the first step. The figure darted to one side like a deer. He automatically ran after it, but by the time he'd reached the end of the aisle, it was nowhere to be seen.

"Hide and seek," he murmured. "For God's sake, hide and seek."

He rubbed his groin abstractedly, trying to still the flood of excitement rushing into his stomach and chest. His fantasies multiplied, and he bent over double, grunting. He forced himself to straighten up, held out his arms, and concentrated on something distracting.

He saw a head that looked very much like Thinner's. It was wired to a board behind the rack, and fluids pulsed up tubes into its neck. The eyes were open but glazed, and the flesh was ghostly. Jeshua reached out to touch it. It was cold, lifeless.

He examined other bodies more closely. Most were naked, complete in every detail. He hesitated, then reached down to touch the genitals of a male. The flesh was soft and flaccid. He shuddered. His fingers, as if working on their own, went to the pubic mound of a female figure. He grimaced and straightened, rubbing his hand on his pants with automatic distaste. A tremor jerked up his back. He was spooked now, having touched the lifeless forms, feeling what seemed dead flesh.

What were they doing here? Why was Mandala manufacturing thousands of surrogates? He peered around the racks of bodies, this way and behind, and saw open doors far beyond. Perhaps the girl—it must have been the girl—had gone into one of those.

He walked past the rows. The air smelled like cut grass and broken reed stems, with sap leaking. Now and then it smelled like fresh slaughtered meat, or like oil and metal.

Something made a noise. He stopped. One of the racks. He walked slowly down one aisle, looking carefully, seeing nothing but stillness, hearing only the pumping of fluids in thin pipes and the clicks of small valves. Perhaps the girl was pretending to be a cyborg. He mouthed the word over again.

Cyborg. He knew it from his schooling. The cities themselves were cybernetic organisms.

He heard someone running away from him, slap of bare feet on floor. He paced evenly past the rows, looking down each aisle, nothing, nothing, stillness, there! The girl was at the opposite end, laughing at him. An arm waved. Then she vanished.

He decided it was wise not to chase anyone who knew the city better than he did. Best to let her come to him. He left the room through an open door.

A gallery outside adjoined a smaller shaft. This one was red and only fifty or sixty feet in diameter. Rectangular doors opened off the galleries, closed but unlocked. He tested the three doors on his level, opening them one at a time with a push. Each room held much the same thing—a closet filled with dust, rotting and collapsed furniture, emptiness and the smell of old tombs. Dust drifted into his nostrils, and he sneezed. He went back to the gallery and the hexagonal door. Looking down, he swayed and felt sweat start. The view was dizzying and claustrophobic.

A singing voice came down to him from above. It was feminine, sweet and young, a song in words he did not completely catch. They resembled Thinner's chaser dialect, but echoes broke the meaning. He leaned out over the railing as far as he dared and looked up. It was definitely the girl—five, six, seven levels up. The voice sounded almost childish. Some of the words reached him clearly with a puff of direct breeze:

"Dis em, in solit lib, dis em . . . Clo'ed in clo'es ob dead . . ."

The red shaft vanished to a point without skylight. The unfamiliar glare hurt his eyes. He shaded them to see more clearly. The girl backed away from the railing and stopped singing.

He knew by rights he should be angry, that he was being teased. But he wasn't. Instead he felt a loneliness too sharp to sustain. He turned away from the shaft and looked back at the door to the room of cyborgs.

Thinner stared back at him, grinning crookedly. "Didn't have chance to welcome," he said in Hebrew. His head was mounted on a metal snake two feet long; his body was a rolling green car with three wheels, a yard long and half a yard wide. It moved silently. "Have any difficulty?"

Jeshua looked him over slowly, then grinned. "It doesn't suit you," he said. "Are you the same Thinner?"

"Doesn't matter, but yes, to make you comfortable."

"If it doesn't matter, then who am I talking to? The city computers?"

"No, no. They can't talk. Too concerned with maintaining. You're talking with what's left of the architect."

Jeshua nodded slowly, though he didn't understand.

"It's a bit complicated," Thinner said. "Go into it with you later. You saw the girl, and she ran away from you."

"I must be pretty frightening. How long has she been here?"

"A year."

"How old is she?"

"Don't know for sure. Have you eaten for a while?"

"No. How did she get in?"

"Not out of innocence, if that's what you're thinking. She was already married before she came here. The chasers encourage marriage early."

"Then I'm not here out of innocence, either."

"No."

"You never saw me naked," Jeshua said. "How did you know what was wrong with me?"

"I'm not limited to human senses, though El knows what I do have are bad enough. Follow me, and I'll find suitable quarters for you."

"I may not want to stay."

"As I understand it, you've come here to be made whole. That can be done, and I can arrange it. But patience is always a virtue."

Jeshua nodded at the familiar homily. "She speaks Chaser English. Is that why you were with the chasers, to find a companion for her?"

The Thinner-vehicle turned away from Jeshua without answering. It rolled through the cyborg chamber, and Jeshua followed. "It would be best if someone she was familiar with would come to join her, but none could be persuaded."

"Why did she come?"

Thinner was silent again. They took a spiral moving walkway around the central shaft, going higher. "It's the slow, scenic route," Thinner said, "but you'll have to get used to the city and its scale."

"How long am I going to stay?"

"As long as you wish."

They disembarked from the walkway and took one of the access halls to an apartment block on the outer wall of the city. The construction and colors here were more solid. The bulkheads and doors were opaque and brightly colored in blue, burnt orange, and purple. The total effect reminded Jeshua of a sunset. A long balcony in the outer wall gave a spectacular view of Arat and the plains, but Thinner allowed him no time to sightsee. He took Jeshua into a large apartment and made him familiar with the layout.

"It's been cleaned up and provided with furniture you should be used to. You can trade it in for somewhere else whenever you want. But you'll have to wait until you've been seen to by the medical units. You've been scheduled for work in this apartment." Thinner showed him a white-tile and stainless-steel kitchen, with food dispensers and basic utensils. "Food can be obtained here. There's enough material to customize whatever comes out of the dispensers. Sanitary units are in here and should explain themselves—"

"They talk?"

"No. I mean their use should be self-evident. Very few things talk in the city."

"We were told the cities were commanded by voice."

"Not by most of the citizens. The city itself does not talk

back. Only certain units, not like myself—none of the cyborgs were here when humans were. That's a later development. I'll explain in time. I'm sure you're more used to books and scrolls than tapes or tridvee experiences, so I've provided some offprints for you on these shelves. Over here—"

"Seems I'm going to be here for a long time."

"Don't be worried by the accommodations. This may be fancy by your standards, but it certainly isn't by Mandala's. These used to be apartments for those of an ascetic temper. If there's anything you want to know when I'm not here, ask the information desk. It's hooked to the same source I am."

"I've heard of the city libraries. Are you part of them?"

"No. I've told you, I'm part of the architect. Avoid library outlets for the moment. In fact, for the next few days, don't wander too far. Too much too soon, and all that. Ask the desk, and it will give you safe limits. Remember, you're more helpless than a child here. Mandala is not out-and-out dangerous, but it can be disturbing."

"What do I do if the girl visits me?"

"You anticipate it?"

"She was singing to me, I think. But she didn't want to show herself directly. She must be lonely."

"She is." Thinner's voice carried something more than a tone of crisp efficiency. "She's been asking a lot of questions about you, and she's been told the truth. But she's lived without company for a long time, so don't expect anything soon."

"I'm confused," Jeshua said.

"In your case, that's a healthy state of mind. Relax for a while; don't let unknowns bother you."

Thinner finished explaining about the apartment and left. Jeshua went out the door to stand on the terrace beyond the walkway. Light from God-Does-Battle's synchronous artificial moons made the snows of Arat gleam like dull steel in the distance. Jeshua regarded the moons with an understanding he'd never had before. Humans had brought them from the orbit of another world, to grace God-Does-Battle's nights.

The thought was staggering. People used to live there, a thousand years ago. What had happened to them when the cities had exiled their citizens? Had the lunar cities done the same thing as the cities of God-Does-Battle?

He went to his knees for a moment, feeling ashamed and primitive, and prayed to El for guidance. He was not convinced his confusion was so healthy.

He ate a meal that came as close as amateur instructions could make it to the simple fare of Bethel-Japhet. He then examined his bed, stripped away the covers—the room was warm enough—and slept.

Once, long ago, if his earliest childhood memories were accurate, he had been taken from Bethel-Japhet to a communion in the hills of Kebal. That had been years before the Synedrium had stiffened the separation laws between Catholic and Habiru rituals. His father and most of his acquaintances had been Habiru and spoke Hebrew. But prominent members of the community, such as Sam Daniel, had by long family tradition worshipped Jesus as more than a prophet, according to established creeds grouped under the title of Catholicism. His father had not resented the Catholics for their ideas.

At that communion, not only had Habiru and Catholic worshipped, but also the now-separate Muslims and a few diverse creeds best left forgotten. Those had been difficult times, perhaps as hard as the times just after the Exiling. Jeshua remembered listening to the talk between his father and a group of Catholics—relaxed, informal talk, without the stiffness of ceremony that had grown up since. His father had mentioned that his young son's name was Jeshua, which was a form of Jesus, and the Catholics had clustered around him like fathers all, commenting on his fine form as a six-year-old and his size and evident strength. "Will you make him a carpenter?" they asked jokingly.

"He will be a cain," his father answered.

They frowned, puzzled.

"A maker of tools."

"It was the making of tools that brought us to the Exiling," Sam Daniel said.

"Aye, and raised us from beasts," his father countered.

Jeshua remembered the talk that followed in some detail. It had stuck with him and determined much of his outlook as an adult, after the death of his father in a mining accident.

"It was the shepherd who raised us above the beasts by making us their masters," another said. "It was the maker of tools and tiller of the soil who murdered the shepherd and was sent to wander in exile."

"Yes," his father said, eyes gleaming in the firelight. "And later it was the shepherd who stole a birthright from his nomad brother—or have we forgotten Jacob and Esau? The debt, I think, was even."

"There's much that is confusing in the past," Sam Daniel admitted. "And if we use our eyes and see that our exile is made less difficult by the use of tools, we should not condemn our worthy cains. But those who built the cities that exiled us were also making tools, and the tools turned against us."

"But why?" his father asked. "Because of our degraded state as humans? Remember, it was the Habirus and Catholics—then Jews and Christians—who commissioned Robert Kahn to build the cities for God-Does-Battle and to make them pure cities for the best of mankind, the final carriers of the flame of Jesus and the Lord. We were self-righteous in those days and wished to leave behind the degraded ways of our neighbors. How was it that the best were cast out?"

"Hubris," chuckled a Catholic. "A shameful thing, anyway. The histories tell us of many shameful things, eh, lad?" He looked at Jeshua. "You remember the stories of the evil that men did."

"Don't bother the child," his father said angrily.

Sam Daniel put his arm around the shoulder of Jeshua's father, "Our debater is at it again. Still have the secret for uniting us all?"

Half-asleep, he opened his eyes and tried to roll over on the bed.

Something stopped him, and he felt a twinge at the nape of his neck. He couldn't see well—his eyes were watering and everything was blurred. His nose tickled and his palate hurt vaguely, as if something were crawling through his nostrils into the back of his throat. He tried to speak but couldn't. Silvery arms weaved above him, leaving grey trails of shadow behind, and he thought he saw wires spinning over his chest. He blinked. Liquid drops hung from the wires like dew on a web. When the drops fell and touched his skin, waves of warmth and numbness radiated.

He heard a whine, like an animal in pain, It came from his own throat. Each time he breathed, the whine escaped. Again the metal things bobbed above him, this time unraveling the wires. He blinked, and it took a long time for his eyelids to open again. There was a split in the ceiling, and branches grew down from it, one coming up under his vision and reaching into his nose, others holding him gently on the bed, another humming behind his head, making his scalp prickle. He searched for the twinge below his neck. It felt as if a hair was being pulled from his skin or a single tiny ant was pinching him. He was aloof; far above it, not concerned; but his hand still wanted to scratch and a branch prevented it from moving. His vision cleared for an instant, and he saw green enameled tubes, chromed grips, pale blue ovals being handed back and forth.

"A anna eh uh," he tried to say. "Eh ee uh." His lips wouldn't move. His tongue was playing with something sweet. He'd been given candy. Years ago he'd gone for a mouth examination—with a clean bill of health—and he'd been given a roll of sugar gum to tongue on the way home.

He sank back into his skull to listen to the talk by the fireside again. "Hubris," chuckled a Catholic.

"Habirus," he said to himself. "Hubris."

"A shameful thing, anyway—"

"Our debater is at it again. Still have the secret for uniting us all?"

"And raised us from beasts."

Deep, and sleep.

He opened his eyes and felt something in bed with him. He moved his hand to his crotch. It felt as if a portion of the bed had gotten loose and was stuck under his hip, in his shorts. He lifted his hips and pulled down the garment, then lay back, a terrified look coming into his face. Tears streamed from his eyes.

"Thanks to El," he murmured. He tried to back away from the vision, but it went with him, was truly a part of him. He hit the side of his head to see if it was still a time for dreams. It was real.

He climbed off the bed and stripped away his shirt, standing naked by the mirror to look at himself. He was afraid to touch it, but of itself it jerked and nearly made him mad with desire. He reached up and hit the ceiling with his fists.

"Great El, magnificent Lord," he breathed. He wanted to rush out the door and stand on the balcony, to show God-Does-Battle he was now fully a man, fully as capable as anyone else to accomplish any task given to him, including—merciful El!—founding and fathering a family.

He couldn't restrain himself. He threw open the door of the apartment and ran naked outside.

"BiGod!"

He stopped, his neck hair prickling, and turned to look.

She stood by the door to the apartment, poised like a jacklighted animal. She was only fourteen or fifteen, at the oldest, and slender, any curves hidden beneath a sacky cloth of pink and orange. She looked at him as she might have looked at a ravening beast. He must have seemed one. Then she turned and fled.

Devastated in the midst of his triumph, he stood with shoulders drooped, hardly breathing, and blinked at the afterimage of brown hair and naked feet. His erection subsided into a morning urge to urinate. He threw his hands up in the air, returned to the apartment, and went into the bathroom.

After breakfast he faced the information desk, squatting uncomfortably on a small stool. The front of the desk was paneled with green slats, which opened as he approached. Sensor cells peered out at him.

"I'd like to know what I can do to leave," he said.

"Why do you want to leave?" The voice was deeper than Thinner's, but otherwise much the same.

"I've got friends elsewhere, and a past life to return to. I don't have anything here."

"You have all of the past here, an infinite number of things to learn."

"I really just want out."

"You can leave anytime."

"How?"

"This is a problem. Not all of Mandala's systems cooperate with this unit—"

"Which unit?"

"I am the architect. The systems follow schedules set up a thousand years ago. You're welcome to try to leave—we certainly won't do anything to stop you—but it could be difficult."

Jeshua drummed his fingers on the panel for a minute. "What do you mean, the architect?"

"The unit constructed to design and coordinate the building of the cities."

"Could you ask Thinner to come here?"

"Thinner unit is being reassembled."

"Is he part of the architect?"

"Yes."

"Where are you?"

"If you mean, where is my central position, I have none. I am part of Mandala."

"Does the architect control Mandala?"

"No. Not all city units respond to the architect. Only a few."

"The cyborgs were built by the architect," Jeshua guessed.

"Yes."

Jeshua drummed his fingers again, then backed away from the desk and left the apartment. He stood on the terrace, looking across the plains, working his teeth in frustration. He seemed to be missing something terribly important.

"Hey."

He looked up. The girl was on a terrace two levels above him, leaning with her elbows on the rail.

"I'm sorry I scared you," he said.

"Dis me, no' terrafy. Li'l shock, but dat all mucky same-same 'ereber dis em go now. Hey, do, I got warns fo' you."

"What? Warnings?"

"Dey got probs here, 'tween Mandala an' dey 'oo built."

"I don't understand."

"No' compree? Lissy dis me, close, like all dis depen' on't: Dis em, was carry by polis 'en dis dey moob, week'r two ago. Was no' fun. Walk an' be carry, was I. No' fun."

"The city moved? Why?"

"To leeb behine de part dis dey call builder."

"The architect? You mean, Thinner and the information desks?"

"An' too de bods 'ich are hurt."

Jeshua began to understand. There were at least two forces in Mandala that were at odds with each other—the city and something within the city that called itself the architect.

"How can I talk to the city?"

"De polis no' talk."

"Why does the architect want us here?"

"Don' know."

Jeshua massaged his neck to stop a cramp. "Can you come down here and talk?"

"No' now dis you are full a man . . . Too mucky for dis me, too cashin' big."

"I won't hurt you. I've lived with it for all my life—can live a while longer."

"Oop!" She backed away from the rail.

"Wait!" Jeshua called. He turned and saw Thinner, fully corporeal now, leaning on the rounded corner of the access hall.

"So you've been able to talk to her," Thinner said.

"Yes. Made me curious, too. And the information desk."

"We expected it."

"Then can I have some sound answers?"

"Of course."

"Why was I brought here—to mate with the girl?"

"El! Not at all." Thinner gestured for him to follow. "I'm afraid you're in the middle of a pitched battle. The city rejects all humans. But the architect knows a city needs citizens. Anything else is a farce."

"We were kicked out for our sins," Jeshua said.

"That's embarrassing, not for you so much as for us. The architect designed the city according to the specifications given by humans—but any good designer should know when a program contains an incipient psychosis. I'm afraid it's set this world back quite a few centuries. The architect was made to direct the construction of the cities. Mandala was the first city, and we were installed here to make it easier to supervise construction everywhere. But now we have no control elsewhere. After a century of building and successful testing, we put community control into the city maintenance computers. We tore down the old cities when there were enough of the new to house the people of God-Does-Battle. Problems didn't develop until all the living cities were integrated on a broad plan. They began to compare notes, in a manner of speaking."

"They found humanity wanting."

"Simply put. One of the original directives of the city was that socially destructive people—those who did not live their faith as Jews or Christians—would be either reformed or exiled. The cities were constantly aware of human activity and motivation. After a few decades they decided everybody was socially destructive in one way or another."

"We are all sinners."

"This way," Thinner directed. They came to the moving walkway around the central shaft and stepped onto it. "The cities weren't capable of realizing human checks and balances. By the time the problem was discovered, it was too late. The cities went on emergency systems and isolated themselves, because each city reported that it was full of antisocials. They were never coordinated again. It takes people to reinstate the interurban links."

Jeshua looked at Thinner warily, trying to judge the truth of the story. It was hard to accept—a thousand years of self-disgust and misery because of bad design! "Why did the ships leave the sky?"

"This world was under a colony contract and received support only so long as it stayed productive. Production dropped off sharply, so there was no profit, and considerable expense and danger in keeping contact. There were tens of millions of desperate people here then. After a time, God-Does-Battle was written off as a loss."

"Then we are not sinners, we did not break El's laws?"

"No more than any other living thing."

Jeshua felt a slow hatred begin inside. "There are others who must learn this," he said.

"Sorry," Thinner said. "You're in it for the duration. We'll get off here."

"I will not be a prisoner," Jeshua said.

"It's not a matter of being held prisoner. The city is in for another move. It's been trying to get rid of the architect, but it can't—it never will. It would go against a directive for city cohesion. And so would you if you try to leave now. Whatever is in the city just before a move is catalogued and kept careful track of by watcher units."

"What can any of you do to stop me?" Jeshua asked, his face set as if he'd come across a piece of steel difficult to hammer. He walked away from the shaft exit, wondering what Thinner would try.

The floor rocked back and forth and knocked him on his hands and knees. Streamers of brown and green crawled over a near wall, flexing and curling. The wall came away, shivered as if in agony, then fell on its side. The sections around it did likewise until a modular room had been disassembled. Its contents were neatly packed by scurrying coat-trees, each with a fringe of arms and a heavier frame for loads. All around the central shaft, walls were being plucked out and rooms dismantled. Thinner kneeled next to Jeshua and patted him on the shoulder.

"Best you come with this unit and avoid the problems here. I can guarantee safe passage until the city has reassembled."

Jeshua hesitated, then looked up and saw a cantilever arch throwing out green fluid ropes like a spider spinning silk. The ropes caught on opposite bracings and the arch lowered itself. Jeshua stood up on the uncertain flooring and followed Thinner.

"This is only preliminary work," Thinner said as he took him into the cyborg room. "In a few hours the big structural units will start to come down, then the bulkheads, ceiling, and floor pieces, then the rest. By this evening, the whole city will be mobile. The girl will be here in a few minutes—you can travel together if you want to. This unit will give you instructions on how to avoid injury during reassembly."

But Jeshua had other plans. He did as Thinner told him, resting on one of the racks like a cyborg, stiffening as the girl came in from another door and positioned herself several aisles down. He was sweating profusely, and the smell of his fear nauseated him.

The girl looked at him curiously. "You know 'at dis you in fo'?" she asked.

He shook his head.

The clamps on the rack closed and held him comfortably but securely. He didn't try to struggle. The room was disassembling itself. Panels beneath the racks retracted, and wheels jutted out. Shivering with their new energy, the racks elevated and wheeled out their charges.

The racks formed a long train down a hall crowded with

scurrying machines. Behind them, the hall took itself apart with spewed ropes, fresh-spouted grasping limbs and feet, wheels and treads.

It was a dance. With the precision of a bed of flowers closing for the night, the city shrank, drew in, pulled itself down from the top, and packed itself onto wide-tread beasts with unfathomable jade eyes. The racks were put on the backs of a trailer like a flat-backed spider, long multiple legs pumping up and down smoothly. A hundred spiders like it carried the remaining racks, and thousands of other choreographed tractors, robots, organic cranes, cyborg monsters, waited in concentric circles around Mandala. A storm gathered to the south about Arat's snowy peaks. As the day went on and the city diminished, the grey front swept near, then over. A mantle of cloud hid the disassembly of the upper levels. Rain fell on the ranks of machines and half-machines, and the ground became dark with mud and trampled vegetation. Transparent skins came up over the backs of the spider-trailers, hanging from rigid foam poles. Thinner crawled between the racks and approached Jeshua, who was stiff and sore by now.

"We've let the girl loose," Thinner said. "She has no place to go but with us. Will you try to leave?"

Jeshua nodded.

"It'll only mean trouble for you. But I don't think you'll get hurt." Thinner tapped the rack, and the clamps backed away. Night was coming down over the storm. Through the trailer skin, Jeshua could see the city's parts and vehicles switch on interior lights. Rain streaks distorted the lights into ragged splashes and bars. He stretched his arms and legs and winced.

A tall tractor unit surmounted by a blunt-nosed cone rumbled up to the trailer and hooked itself on. The trailer lurched and began to move. The ride on the pumping man-thick legs was surprisingly smooth. Mandala marched through the rain and dark.

By morning, the new site had been chosen.

Jeshua lifted the trailer skin and jumped into the mud. He had slept little during the trek, thinking about what had happened and what he had been told. He was no longer meek and ashamed.

The cities were no longer lost paradises to him. They now had an air of priggishness. They were themselves flawed. He spat into the mud.

But the city had made him whole again. Who had been more responsible: the architect or Mandala itself? He didn't know and hardly cared. He had been taken care of as any unit in Mandala would have been, automatically and efficiently. He coveted his new wholeness, but it didn't make him grateful. It should have been his by a birthright of ten centuries. It had been denied by incompetence—and whatever passed as willful blindness in the cities.

He could not accept it as perpetual error. His people tended to think in terms of will and responsibility.

The maze of vehicles and city parts was quiet now, as if resting before the next effort of reassembly. The air was misty and grey with a heaviness that lowered his spirits.

" 'Ere dis you go?"

He turned back to the trailer and saw the girl peering under the skin. "I'm going to try to get away," he said. "I don't belong here. Nobody does."

"Lissy. I tol' de one, T-*Thi*nner to teach dis me . . . teach me how to spek li' dis you. When you come back, I know by den."

"I don't plan on coming back." He looked at her closely. She was wearing the same shift she wore when he first saw her, but a belt had tightened it around her waist. He took a deep breath and backed away a step, his sandals sinking in the mud.

"I don' know 'oo you are . . . who you are . . . but if Th-Thinner brought you, you must be a good person."

Jeshua widened his eyes. "Why?"

She shrugged. "Dis me just know." She jumped down

from the trailer, swinging from a rain-shiny leg. Mud splattered up her bare white calves.

"If you, dis me, t'ought . . . thought you were bad, I'd expec' you to brute me right now. But you don'. Even though you neba—never have a gol before." Her strained speech started to crack, and she laughed nervously. "I was tol' abou' you 'en you came. About your prob—lem." She looked at him curiously. "How do you feel?"

"Alive. And I wouldn't be too sure I'm not a danger. I've never had to control myself before."

The girl looked him over coquettishly.

"Mandala, it isn't all bad, no good," she said. "It took care ob you. Dat's good, is it no'?"

"When I go home," Jeshua said, drawing a breath, "I'm going to tell my people we should come and destroy the cities."

The girl frowned. "Li' take down?"

"Piece by piece."

"Too much to do. Nobod can do dat."

"Enough people can."

"No' good to do in firs' place. No' tall."

"It's because of them we're like savages now."

The girl shimmied up the spider's leg again and motioned for him to follow. He lifted himself and stood on the rounded lip of the back, watching her as she walked with arms balancing to the middle of the vehicle. "Look dis," she said. She pointed to the ranked legions of Mandala. The mist was starting to burn off. Shafts of sunlight cut through and brightened wide circles of the plain. "De polis, dey are li' not'ing else. Dey are de . . ." She sighed at her lapses. "They are the fines' thing we eba put together. We should try t'save dem."

But Jeshua was resolute. His face burned with anger as he looked out over the disassembled city. He jumped from the rim and landed in the pounded mud. "If there's no place for people in them, they're useless. Let the architect try to reclaim. I've got more immediate things to do."

The girl smiled slowly and shook her head. Jeshua stalked off between the vehicles and city parts.

Mandala, broken down, covered at least thirty square miles of the plain. Jeshua took his bearings from a tall rock pinnacle, chose the shortest distance to the edge, and sighted on a peak in Arat. He walked without trouble for a half hour and found himself approaching an attenuated concentration of city fragments. Grass grew up between flattened trails. Taking a final sprint, he stood on the edge of Mandala. He took a deep breath and looked behind to see if anything was following.

He still had his club. He held it in one hand, hefted it, and examined it closely, trying to decide what to do with it if he was bothered. He put it back in his belt, deciding he would need it for the long trip back to his expolis. Behind him, the ranks of vehicles and parts lurched and began to move. Mandala was beginning reconstruction. It was best to escape now.

He ran. The long grass made speed difficult, but he persisted until he stumbled into a burrow and fell over. He got up, rubbed his ankle, decided he was intact, and continued his clumsy springing gait.

In an hour he rested beneath the shade of a copse of trees and laughed to himself. The sun beat down heavily on the plain, and the grass shimmered with a golden heat. It was no time for travel. There was a small puddle held in the cup of a rock, and he drank from that, then slept for a while.

He was awakened by a shoe gently nudging him in the ribs.

"Jeshua Tubal Iben Daod," a voice said.

He rolled from his stomach and looked into the face of Sam Daniel the Catholic. Two women and another man, as well as three young children, were behind him jockeying for positions in the coolest shade.

"Have you calmed yourself in the wilderness?" the Catholic asked. Jeshua sat up and rubbed his eyes. He had nothing to fear. The chief of the guard wasn't acting in his professional capacity—he was traveling, not searching. And besides, Jeshua was returning to the expolis.

"I am calmer, thank you," Jeshua said. "I apologize for my actions."

"It's only been a fortnight," Sam Daniel said. "Has so much changed since?"

"I . . ." Jeshua shook his head. "I don't think you would believe."

"You came from the direction of the traveling city," the Catholic said, sitting on the soft loam. He motioned for the rest of the troop to rest and relax. "Meet anything interesting there?"

Jeshua nodded. "Why have you come this far?"

"For reasons of health. And to visit the western limb of Expolis Canaan, where my parents live now. My wife has a bad lung ailment—I think an allergic reaction to the new strain of sorghum being planted in the ridge paddies above Bethel-Japhet. We will stay away until the harvest. Have you stayed in other villages near here?"

Jeshua shook his head. "Sam Daniel, I have always thought you a man of reason and honor. Will you listen with an open mind to my story?"

The Catholic considered, then nodded.

"I have been inside a city."

He raised his eyebrows. "The one on the plain?"

Jeshua told him most of the story. Then he stood. "I'd like you to follow me. Away from the rest. I have proof."

Sam Daniel followed Jeshua behind the rocks, and Jeshua shyly revealed his proof. Sam Daniel stared. "It's real?" he asked. Jeshua nodded.

"I've been restored. I can go back to Bethel-Japhet and become a regular member of the community."

"No one has ever been in a city before. Not for as long as any remember."

"There's at least one other, a girl. She's from the city chasers."

"But the city took itself apart and marched. We had to change our course to go around it or face the hooligans following. How could anyone live in a rebuilding city?"

"I survived its disassembly. There are ways." And he told about the architect and its extensions. "I've had to twist my thoughts to understand what I've experienced," he said. "But I've reached a conclusion. We don't belong in the cities, any more than they deserve to have us."

"Our shame lies in them."

"Then they must be destroyed."

Sam Daniel looked at him sharply. "That would be blasphemous. They serve to remind us of our sins."

"We were exiled not for our sins, but for what we are—human beings! Would you kick a dog from your house because it dreams of hunting during Passover—or Lent? Then why should a city kick its citizens out because of their inner thoughts? Or because of a minority's actions? They were built with morals too rigid to be practical. They are worse than the most callous priest or judge, like tiny children in their self-righteousness. They've caused us to suffer needlessly. And as long as they stand, they remind us of an inferiority and shame that is a lie! We should tear them down to their roots and sow the ground with salt."

Sam Daniel rubbed his nose thoughtfully between two fingers. "It goes against everything the expolises stand for," he said. "The cities are perfect. They are eternal, and if they are self-righteous, they deserve to be. You of all should know that."

"You haven't understood," Jeshua said, pacing. "They are not perfect, not eternal. They were made by men—"

"Papa! Papa!" a child screamed. They ran back to the group. A black tractor-mounted giant with an angular bird-like head and five arms sat ticking quietly near the trees, Sam Daniel called his family back near the center of the copse and looked at Jeshua with fear and anger. "Has it come for you?"

He nodded.

"Then go with it."

Jeshua stepped forward. He didn't look at the Catholic as he said, "Tell them what I've told you. Tell them what I've done, and what I know we must do."

A boy moaned softly.

The giant picked Jeshua up delicately with a mandibled arm and set him on its back. It spun around with a spew of dirt and grass, then moved quietly back across the plain to Mandala.

When they arrived, the city had almost finished rebuilding. It looked no different from when he'd first seen it, but its order was ugly to him now. He preferred the human asymmetry of brick homes and stone walls. Its noises made him queasy. His reaction grew like steam pressure in a boiler, and his muscles felt tense as a snake about to strike.

The giant set him down in the lowest level of the city. Thinner met him there. Jeshua saw the girl waiting on a platform near the circular design in the shaft.

"If it makes any difference to you, we had nothing to do with bringing you back," Thinner said.

"If it makes any difference to you, I had nothing to do with returning. Where will you shut me tonight?"

"Nowhere," Thinner said. "You have the run of the city."

"And the girl?"

"What about her?"

"What does she expect?"

"You don't make much sense," Thinner said.

"Does she expect me to stay and make the best of things?"

"Ask her. We don't control her, either."

Jeshua walked past the cyborgs and over the circular design, now disordered again. The girl watched him steadily as he approached. He stopped below the platform and looked up at her, hands tightly clenched at his waist.

"What do you want from this place?" he asked.

"Freedom," she said. "The choice of what to be, where to live."

"But the city won't let you leave. You have no choice."

"Yes, the city, I can leave it whenever I want."

Thinner called from across the mall. "As soon as the city is put together, you can leave, too. The inventory is policed only during a move."

Jeshua's shoulders slumped, and his bristling stance softened. He had nothing to fight against now, not immediately. He kept his fists clenched, even so.

"I'm confused," he said.

"Stay for the evening," she suggested. "Then will you make thought come clear of confusion."

He followed her to his room near the peak of the city. The room hadn't been changed. Before she left him there, he asked what her name was.

"Anata," she said. "Anata Leucippe."

"Do you get lonely in the evenings?" he asked, stumbling over the question.

"Never," she said. She laughed and turned half-away from him. "An' now certes am dis em, you no' trustable!"

She left him by the door. "Eat!" she called from the corner of the access hall. "I be back, around mid of the evening."

He smiled and shut his door, then turned to the kitchen to choose what he was going to eat.

Being a whole man, he now knew, did not stop the pain of fear and loneliness. The possibility of quenching was, in fact, a final turn of the thumbscrew. He paced like a caged bear, thinking furiously and reaching no conclusions.

By midnight he was near an explosion. He waited in the viewing area of the terrace, watching the moonlight bathe God-Does-Battle like milk, gripping the railing with a strength that could have crushed wood. He listened to the noise of the city. It was less soothing than he remembered, neither synchronous nor melodic.

Anata came for him half an hour after she said she would. Jeshua had gone through so many ups and downs of despair and aloofness that he was exhausted. She took his hand and led him to the central shaft on foot. They found hidden curved stairwells and went down four levels to a broad promenade that circled a widening in the shart. "The walkway, it doesn't work yet," she told him. "My tongue, I'm getting it down. I'm studying."

"There's no reason you should speak like me," he said.

"It is difficult at times. Dis me—I cannot cure a lifetime ob—of talk."

"Your own language is pretty," he said, half-lying.

"I know. Prettier. Alive-o. But—" She shrugged.

Jeshua thought he couldn't be more than five or six years older than she was, by no means an insurmountable distance. He jerked as the city lights dimmed. All around, the walls lost their bright glow and produced in its stead a pale lunar gleam, like the night outside.

"This is what I brough' you here for," she said. "To see."

The ghost-moon luminescence made him shiver. The walls and floor passed threads of light between them, and from the threads grew spirits, shimmering first like mirages, then settling into translucent sharpness. They began to move.

They came in couples, groups, crowds, and with them were children, animals, birds, and things he couldn't identify. They filled the promenade and terraces and walked, talking in tunnel-end whispers he couldn't make out, laughing and looking and being alive, but not in Jeshua's time.

They were not solid, not robots or cyborgs. They were spirits from ten centuries past, and he was rapidly losing all decorum watching them come to form around him.

"Sh!" Anata said, taking his arm to steady him. "They don't hurt anybody. They're no' here. They're dreams."

Jeshua clasped his hands tight and forced himself to be calm.

"This is the city, what it desires," Anata said. "You want to kill the polis, the city, because it keeps out the people, but look—it hurts, too. It wants. What's a city without its people? Just sick. No' bad. No' evil. Can't kill a sick one, can you?"

Each night, she said, the city reenacted a living memory of the past, and each night she came to watch.

Jeshua saw the pseudolife, the half-silent existence of a billion recorded memories, and his anger slowly faded. His hands loosened their grip on each other. He could never sustain hatred for long. Now, with understanding just out of reach, but obviously coming, he could only resign himself to more confusion for the moment.

"It'll take me a long, long time to forgive what happened," he said.

"This me, too." She sighed. "When I was married, I found I could not have children. This my husband could not understand. All the others of the women in the group could have children. So I left in shame and came to the city we had always worshipped. I thought it would be, the city, the only one to cure. But now I don't know. I do not want another husband, I want to wait for this to go away. It is too beautiful to leave while it is still here."

"Go away?"

"The cities, they get old and they wander," she said. "Not all things work good here now. Pieces are dying. Soon it will all die. Even such as Thinner, they die. The room is full of them. And no more are being made. The city is too old to grow new. So I wait until the beauty is gone."

Jeshua looked at her more closely. There was a whitish cast in her left eye. It had not been there a few hours ago.

"It is time to go to sleep," she said. "Very late."

He took her gently by the hand and led her through the phantoms, up the empty but crowded staircases, asking her where she lived.

"I don't have any one room," she said. "Sleep in all of them at some time or another. But we can't go back dere." She stopped. "There. Dere. Can't go back." She looked up at him. "Dis me, canno' spek mucky ob—" She held her hand to her mouth. "I forget. I learned bu' now—I don't know . . ."

He felt a slow horror grind in his stomach.

"Something is going wrong," she said. Her voice became deeper, like Thinner's, and she opened her mouth to scream but could not. She tore away from him and backed up. "I'm doing something wrong."

"Take off your shirt," Jeshua said.

"No." She looked offended.

"It's all a lie, isn't it?" he asked.

"No."

"Then take off your shirt."

She began to remove it. Her hands hesitated.

"Now."

She peeled it over her head and stood naked, with her small breasts outthrust, narrow hips square and bonily dimpled, genitals flossed in feathery brown. A pattern of scars on her chest and breasts formed a circle. Bits of black remained like cinders, like the cinders on his own chest—from a campfire that had never been. Once, both of them had been marked like Thinner, stamped with the seal of Mandala.

She turned away from him on the staircase, phantoms drifting past her and through her. He reached out to stop her but wasn't quick enough. Her foot spasmed and she fell, gathering into a twisted ball, down the staircase, up against the railings, to the bottom.

He stood near the top and saw her pale blue fluid and red skinblood and green tissue leaking from a torn leg. He felt he might go insane.

"Thinner!" he screamed. He kept calling the name. The lunar glow brightened, and the phantoms disappeared. The halls and vaults echoed with his braying cry.

The cyborg appeared at the bottom of the staircase and knelt down to examine the girl.

"Both of us," Jeshua said. "Both lies."

"We don't have the parts to fix her," Thinner said.

"Why did you bring us back? Why not let us stay? And why not just tell us what we are?"

"Until a few years ago there was still hope," Thinner said. "The city was still trying to correct the programs, still trying to get back its citizens. Sixty years ago it gave the architect more freedom to try to find out what went wrong. We built ourselves—you, her, the others—to go among the humans and see what they were like now, how the cities could accommodate. And if we had told you this, would you have believed? As humans, you were so convincing you couldn't even go into cities except your own. Then the aging began, and the sickness. The attempt finally died."

Jeshua felt the scars on his chest and shut his eyes, wishing, hoping it was all a nightmare.

"David the smith purged the mark from you when you were a young cyborg, that you might pass for human. Then he stunted your development that you might someday be forced to come back."

"My father was like me."

"Yes. He carried the scar, too."

Jeshua nodded. "How long do we have?"

"I don't know. The city is running out of memories to repeat. Soon it will have to give up . . . less than a century. It will move like the others and strand itself someplace."

Jeshua walked away from Thinner and the girl's body and wandered down an access hall to the terraces on the outer wall of the city. He shaded his eyes against the rising sun in the east and looked toward Arat. There, he saw the city that had once occupied Mesa Canaan. It had disassembled and was trying to cross the mountains.

"Kisa," he said.

Many of the cities did not die quickly. They lingered on for more years, some as if by force of will, others by the fortune of their kind environments. Wherever they stood, the humans in their shadows lived with their minds fixed on a past splendor they could never have again . . . so they believed, for the universe was a hard place, and God's judgement harsh.

But not all exiles accepted that judgement.

And not all the cities, either, for a few were decaying in quite unexpected ways . . .

BOOK TWO
3460 A.D.

Resurrection

IT was the middle of the month Tammuz, and drought was on the land. The village of Akkabar squatted near the confluence of two streams normally deep enough for commerce, in an otherwise barren and featureless expanse where a single broad river had once flowed into the sea. The streams were now cracked mud. Some villagers thought the water table had dropped below most of the town's wells; others thought it was punishment from Allah for a multitude of sins. Yet where could one direct his prayers for forgiveness? They had all foresaken the Earth over a thousand years ago. Under the hot blue skies of God-Does-Battle, none could remember which direction Mecca was.

At forty, Reah was an ill-favored picker of rags and bagger of bones. She had decided, quite rationally, to take the way of the ghouls, trod only by nightmares and *ifrits*, of whom she might be one: a singularly well-disguised *ifrit*. Gradually her mind clouded in earnest and she went about scavenging trash. All this had come to pass in the ten years since the death of her husband and daughter in a fire.

Leavings in the town dump were sparse. She stood in her black cloak, face veiled against the dust and sun, dark eyes looking over the piles of broken rock, dry-dead livestock, broken pottery, old splintered boxes and a digging cat. Her worn sandals scuffed the baked dirt uncertainly. She turned and looked back at the northern gate of Akkabar. There was no longer enough here to keep her alive. People weren't throwing enough away.

She shuffled through the town gates, passing between sleepy guards too tired to kick her. She could satisfy her thirst at one of the few public wells still producing water, but hunger was pushing her hard. Drawing from her last resources of wit she waited for nightfall, stripped down in the moonlit empty square, and washed her only robe until it looked presentable enough to be worn by a poor wife. She affixed the cowl and veil so her scraggly hair wouldn't show through. With morning she waited on the outskirts of the market.

After the town dealers had set up their booths, she walked between the rows and pretended to examine the half-empty bins of produce. Boys with fly-whips watched her through slitted eyes as she looked at this shriveled fruit, then that. When she thought they weren't paying close attention, she withdrew one hand into a sleeve, clutching a half-rotten orange. The hand emerged empty.

She had palmed three pieces of fruit and was looking for the best route to leave when the market square manager appeared in front of her like a djinn out of the dust. "Who are you, woman?" he asked. She looked up and shook her head.

"You know what it means to steal?"

Reah turned and tried to shuffle away. The manager grabbed her arm and an orange fell from the sleeve. One of the boys laughed and retrieved the fruit. "These are hard times," the manager said. "We all need to eat." Reah looked at him hopefully. "Those who steal, steal from the mouths of our children. You know that?" His face was reddening and his eyes were elsewhere. Some inner fury was building and all of Reah's humble slouch and scared eyes couldn't satisfy it.

"Thieves have their hands cut off," he growled. "So it is

written, *billah*! So our fathers would have done it long ago. But in our misery and exile we've forgotten these laws. Now it is time to remember!"

Reah shook her head again, afraid to speak.

"I stoned a thief here last week!" the manager shouted, raising his hand. He brought it down on her head and she sprawled in the dirt. "Brothers, here's a thief! Spawn of *Iblis*, a stealer of food!"

The morning shoppers crowded around. Reah found no sympathy in their eyes. She stood and raised her hands defiantly, swaying back and forth, trying to make them go away with her power. They would learn better, tangling with an *ifrit*.

A rock whistled from the circle and struck her on the back. She forgot her fear and hunger and ran. The crowd followed like a single beast. She dodged a stone and fell against a slow-moving cart, then to the ground. The crowd circled again. She looked at their feet swinging under their robes and heard bells. A crowd of bronze bells circled her, ringing, buzzing like insects. Among them she saw a man with a strong face, a muezzin perhaps but still part of the crowd, eyes pitiless and glazed, slightly upturned, looking at the sky, stone clutched in his hand. He raised the hand.

She stood and clung to him. "I am thy suppliant," she rasped. "No one can deny my need."

He looked down on her and the crowd stopped. His eyes cleared and he cursed under his breath.

"*Ullah yáfukk' ny minch!*" the strong man exclaimed. Only a muezzin or a scholar would speak the old tongue so well.

"Allah wills it," she whispered, eyes almost commanding him. "You cannot refuse."

The man shook his head and raised his hand to stop the crowd. So was the custom—he could not deny a suppliant. She was in his care now and by his faith he must keep her from harm, at least for the moment. The crowd paced around them restlessly. Reah looked over his shoulder at the stones and hands and cold faces. "Wolves," she said. "I will fly before wolves."

"Stop," the man said. "She's not in her right mind. It isn't just to stone the sick—"

"Even the sick must obey the law," the manager said. She looked up into the strong man's face.

"He's right," he said. "You have to leave the town or they'll stone you."

She nodded. There was little about the next hour that she remembered. Only the dipper of water, the giving of a knapsack filled with stale bread and a few figs, the cup of *leban* from the near-empty jar of the muezzin's wife. He brought out a worn water-skin and took her to the south gate, pointing her direction. She must circle around Akkabar and head north, but not until dusk. Her life in Akkabar was over. He said a prayer for her and sat under the shadow of an abandoned lean-to by the gate.

"At night," he said. "When it is cool. *Shalaym alaycham*." For the prayer and the farewell he fell into the more colloquial tongue of the city politicians. He gave her the skin of water and returned through the gate.

Reah looked out steadily at the flat river plain until her eyes watered. She slept for a while and awoke to the distant sounds of hunting night-insects. Dusk was settling. She stood carefully, dusted her cloak off, and began to walk around the walls until she was going north.

To the north lived the Habiru, more prosperous than the Moslems but still cursed. They might give her food and shelter. She fingered a string of clay beads as she walked, saying scattered prayers, long-engrained thanks for choice rags, clean bones, bits of metal and glass or edible food.

No living city had ever wandered onto the alluvial plain. A thousand years ago, before the Exiling, the old river had flowed across all of this land. In the memory of the cities, water still ran here. They stayed on the other side of the mountains, or in the foothills six kilometers away. Reah shaded her eyes and saw the outline of towers directly north. There was nothing for her in a living city.

She had been close to one of the cities as a young girl, on a trip with her father and mother to barter with the Habiru. That was before trade restrictions had tightened between Christians, Jews, and the few Moslem communities. It had been a glorious thing, its towers glowing and humming in the night, like a magic green tree filled with insects. They had camped under the light of two full moons, sharing a picnic supper with the families of her father's business partners. One of the old women, a spinner of tales to three generations, had told them first about the building of the moons, how trained birds big as mountains had hauled loads of mud-brick into the sky. One of the young men, testing his masculine authority, had offered an alternate version—that the moons had been brought from other worlds. Reah preferred the first version now. The families had gone over the old stories about the living cities, how the prodigal Jew Robert Kahn had designed them to the specifications of the Last of the Faithful . . . how they had been built from the seeds of a thousand altered species, and made to incorporate steel and stone and other materials which were now lost secrets . . . and, as the night grew old and the fires cooled, they listened with damp eyes to the Exiling.

She shuffled under the sun, host to a swarm of unorganized memories. She didn't see the troop of men keeping step with her to one side, laughing and shushing each other.

"Woman, where are you from?" one called.

She turned and squinted at them, then continued walking. They came closer.

"She's from the town," one said. "Durragon's there now . . ."

They blocked her path. The largest of them reached out and pulled back her cowl. "Hag, dis ol' gol, hag all aroun'. Hard by t'use dis ol' gol."

"She's a woman," another said. The older men backed away, smiling and shaking their heads. The younger ones closed in, faces troubled. "Dis em neba had a gol befo', ol', bri' o de skin, nor kine't all!"

"She'll do," another young one said.

They pulled her to the ground, took off her robes, and raped her. She ignored them, dreaming of the living cities and their cool green spires, assuaging her thirst with the memories.

When they were done, they left her in the waning daylight and continued patrolling south. She stood and gathered her supplies, then found a scrawny bush and slept under it. It was harder getting up to the pale dawn, harder to walk under the growing heat. She rationed her water carefully, but ate the food quickly. Different masters controlled her actions. Her stiff, knotted hair crackled in the heat.

Another party of soldiers passed by. She was like a ghost, lurching into the thin breeze, arms held out. Somewhere behind her was the empty water sack and the last of the crumbs. Her clay necklace lay under the bush where she'd slept. The soldiers watched her with mixed fear and disgust, then went south to join their army. Rifle fire echoed across the river plain.

By nightfall she was sitting under cottonwood trees and drinking from a shallow spring. She was sure she had entered the first stage of Paradise. Still, the men said that in Paradise women served, and she didn't like that idea. *Ifrits* did not serve. They were mean as scorpions when crossed.

In the morning she ate a few shreds of grass and nuts dug from a seed-pod, which made her faintly ill. By afternoon, following an overgrown dirt path, she found a Habiru village. It had been burned to the ground and the stone walls knocked over, probably by evil giants. The village overlooked the plain and from its southern end she had a good view of the two river beds and Akkabar. Holding her nose against the lingering smell of dead flesh, she looked back at her home and squinted. Smoke was rising from the center of the town. A grey mass of specks surrounded the mud and stone walls. In an hour, the pillar of smoke was black and tall. "I really *am* an *ifrit*," she murmured. "Soldiers rub the walls and out I pour in a cloud of soot, to sit in the hills and laugh."

She left the dead Habiru village and followed the road to a high grassland beyond, swatting at the insects which clung to her bare, peeling arms. Her strength was rapidly fading. She managed to keep walking until her feet struck clear, glass pavement. Her legs still kicked after she fell.

An hour passed and she lay motionless under the stars, eyes closed, lulled by a pleasant hum. Something beautiful was near. She opened her eyes and pulled a final moment of reason from her reserves. She was on her back, nearly dead. Beyond her feet was a tall, intricate arch, polished and green, glowing with its own light and exhaling a warm wind.

Perhaps she was already dead. She was on the perimeter of a living city. The pavement around her should have bristled into an impenetrable barricade, keeping all humans out. Then her reason slipped away and she sang weakly to herself, until strong mandibles closed around her legs and shoulders and she was taken through the arch, into the pale underwater luminosity.

Durragon the Apostate, commander of three thousand Chasers and a handful of Expolitan grumblers, felt a vague regret about the smoking Moslem town. He kicked aside a pile of rags filled with bloody meat and stood in the middle of the ruin, eyes half-closed, trying to think. The smell was awful. The Chasers were marvelous scrappers but no good at restraint. Still, they were the only thing between him and anonymity. They obeyed his orders with a kind of reverence, if only because he could kill any two of them in combat, and had. But it didn't make much sense, economically speaking, to let them continue. It was time to risk their contempt and demand discretion in the looting.

He put his hand on the bare, scabbed shoulder of his left-flank runner, Breetod, and spoke into his ear. "Take the three torchers into the market. I'm not happy with this, not happy at all. We could have lived here a while. Now even the grain stores are burned."

Breetod's face fell into unhappy creases, but he ran off to carry out the orders. Durragon took out his pistol and loaded it thoughtfully. He walked through the rubble to where the market had been, sidestepping the charred bodies.

The three torchers stood by the jagged black heaps of the market stalls, hands folded, grinning nervously. One of them took a step forward and was restrained by Breetod.

"Dis we, no' try t'—"

"Quiet," Durragon said softly. His stomach twisted. He didn't like this at all, but it was necessary. Without him, they would still be unorganized savages. They were like children. Sometimes their discipline had to be harsh. He took out his pistol. The torchers stopped smiling.

Other Chasers stood around, grim and silent. He motioned them away from his line of fire.

"Day-o," the youngest torcher moaned.

His teeth gritted, Durragon pulled the trigger three times. The Chasers broke up and walked to the outskirts of the ruins, where their camp-followers waited. The rest of the marauders were on the other side of the town, searching the rubble for scraps of molten gold and silver. Akkabar had been a poor town. They weren't likely to find much.

Reah thought a clear, untroubled thought for the first time in ten years. She stood in the middle of a clean white room with a bunk in one corner, a green-tinted window along one wall, and a very strange desk which might have been a wash basin. Something like music came out of the ceiling, which was a flowing, oily gold color. She turned around slowly and saw the open doorway and a hall beyond. Her hair was clean and straight, even faintly scented. She wore a white gown, not flattering—she had let herself go too long to be flattered by clothing—and a pair of sandals made from some soft fiber. It was delightful. She waited a moment for the uncertainties and clouds of insects to rise in her head, but all was still. She had a mild headache and was hungry, but she was no longer an *ifrit*.

She walked out the door and through the clean white hall until she reached a balcony, two floors above a courtyard. The music followed her. She peered over the railing. The floor of the circular mall below was an indescribable gray-green color. Looking closer, she saw it wasn't a solid color at all—the floor was a mosaic of tiny moving patterns, forming geometric forests with the slowness of a burning candle. A hundred meters away, four people dressed in white and orange robes strolled on the edge of the mall. Birds flew over them, through a wide gateway flanked by green arches. Her throat seized up and she thought she was going to cry.

"Hello," a male voice said behind her. She turned to look, lower lip quivering. He was about thirty, with black hair and dark, tan skin, a few centimeters taller than Reah but not much stockier. His nose was small with delicate nostrils, and his eyes were gray like fine clay dirt. He looked well-fed and healthy.

"I'm in a city, aren't I?" she said. "But it's supposed to be empty." Her hands fluttered nervously across the front of her robe, reaching for frayed ends of a shawl she no longer wore.

"This one doesn't have much control any more. It's dying, like an old person. Some parts still work, others don't. It lets sick people in. Can we help you?"

"I'm better now . . . I can feel it. Is this a hospital?"

"All cities were made to treat their citizens. You're the one found on the paving outside—from a Moslem town, right?"

"I saw Akkabar burning. My town. Was I dreaming?"

The man shook his head. "Akkabar was destroyed two weeks ago. We watched it from the Tower Plaza, near the top. I don't think many escaped. You're the only one in Resurrection. That's what this city is called. You must have walked fifty, sixty kilometers."

She thought that over for a moment, then held her hand out to touch him and see if he was real. He looked down at her fingers on his arm and she withdrew them quickly, backing away. "I—we heard stories that the cities made things like people . . . shaped like us. There was one in Akkabar when I was a girl. Someone killed him in a duel. He was like a plant and a machine inside. Are you human?"

"Flesh and blood. All of us are. Most of us come from Bethel-Yakob. Why don't you go back to your room—"

"I'd rather stay here."

"Whatever you want."

"Did the city fix you, too?"

He nodded. "Most of Expolis Capernahum was slaughtered by Durragon and his Chasers. We were wounded."

Reah shook her head slowly, not knowing what to believe. "I remember walking through a Habiru village. Yours?"

"Probably not. I'm from twenty kilometers northeast of here."

"When will Durragon come for us?"

The man smiled. "He won't. The city only lets injured people in. We're all of a kind here. Patients." He pulled up a sleeve and showed her his upper arm. It was covered with a milky-white, skin-tight bandage.

Reah looked up and closed her eyes. Above the mall, a shaft of orange and red and white seemed to extend to infinity. She looked again and saw that the white bands were circles of rectangular balconies, and the red horizontal strips were massive support beams. Orange trim relieved the red with abstract and geometric designs. It was pure magic, an air shaft in a living city. She was no longer an *ifrit*, but she was still surrounded by the stuff of legends. "Who is Durragon?"

"A tyrant, a butcher." The man's lips curled, almost theatrically. "He wants to be a new Herod, a Caesar."

Her thoughts seemed to hiccup. She wasn't used to thinking clearly. How much easier to drift from distortion to distortion . . . and how much more terrifying! She remembered nothing but fear. She followed the man back to her room and sat on the bunk, smelling the cleanness, the order, the kindness. "You," she called as the man started to leave. He turned and raised an eyebrow. "You know . . ." She paused. "I'll never be afraid again, not that way."

He nodded. "My name is Belshezar Iben Sulaym. And yours?"

"Reah," she replied. "Wife to Abram Khaldun."

"Is he dead?"

"Years dead," she said.

"You were still weeping for him, three nights ago."

"No more. Nothing is worth that much grief."

He smiled sympathetically and left.

"Gerat, Manuay, Persicca and Tobomar; they have sacked four towns and found sixteen hundred head of cattle. Captured three hundred women and young boys, recovered three hundred tons of various grains, and some weapons which I let them keep." Breetod read the list slowly, squinting at the scrawled figures. His opposite, the right flank runner Nebeki, sat chewing a flap of giant snail flesh, nodding as the names of the troop leaders were read off.

"Ferda, Comingory and Flavin; they have sacked two co-op farms and a village. Fifty cattle, twenty-seven women, ten tons of grain."

"They killed too many," Durragon said. His leather camp chair creaked as he leaned forward in the hot shadow. A bead of sweat fell from his nose and splashed on the leather floor. "Cut their share by a tenth and lash Comingory across the open palm, twice."

"Too much shame," Nebeki advised. "A tenth cut is enough, sir, if I may speak."

Durragon shrugged. "Tell him he deserves the lash, but I have high hopes for his strength in future raids, and graciously spare him. Is that all?"

Breetod assented and looked at Durragon with crazed, dogs-blue eyes as the Apostate walked to the tent flap and lifted it. "No more towns left," he said. "And I always wanted to put my capitol here. Now, because of our . . . perhaps it is best to say *enthusiasm*, I can't even support my army here. Not for another three or four years. So where next?''

Nebeki dropped his scraps into a wooden bowl and wiped his hands on a towel hung from a tent-pole. ''Before we go, sir, we can try the city on the high plain.''

''We can't get in.''

''My runners passed it a week ago. They say it's dying fast. A third of its towers are grey. Soon the spikes will go down and we can hunt for weapons and jewelry, even machinery if we can tame it.''

Durragon scowled. He had lost a finger to a marauding city part as a child. The beasts that poured out of a dead city were too unpredictable for his taste; his father had made a living taming them, but the predilection wasn't hereditary.

''Water supply and good land,'' Breetod said. ''A city always puts its roots down in fine soil. We can settle around it and wait a few months for it to die.'' He savored the idea of a rest.

Durragon cocked his head to one side, thinking hard for several minutes while his flank runners were respectfully silent, then agreed with a barely perceptible nod. ''Breetod will keep track of the bearers and the loot. We'll return to Expolis Capernahum. Maybe a few of the Habiru have rebuilt and we can trade with them for seed, plant a crop while we sit.''

Nebeki looked at Breetod, who returned his glance with a warning purse of the lips. Despite Durragon's ancestry, he knew little about either the Habiru or farming. Neither the survivors nor the land they were in would be tractable, but there was little chance of danger—just boredom.

Reah sat before the console with a grim expression. She knew she was ignorant, and therefore helpless, but the idea of talking with something not human was more than she could calmly accept. Belshezar watched from the other side of the apartment, leaning against a white ceramic ovoid half-buried in the floor. Beside him was a black-haired, sharp-faced woman named Rebecca. Behind them, under the broad picture-window which overlooked a promenade and indoor park, was a pile of rubble which had once been furniture. Reah swiveled on her bench.

"Everyone in Resurrection had one of these?"

"Every apartment," Belshezar said. "They were as common as windows and more important. Children learned from them, the people saw what was happening to their world in them."

Green louvres on the console swung open at her touch and a fluid turquoise triangle shimmered on the flat screen. Beneath the screen was a plate about thirty centimeters across with two keyboards on either side, designed to fit the viewer's fingers with a minimum of effort. She touched the index finger button and a human image appeared on the plate, palm-high, a sexless homunculus dressed in skin-tight black.

"May I answer?" it asked, speech thickly accented.

"It's hard to understand," Reah said, looking back at them. Belshezar was tapping his fingers on the ovoid, looking across at Rebecca with a tolerant smile. "It's English the way they spoke it a thousand years ago," Rebecca said.

"What do I do now?"

"Ask it questions." She tossed back her red hair. "It'll answer your question."

"Not just any question," Belshezar corrected. "Remember—the cities haven't been inhabited for centuries. The memory files aren't up to date. It doesn't know about a lot of outside events—though it does seem to know a few things about other cities. We suppose they talk to each other now and then. Excuse us, we have to meet friends elsewhere—can you take care of yourself here?"

Reah nodded hesitantly. "Good," Belshezar said. He patted her lightly—almost condescendingly—on the shoulder and left her alone in the apartment. She sniffed the cool air and bent closer to examine the homunculus. It returned her gaze steadily. She couldn't tell if it was male or female, and the voice was no clue. The people in those times, before the Exiling, must have been very different, even though they shared the faiths of Yahweh and Allah. "I'm ignorant," she said hesitantly. "That makes me weak. I need to learn."

"Where shall we begin?" the homunculus asked.

"I wish to know what happened. History. Then I'd like to be generally educated."

"We'll mix them, okay? Listen and watch close, pupil."

For the first day's lessons, the console taught her in real time, and it went slowly. The next day, it told her to insert her fingers into the accelerated transfer terminals, little depressions above the keyboards. She felt a prickly sensation, then a warmth up her backbone and a bright spot between her eyes. The learning went more rapidly. On the third day, it told her how to look into patterns generated by special projectors around the screen. On the fourth day she was much less weak, and very little like the old Reah.

Breetod presented the tamed city part to Durragon on his birthday. It had been captured a week earlier by a band of Chasers hunting on a mountain ridge fifteen miles north. It wasn't graceful—it looked more like a sawhorse than a real horse—but it was large and fast and obeyed well enough. Durragon walked around it and looked it over without enthusiasm. He mounted and sat uncomfortably in the makeshift saddle.

"We were thinking it should be called Bucephalus," Breetod said. Nebeki smiled. The bodyguards and Durragon's personal troops looked on, weary from the march.

The thing's back was smooth and soft as leather, but translucent and green like a young tree stem. Under the skin blue veins gathered in squares, and beneath them shone the paleness of metal parts and colloid bones. Its head was a cluster of eyes on flexible stalks. Its mouth was a tube through which it absorbed water and soil nutrients. There was a plug in one leg, now corroded over; it hadn't had a city-provided meal in at least twenty years. Its gait was regular and comfortable. "I don't like the name," Durragon said, dismounting. "What was it used for?"

"In the cities, sir?" Nebeki asked hesitantly. "It was a toy for children, I think."

"I want another name." He walked toward the shade of a cluster of mulcet trees. A table had been set up there, with charts spread across it, held down by stones. On one side of the table was an advisor, the old Habiru, Ezeki Iben Tav. Ezeki was lean and wrinkled, his forehead burned leather-brown by the sun, but his bald pate fading to almost white where it was usually covered by a ragged knit cap. He claimed to have been a teacher years before. He was using the cap to fan himself now as he traced a course on one map with his sharp-nailed finger. "What was Bucephalus?" Durragon asked him.

"A brain disorder among the Politans in the early years of this planet," Ezeki said. Durragon humphed and looked at the charts.

"Why would anyone name a mount that?" he wondered.

Sweating under the hot sun, Nebeki and Breetod were arguing. "I only spoke the truth," Nebeki said. "And the name was yours, besides."

"Ezeki told me about Alexander. You shouldn't have told him it was a toy. It'll make him reluctant to use it and we'll have to lead the litter."

What to do with a fabled city . . .

She took a drink of clear, cold water from a fountain in an upper-level park. The grass was tended by organic machines which ate the cuttings and fertilized the lawns. Irrigation hoses wormed underground and aerated the soil at the same time. The trees were trimmed by things with the attributes of giraffes, rose bushes and silvery shears. What struck her most of all was the coherent motif. Each part obviously belonged to the city as a whole, wearing just the right shapes with the proper angles and curves, carrying a certain neatness in every portion. Those places in the city which were completely healthy were like a child's dream as imagined by civic-minded adults—beauty mixed with fantasy, utility with crazy ingenuity.

The loss of the cities must have driven the Expolitans nearly mad. God-Does-Battle was a fine world, capable of supporting as wide a variety of life as old Earth, but it was a hard, nature-bound place. She shook her head. The planet had adapted to humanity long generations ago, after the artificial controls had failed. Misery and despair and disease had returned; at times, it seemed God-Does-Battle was trying to eat them alive. Against these odds, the Expolitans had made a place for themselves, blunted the planet's attacks, and settled down to the sort of catch-as-catch-can existence that Reah and nine or ten generations before her grew familiar with. All that time, the cities had seemed to mock them.

But what could she do about it?

All the cities had been connected by formal communications links. Though each city had been autonomous, they had shared in the spiritual policing and had reported their progress to each other, hour by hour.

It had taken less than a century for the cities to make their final decision. One awful morning, the cities coordinated and cast out all their citizens. In accord with emergency procedures guaranteeing the ostracism of spiritually diseased communities, the links between the cities broke down. The people wandered homeless through the park-like forests and fields. There was wide-spread starvation, violence. No ship from outside dared to land, lest the cities commandeer their vehicles or the citizens destroy them in a frenzy.

By themselves, the cities could do nothing to change things. Some had apparently tried and failed. People would have to take the initiative. But for a thousand years they had tried and failed, too.

Could she manage any better?

Reah looked back on her life and saw herself as three

different people: first, the contented, ignorant wife of the Moslem blacksmith; second, the insane harridan; and third, the comfortable, sane and very educated . . . what? Redeemer of Resurrection?

None of the other inhabitants paid much attention to her, and on the whole she distrusted them. They were friendly but didn't seem to appreciate what had been given to them. They were almost irresponsible in the way they enjoyed Resurrection. Once, while walking, she caught Rebecca and Belshezar making love in an upper-level fountain. She shuddered. And yet . . . They were only enjoying themselves after years of deprivation and past months of battle and agony. She felt the temptation to let loose, too, but laxity of body and character was not that far from laxity of mind, which she found abhorrent. Never again the fear.

As she sat on a bench in the park, near a sparkling column of glass carrying fluid nutrients to the highest reaches of the city, she began to fall in love again, not with luxury and ease, but with the idea her ancestors had once had. Outside there was no holiness in the suffering, and nothing to look forward to but a long, grinding crawl back to the level of society which had made the cities. Inside, there was hope of a sudden leap, benefiting from past experience.

To realize that, she had to learn how to control the city, and how to doctor it. Somewhere in the city's memory there had to be instructions. She stood on the grass and put her arms around the fluid-rushing column, eyes wet. "Allah, Allah," she said. "Preserve me! This is madness again, I can't dream such things. Only days ago I was filthy and near death. Who am I to wish to control Paradise?"

Then she wiped her eyes and stepped back, hands tingling from the living sound of the city's blood. This wasn't madness returning, or at least it was only madness fighting more madness—the demented exile of a thousand years.

"It's time to go back," she whispered, uneasy about talking to herself. "We have fallen below humanity, and now we must return."

* * *

Durragon looked across the field at the tide of the marching city. His neck hair was on end. "It came out of the western hills three hours ago," Breetod said. Now it was blocking the army's path.

"It's very sick," Nebeki said. "It moves slow. A lot of the pieces are dead."

"It's like a woman without a man," Durragon said. "A ghost wandering from place to place."

Nebeki glanced at Breetod and raised an eyebrow. Durragon was seldom poetic; the sight of the old city obviously moved him.

"We think it is the city called Tomoye," Breetod said. "It sat on a hill to the west for sixty years while most of the other cities killed themselves on the razor-ridge mountains." Two years before, Durragon's armies had crossed the mountains and seen the ruins.

"Bring me the Habiru," Durragon said. Nebeki trotted off to fetch the teacher. The old thin man complained beneath his breath as he was prodded up the sandy hummock to where Durragon sat on his green mount.

"What is it, General?" he asked, suddenly obsequious. He bowed before the multi-eyed head of the city part.

"How many cities are there now?"

"A handful, General. Most are dissolved, dead or with their parts gone rogue."

"How many?"

Ezeki Iben Tav pursed his lips. "In this area, three perhaps. The closest is the city on the high plain. I saw it many times as a youngster. No doubt it's dying as fast as this one." He pointed to the marching columns, supports, and bulkheads, with their attendant carriers and spider-leg guides. "I don't know if it will ever come together again, when it reaches its destination. It doesn't look very organized."

Grey clouds were spilling over the mountains to the east and the air was thick with humidity. Durragon had difficulty getting a satisfactory breath. He was used to colder southern climes. "Do you recommend capturing any of the parts?"

The Habiru squinted at the procession and shook his head. Always better to be cautious; one seldom lost one's head by being conservative. "No," he said. "Too many guides and defenders. Chop up the army like blades of grass."

Durragon stood up in the saddle and sniffed the breeze blowing west. Breetod did likewise but smelled nothing unusual.

"I disagree. Nebeki, move the runners and their divisions into formation this side of the city. Breetod, put half your runners and men to harrying to rear and picking up stragglers. Caution them that no parts are to be injured. Take the other half and see if you can stop the city—you personally in the lead. What are you waiting for?"

"I'm off," Breetod said, turning on his heel and running. Durragon sat back in the saddle and sighed. The old Habiru caught an acrid smell and thought, "The man's scared."

Durragon was remembering the loss of his finger many years ago. A rogue city part, like a butcher shop's rack of knives set on cylinder, had fled a band of his father's hunters and run Durragon down. He had been lucky to survive.

"Something that big must have a thinking part," he said to the Habiru. "Something to keep it organized. Catch the brain, and we will know how a city works. Maybe then . . ."

"It's been tried," the old man snapped. He bowed and said, more softly, "Many times others have tried, but the cities were too strong."

"This city isn't strong any more, you said so yourself. We'll treat it just like we'd treat an army."

The Habiru held his counsel. He wanted to mention that all the armies they had fought this far had been poorly equipped and weakened by drought and hunger. He watched the clouds boiling above the mountains, spinning in the hot updrafts of air from the lower hills.

Perhaps Durragon was right. No city had ever come this

close to the old alluvial plain. But then, would the brain of a city so foolish be worth capturing?

"Will it rain?" Durragon asked.

"No," the old man said wearily. "Not here. Look at the clouds. They're starting to break up already." They could both feel the humidity decreasing, being sucked out of the air.

"None of us gives any thought to it," Rebecca said, clinging to Belshezar's arm. She sounded resentful. "We're not sure how much Resurrection will put up with . . . we're mostly healed now. It could throw all of us out any minute." There was going to be a dance. Already the patients were arriving in clothes designed a thousand years ago, but created only a few hours before.

"Have you found instructions, though?" Reah asked. "On how to run the city, keep it clean . . ."

"It does all that all by itself," Belshezar said. "It doesn't need anything."

"But it's dying." Reah pointed to a broad grey spot on the atrium ceiling. The rows and rows of empty seats were browning and spotting like handfuls of autumn leaves. "Perhaps we can save it."

"It takes thousands of years for a city to die," Rebecca said. "We'll all be dust before that happens."

"Well," Belshezar said, "that's not exactly true. A city can die in a few decades. But this one—the parts we live in, anyway—will last out our lifetimes easily."

"We should just stay here and not interfere, then," Reah mused.

"Would it be better to live outside?" Rebecca asked, her eyes wide and lips thinned. "You came here by the grace of God, to live in luxury as one of the chosen—"

"No," Reah interrupted firmly. "Not chosen. I came here perhaps by Allah's will, but not to sit and watch everything rot. You won't help?"

Belshezar looked at the floor. "Too much risk. You shouldn't interfere. Haven't we been good to you, helped you?"

Reah stood silent in front of them for a few seconds. "There aren't many of you," she said. "You could spend days finding me if I wanted to get lost."

Rebecca's mouth dropped open, showing her bottom teeth. "What . . ." Her eyes narrowed, as if she had suddenly seen Reah in a clear light. "We've been here longer. We know the city better. Don't make us throw you out."

"You don't have the power to throw anyone out!" Reah spat. Belshezar reached out to take her arm but she backed away, soft dress swirling.

"Then leave by yourself," Rebecca said. "Leave us alone!"

Reah shook her head. She turned away and Belshezar began to follow. "Wait a moment," he said. "Let's talk about this—" She ran. Before he could reach her she clambered into a bee-shaped flier and told it to take her to the city's peak.

As the flier rose in a slow spiral, Belshezar and Rebecca stood on the floor below, finally merging into the grand lily design which folded and unfolded in the cool green light.

The city's peak rose twelve hundred meters above the high plains. The air was colder and thinner so high, making it hard for her to breathe. She left the vehicle at the landing platform with orders to stay and walked through the arched buttresses which supported the city's crest. Above and below the porch surrounding the shaft were garden levels, terraced and provided with waterfalls and streams. The air smelled of flowers, but half the gardens were a riot now, untended by organic machines which lay in moldering ruins. God-Does-Battle's wildlife was already finding sanctuary up here, away from the more vigilant defenses below. Birds nested in the trees or on splintered columns, and insects scampered across the pathways at her approach. A giant moth broad as her shoulders swooped by with a tiny squeak and lighted on a closed bud. She stopped to look at it, then hurried on and lost herself in the peak's central forest.

The trees had once been part of the city itself, but with the failing systems, some had germinated on their own and left generations of independent offspring. Now the forest was little different from natural woods below, but there were no large animals. As she walked, she discovered that a few houses still functioned in the middle of the trees, and she decided to stay in one for the rest of the night.

The furniture was scattered through the rooms, bent and crumbling, cloth in rotting tatters. Dust covered the floor and made her cough. The insect life was profuse. She had second thoughts—but then she saw the console and covered screen. The bench in front of the console was solid. She sat on it and requested information. With a rustle of dust, the louvres opened and a homunculus appeared on the plate.

"Are there any facilities for cleaning this place?" she asked. The figure appeared to think the question over for a moment. "One machine replies; would you like it activated and put to work?"

"Yes. Also, I'd like fresh bedclothes and furniture manufactured."

"They will be transported from factories in the lower levels."

"That's fine. Now, while I wait, I want to be connected to the city archives."

"Archives are closed. Only city managers may see—"

"I am a city manager," Reah said, tensing with her lie.

The homunculus wavered for a moment, then became solid again. "City manager—status, please."

"Retired. Listen, the city is in need of organization—"

"That is the status," the homunculus said. "Pardon this unit. Not all portions function as well as they should. Which archives do you wish to see?"

"Records of previous managers."

She felt a presence behind her and jumped, then screamed. A man dressed in black was walking out of the wall. He raised one hand and moved his lips silently, beckoning her to follow.

The army was arranged as Durragon had ordered. The first group of city parts was coming up against the forward line. He could see the Chasers running in and out like reckless children at play. Big machines rolled out of the group on tractor treads, forcing the marauders back, while the smaller parts moved toward the center.

The rear lines faced similar problems, but they had already cut out a score of stragglers and were tying them down with ropes and stakes. Periodically one of the bound parts would break loose and a knot of men would gather around it again. The struggle reminded him of a formation of ants trying to stop a burst of water. The beleaguered city seemed to run over itself at certain points, and pieces would reassemble, forming nightmare castles and towers which dissolved into the common mass minutes after. Breetod stood by Durragon, leaning on the flank of the green mount, chewing on a piece of sweet grass. They both turned at once when rising smoke caught their eyes.

"What's that?" Durragon asked.

"Bastards have set a grass fire," Breetod said. "They're trying to stop the advance with a fire!"

"Tell the rest of the troops to start cutting into the rear. I want them to find anything that looks like it's in command—anything! Cut it out of the formation and bring it here. And whoever set that fire—shoot them on the spot."

Breetod ran off. Nebeki came up on his other side, breathing hard, face smudged with dirt. He was smiling until he saw the trickle of smoke on the plain. "What's that?"

"Never mind. Take all the captured parts and get them off the plain, away from the grass. Take them into the hills on the other side."

In an hour, the fire raged out of control. Smoke reached up to the blue sky and streamed to the west. The city had stopped. Durragon could see that large sections of it were already on fire. Before long at least a third of the mass was blazing, but the city would not retreat. Breetod returned, gasping and exhausted, face smoke-darkened and hair snagged with burrs and bits of grass. "Sir, we're going to lose the whole city. There aren't any defenses left to put out the fire. It's just waiting to die."

"Follow," Durragon said, urging the mount forward.

The next few hours blurred in his memory. He rode out among the burning city parts, coughing in the smoke. The night sky descended and the plain and surrounding hills were lit up by the central blaze. Many of the Chasers were trapped and burned to death, or so badly burned they had to be put out of their agony. The rest of the army herded captured parts across the plain into the hills, tying them to the thickest trees and cutting down the brush behind them to form a firebreak. Breetod was almost trampled by a transport unit which rumbled over him, undercarriage passing a scant finger's breadth above his back.

When the fire showed no signs of abating, they untied the captured parts and herded them still higher, into the rock columns which had fallen away from some of the sheer hill ledges.

Durragon wandered through the assembly on foot, with the Habiru teacher following several steps behind. A few suspect parts were isolated and a rough fence built around them. One—a drum that had been carried by a transport until the transport burned—had no obvious purpose, and Ezeki Iben Tav examined it closely. "This may be a control," he said.

By morning the plain was a smoldering expanse of the char. The fire had passed to east and west, ending at the dust of the river bottom and the rocks of the higher hills. After a few hours of fitful, coughing-racked sleep, Durragon took his mount out to survey the remains of the city.

"So passes the city of Tomoye," the old Habiru said, bending down to rescue a small water-spreader lacking its hose. It wriggled in his arms and tried to spurt dry air.

* * *

The ghost's path was old; he went through houses and walls and walked along upper levels which had long since collapsed. She followed as best she could, hair on end, muttering automatic prayers. The figure was not supernatural—it was a normal function of the city to project guides and teachers—but she wasn't immune to awe.

The figure stopped at a tower which rose thirty-five meters above the city crest, on the outer circuit of walkways. He pointed at an eroded panel and she reached out to touch it. Then he vanished.

A door slid aside and Reah stepped into a brightly lit room. The walls were covered with glowing charts and diagrams. In the center, on a raised pedestal, was a chair and a console larger than any she had seen. She stepped up to the chair and stood behind it, looking at the board's soft green luminosity. She recognized the three louvred screens and an array of knobs which were retinal projectors. Reah didn't completely understand the technology of the past, but it wasn't hard to guess that whoever sat in the chair would have a great deal of information at her fingertips.

She sat. The cushion crumpled like pastry under her weight, but the solid body of the chair adjusted to fit.

"May we help you?" a voice from the ceiling asked.

"Where is this?"

"This is one of five city surveillance centers."

Reah nodded absently and looked at the charts more closely. The city was huge. She had hardly had time to become familiar with it, but she recognized many of the larger features. "Are you . . ." She hesitated, still not used to speaking to voices without humans behind them. "Are you aware the city is dying?"

"We are. Our regeneration facilities have been depleted and there is a breakdown in reproduction memory."

"You answer more than my question. Are you a simple machine?"

"We are the architect. We coordinate the city."

"I mean—do you think, are you alive?"

"Yes. But we are not aware in the same way you are."

Reah touched a louvred screen. "But you want to stay alive, don't you?"

"At one time this city had a purpose, and that made it pleasant to exist. There is no purpose now."

"Why?"

"A city is nothing without citizens."

"But you kicked them out."

"They were not worthy."

She didn't feel like arguing the point. "Still, you've let people in now—injured people."

"If we were in complete control, we would not allow that. The city defenses are weakened and many functions have been turned over to medical units."

"Then you don't control everything," Reah said.

"No. Authority has been crumbling for a century."

"Is there any way to get it back?"

"The architect is an incomplete unit now and cannot control all city functions. Authority has been delegated to best serve the city."

"Can you . . . delegate authority to me?"

"No," the architect said, "but there is a unit which can."

"Will you put me in touch with that unit?"

A different voice spoke. "Religious coordinator. May we help you?"

She sat silent for several seconds, biting her lower lip. "What's your function?"

"Scheduling the sacred activities and organizing spiritual exercises."

"Can you give me control of the city?"

"This unit is no longer complete and lacks motivation. For that reason, it is desirable to find a unit or individual with motivation. Do you qualify?"

"I . . . yes."

"Will you reject those who do not meet the spiritual standards of the city, who do not believe in the Resurrection and the Life, in Beauty Eternal and the dominance of the Almighty Lord our God?''

"Yes,'' she said, "but Allah is all-knowing.'' She didn't feel the least twinge of guilt; the city was insane. Having been insane once herself, she knew how necessary it was to exercise discretion.

"You are a retired city manager. Now you are reinstated. The penalty for failing to meet the standards is rejection. The city is under your control.''

Reah smiled and wiped her damp palms on her dress.

In the shadow of Resurrection, after a day's hot march, Durragon relaxed and drank a cup of stale water proferred by Breetod. He looked over the mottled towers and walls with a speculative eye, then ordered the Habiru brought to him. The teacher came with wary eyes and stooped shoulders.

"How much is alive in there, and how much dead?'' Durragon asked.

Ezeki shrugged. "Perhaps a fourth is dead.''

"How soon before it all dies?''

"Decades. Or only years. It isn't the outward decay which counts, but the decay of the city's control and regeneration facilities.''

"Is it worth trying to get inside?''

"If the city doesn't want you in, you won't get in.''

"I think there are ways,'' Durragon said. "You saw what happened to Tomoye. We could burn our way into this one.''

"You—and pardon my bluntness, but you employ me to save you trouble—you don't know the ways of cities. I have observed them for years, decades, and learned about them at the feet of men who have studied them far longer than that. There are defenses within the city which can decimate your men. You lost many to Tomoye, and it was weak.''

Durragon motioned for Nebeki to bring up a chart. "The city's empty, dying. Those spines can't hold us back for long. A party of men will get through—I'll gamble on that—and you'll be among them.''

"It's been tried before."

"On healthy cities, yes. But this one is weak and feeble-minded. I can smell it, like a dying jungle. There's a chance we can take it."

The Habiru shrugged and picked up a chart to examine it. "You'll lose many men."

"They're Chasers. They won't complain because I'll be with them every step. I've heard cities contain knowledge useful to a man with my ambitions. Such knowledge could give me a terrific advantage. After a millennium of strife, don't you think it's time for one leader to emerge?"

The Habiru nodded. "Perhaps. But are you equipped to be that leader?" He felt a thrill of fear, being so bold.

Durragon's smile didn't waver. "Yes. If I wasn't, I'd have you put to death right now for insolence. But there's a place for insolence in my plans. I'm insolent myself. I threaten to end an age of decline. I sneer at the weakness of my forebears."

"The plan is no more foolish than any other," Ezeki said. "My life is no more valuable than any other. I'll go."

"Just for a chance to see what's in the city?"

"For that chance . . . yes." The Habiru's eyes closed.

Reah stepped out of the control chamber and was confronted by three monsters. One was built like a rolling coat-rack, with antennae stuck on its small round head. The second in size was a squat cubic thing which walked on insect legs. The smallest was a translucent-winged bug which lighted on her shoulder and touched her cheek with fine, wiry palps.

"We are to serve you," the coat-rack said. "I am assigned to the architect to report on your position and activities, this box is to protect you, and this insect is your personal link with the religious coordinator. May we, as simple units, warn you—avoid sin?"

"I stand warned," she said. "Where are the patients?"

"Still on the lower levels."

"Guide me to a transport and let's visit them."

She rode a flier in a slow spiral down a heat shaft and came to rest on the flowing design at the base. As she stepped down from the humming vehicle, she saw a crowd of officious city-parts much like her coat-rack rushing from corridor to corridor, whistling shrilly.

Rebecca ran under the heat-shaft arch and saw Reah standing near the center of the design. She stopped, confused, and was grabbed by three flexible metal arms. The device—a mechanical torso mounted on tractor treads—lifted her gently from the floor. "Stop it!" she screamed. "We belong here!"

"What's going on?" Reah asked the coat-rack.

"They are healed now. They must be returned to the outside."

"I want them to stay."

"You have no control," the coat-rack said.

"Why not? I command the city."

"Only those who require medical service are allowed to stay. These people are healthy now. It is the way the city functions."

"Then countermand the orders."

"It cannot be done."

"Reah!" Rebecca screamed. "Stop them!"

Reah watched helpless as the former patients of Resurrection were placed beyond the silicate barriers. She was vaguely disgusted at herself, for she was almost happy they were going. The spines bristled high into the air and the cries diminished.

"No way to bring them back?" she asked.

"None."

"Then it's time to get to work."

Nebeki's chasers brought in the new exiles half an hour after they were put out of the city. Durragon looked them over, saw a mix of peoples from villages and townships he had raided, and asked them pointed questions—what had they seen in the city? Had anyone stayed behind?

A young, dark fellow in a yellow suit said, "There's a woman inside."

"What's your name?" Durragon asked.

"Belshezar."

"What kind of woman?"

"A Moslem," Rebecca spat. "Worse than the worst—a witch! The city didn't throw her out. She has it enchanted."

"How did you get into the city in the first place?" Ezeki asked, walking slowly around the group of twelve. He fingered Belshezar's clothes.

"We were sick," Belshezar said, backing away. "Wounded." He looked around, suddenly frightened. "You're the ones who burned our towns . . ."

"Never mind," the Habiru said. "That's done with for the moment." He glanced sharply at Durragon. "No more left to burn, eh? We need information. Give it to us and you won't have any trouble."

"You want to get into the city?" Belshezar asked.

Durragon raised his riding crop—an affectation, since his city part didn't respond to whipping—and lifted Belshezar's chin with it. "Answer the old man and don't worry about our plans."

"Does it take in all wounded people?" Ezeki asked.

"All that we know of," Belshezar said. "Most of us came by accident. It let us in and we were almost too sick to notice. It sent machines after some of us."

"It actually carried you inside?" Durragon asked.

Belshezar nodded. "It's confused, broken in its . . ." He made a twirling motion with his finger around his ear.

"It's crazy," Ezeki said.

Belshezar agreed.

"Can you draw a map of its insides?" Durragon asked.

"All of us together, maybe." Belshezar looked up defiantly. "If we're treated well."

Ezeki ordered a table and paper brought to them. "I'm sure our general will treat you kindly." He dismissed the women and had the men sit down in the tent. The women were taken to a separate tent and a guard was put around them by Breetod, who disliked the looks on the Chasers' faces.

Into the evening Belshezar, sweating heavily, laid out the city scheme before Durragon and the Habiru, with reluctant help from his comrades.

From the edge of a middle level promenade, Reah watched the tents and fires of the armies massed below. The company of the coat-rack, the box and the bug was beginning to irritate her, but there was no way of getting rid of them. Besides, they answered most of her questions. She was tiring rapidly, however, and her mind still spun with endless schemes, spurred on by the ready information.

It suddenly dawned on her that the army below wasn't made up of simple Chasers. Her dim memories of the raid on Akkabar and the ruins of the Habiru town returned and she rubbed her eyes slowly, as if to scrub the new worries away.

"What are they doing down there?" she asked.

"We do not know," the coat-rack said.

"Can they get inside?"

The device was silent for an unusually long time. "We think they may be able to get in."

"How?"

"Should any of them be injured, portions of the city will allow them in for treatment."

She turned away from the parapet and looked back at the softly glowing gardens beyond the walkways. Smells of orange and cherry blossoms mingled in the moist wind from the higher levels. "If they attack the city, can it hold them off?"

"Yes. If they attack, none of them will get in."

"Will it kill them?"

"Not directly, no."

"What do you mean?"

"In fortifying its outer barriers, it will probably destroy many before they can run far. It's happened before."

She closed her eyes again and enjoyed the dark. "Can you find me a room nearby?"

"Certainly," the coat-rack said. "Please follow."

Resurrection had once housed six hundred thousand people. The variety of living quarters seemed endless to Reah. Her guides led her through meeting halls filled with thousands of now-crumbling desks and chairs. Though there had been no schools as such in Akkabar, she had seen classrooms in one of the Habiru cities. The rooms around the central meeting halls were obviously quarters for children—they were smaller and the furniture, what remained of it, was more delicate. The decors were colorful and simple. Some of the rooms were in good repair and she was taken into one. The bed was small but suitable. She lay down and crawled into a fetal curl.

The three machines lined up near the door and settled down to wait the night out. From all around, like the diminished beating of a sleeping heart, the city sounds subsided and deepened.

She awoke before dawn and ate a quick breakfast at a small metal table. The serving units left their wall nooks and stiffly delivered her food—fruit and a bowl of hot cereal, not unlike the wheat mash served in Akkabar. As she finished, she looked at a large door which hadn't been opened since she arrived. She asked the coat-rack what was behind the door.

"Educational devices, I believe," it answered. "Would you like to see them?"

"Bring them out," she said.

The coat-rack aimed its antennae and the door swung aside, revealing a closet-like interior. Reah peered in and saw several strange machines lining the walls. One looked like a hobby-horse made from garden plants, another was a robot octopus. There was a cluster of dolls no higher than her knee, each meticulously detailed and very life-like. Half the dolls were children, half were adults.

The toy horse stood up stiffly, making a noise like cellophane crackling. One leg fell away and it toppled, cracking its head against the squirming octopus. Both crumpled into glassy bits and a strong odor of resin filled the closet. Two dolls walked out and looked up at her inquisitively.

"Here is how we are played with," the adult doll said, speaking in the old English accent. Reah gasped and backed away—the ghosts of two children had emerged from the wall above her bed and climbed down to kneel beside the dolls. Seeing her shock, the coat-rack immediately made the children vanish and shut off the dolls.

"We regret any alarm," it said, approaching her. She shook her head and held out a hand.

"I'm not used to them—to ghosts."

"We thought you were. You have already seen how such figures are used as guides in the city."

"Yes, but not children. Not the spirits of children. They've been dead . . ."

Her voice trailed off. "My child is dead and can't come back. Why should these children still laugh and play? Take me back to the other house."

The coat-rack hesitated, then complied.

The old Habiru sat on a rock before the spiny barricades of the city, thinking. Breetod stood next to him, looking bored. Durragon considered the old man valuable and kept him guarded. The Chasers were becoming more and more unruly as the months passed.

"Well," the Habiru said, taking a deep breath. "This is the way it should be. Will Durragon come to me, or should I go to him?"

"Better if you go, I think."

The old man pushed on his knees as he stood, and followed Breetod through the camp to Durragon's tent. The first gleam of dawn was driving out the last stars with sweeping orange wolf's-tail clouds. Breetod stood by the flap and drew it aside for the Habiru.

Inside, Durragon was eating an apple picked from one of the wild trees near the camp. The Habiru stood beside him for a moment, waiting to be acknowledged.

"All right, yes?"

"You will wound ten of us and put us by the barricade. I want the Moslem Musa Salih to go with us . . . and Breetod, here."

Breetod raised his eyebrows but said nothing.

"You think the city will let you in?"

"Perhaps."

"What will you do if you get inside?"

"We know what some of the city thinking parts look like. If they don't vanish into the main body when the city is assembled, we might be able to find them and work on them. It'll take time, perhaps years. Ultimately we may be able to make the city drop its barriers and let your army in."

Durragon cringed. "Heaven forbid that. Chasers follow cities—but they wouldn't know how to behave themselves inside one. What will you do with Musa Salih?"

"He will talk to the Moslem woman inside, persuade her we wish no harm."

"Just in case she really does control the city, eh? Why is she still there when the others have been cast out?" Durragon tossed his apple core into a brass chamber pot.

"Perhaps she hasn't fully recovered yet," Nebeki said from the rear of the tent.

"No, she's sound," the old man countered. "This fellow Belshezar says she is, anyway. And Belshezar should go with us too."

"How will I wound you?"

The old man smiled grimly. "Not severely. Cuts across the skin of the legs, the back, the arms perhaps."

"Nothing serious, though, huh? What if the city sees the wounds aren't serious and doesn't let you in?"

"Then we'll heal ourselves. We've managed in the past."

"I don't like the idea," Breetod said, frowning. "Getting chopped in battle is one thing. Standing by without a fight while someone chops me is another."

"Then I'll go," Nebeki said, standing up. "I've always wanted to see the inside of a city."

Breetod glowered at him and shook his head. "Thank you, no. I'll go, but I don't have to enjoy the preparations, do I? Go fetch volunteers-six, right? Besides you, the Moslem and Belshezar."

Ezeki nodded. "We can go this morning, as soon as possible. The city was peaceful last night-you might say it slept well. Most cities are restless even when they've been settled for a long while."

"Some say they have bad dreams," Durragon offered, looking closely at Ezeki. "Do you think they dream, old man?"

He shook his head. "Not of good times. They dream of our manifold sins, General, which so disgusted them they vomited us."

"Then what we plan is like raping a woman who refuses us, eh? Noble plan, I think." Durragon stood and Nebeki brought forward his light armor. When he was suited, Durragon motioned for the runner to leave the tent. "Are you still religious, old man?" he asked. The Habiru shrugged.

"No righteous God would let one like you—or a traitor such as I—live very long. Most of our religion lies buried in cities that won't let us see it any more. We did not take our books with us when we were exiled, General. No Talmud, only a few copies of the Pentateuch, the Histories of Earth. One batch of tapes. Nothing else. Most of those are gone now, or we don't have the machines to read them."

"Ah, to retrieve the knowledge! The information that would let us live as our ancestors did—travelling from star to star, doing things any man today would call sorcery. My religion is man behaving like God. What is yours?"

The old man didn't answer.

"Sometimes I talk to gods in my sleep, auditioning them one by one. 'Come talk, present yourselves!' I say, and watch them stalk past, shadowy, answering me sometimes with my own voice, sometimes with the voice of somebody very like me, but buried deep inside. Never with their own voices. Makes me think all gods must be toadies and servants. Must have been different at one time, eh? Before burning bushes and voices out of mountains became everyday things, and humans took charge."

"Lots of leaders have imagined themselves gods," Ezeki said. "It's a dangerous conceit. Someone might believe you."

"I'm no god; don't ever intend to be one," Durragon said. "No god would put up with troops like the Chasers, and without my troops, what am I? No better than you—perhaps worse. You know why I'm called the Apostate, old man?"

Ezeki stared straight ahead.

"Because I once trained to be a rab. What do you think of that? I was young, but devout. Then I decided the creed of the Catholic was more attractive. Then I joined a group which worshipped a very dark, ugly sort of goddess. None of them satisfied me. From rab to pagan, and then to agnostic."

The old man produced one of his rare smiles.

"You like my revelations, huh?" Durragon asked. "Rare shafts of light between dark curtains. Yes, I know what you think of me. Your hatred invigorates me. We certainly won't grow old together, not when our goals are so far apart. Go and look over Breetod's volunteers. Don't tell Belshezar what I plan until I'm there to see his face."

The city was quiet in the dawn. Mist rose around its base and layers of thin clouds drifted past its upper towers, touching the walls with dew. The morning fires in the camp spread like a carpet of orange stars under the haze. Reah stood on the balcony with the insect lightly clutching her shoulder, the coat-rack behind her and the box at her feet.

"If the city lets any of them in, are there other parts which will obey me and throw them out again?"

The coat-rack didn't answer. The insect shustled its green clockwork body. She reached up to touch its crystalline head, but it flinched under her fingers. "I may explain," the coat-rack said. "The religious coordinator now wishes to treat those in need—"

"They only want in," Reah said.

"We have been watching them, and they behave like other Chasers, though there are more of them."

"They're organized. They burned my town, and they'll destroy this one if they can."

"Many city parts are no longer under control of the architect. Still others—such as defense and medical services—are automatic and cannot be directed by any existing central authority."

"Not even myself?"

The coat-rack considered. "I think not."

"Not even with your help?"

"If these Chasers are actually dangerous to the city—"

"They are."

"But the only way they can get in is to be wounded or disabled."

"They'll hurt themselves deliberately just to get a few inside—and then they'll kill the city."

"How do you know this?"

"It's obvious. They must have captured the others."

The insect was restless. Reah shrugged her shoulder in irritation and it flew away, winding around several buttresses in its flight to the interior.

"Why is the city dying?" she asked. The coat-rack hummed a lowering note but didn't answer. She asked her question again.

"The city no longer picks proper places in which to settle. This area is poor in deep ground-water sources. The soil is adequate only for surface vegetation."

"Would it improve if it found a better area?"

"Probably. Some portions are dead and irreplaceable, but others are not past repair."

"How could we get it to move?"

"That is outside my expertise. I speak to the architect but am not spoken to very often."

"It would know?"

"They. The architect is a consortium of agencies."

"They would know?"

"This unit thinks so."

Reah frowned. "We could do a lot with this city."

"The city is dying," the coat-rack said. "It began to die a long time ago, when it threw out its citizens. A city cannot live uninhabited."

"Children," Reah said. "Children can't survive without a community—not very well, anyway. And sick children—those no one can help. The city could find a place for children—most of them need medical care at one time or another. Resurrection could be a home to them, a school and hospital. Thousands of them . . ." She looked at the clearing mist over the camp.

"Is something wrong?"

"What? Oh, no. I'm just feeling slightly queasy. Too little sleep, I think."

Ezeki gathered the volunteers and told them, in Chaser dialect, what was going to happen.

"Dis you, brayba mans all, be cut undeep—"

The Chasers listened stolidly, then looked at the three runner assistants who sat under a tree, heating their blades in a fire. Ezeki turned to Durragon when he was through explaining. Durragon motioned for the group to approach the tree one by one, Ezeki to go first, Musa Salih second, and Breetod third.

"Dis em, in glow, not bite wid bite ob pus," Ezeki explained. The volunteers watched with squeamish interest as the swordsman laid a shallow cut across the old Habiru's back. Blood dripped down.

"Across my arm now," Ezeki said, wincing. The blade cut lightly from wrist to elbow. "Now put the belt around my upper arm," he said. He swatted at tiny insects gathering around the wounds. One by one, the others were cut, until the last stepped forward with pale face and closed his eyes against the pain.

"Dis we, on now, quicklike," Ezeki said. Breetod motioned for them to follow the old man. They walked through the inner perimeter of the camp and stood by the bristled spines of the city's paving.

"We are hurt!" Ezeki cried, not without conviction.

"We need aid!" Nebeki crouched behind the tents with an extra band of soldiers, waiting for the spines to drop. Durragon watched with legs apart and arms clenched behind his back.

The spines remained erect. Ezeki removed the cord from his arm and squeezed more blood out. "Look, we are hurt!" he shouted, angry this time. "We need medical attention!" He wiped one hand across his arm and smeared the blood on silicate spine. It trembled at his touch.

Durragon shook his head. He turned to his tent aide and ordered the camp herbalists to come forward.

Breetod felt faint and sick. His face was pale and sweat soaked his ragged clothes. The morning air felt cold as ice. Musa Salih slumped to his knees and a Chaser reached down to help him up again. Ezeki cursed under his breath and turned toward the camp. "Bring up the—"

The spines clanged together like bells. Voices rose from the troops a dozen meters away. Ezeki turned and saw an opening form in the barrier—the spines dropped, fitting together to form a section of flat paving. He stumbled forward. Breetod, Musa Salih and Belshezar followed. The wounded Chasers hung back, terrified, until Durragon shouted for them to go. Their blood spattered the ground.

Nebeki watched as the last man passed through. "Now!" Durragon shouted.

The second team rushed from the tents with the general and ran to the gap, trying to push through before it closed. Nebeki was the first to reach the barrier. He jumped over a rising spine. His eyes widened and jaw fell open as a second spine flashed up, catching him in the stomach and lifting him high into the air. The city bellowed as if in anguish, taking Nebeki's scream and amplifying it a thousand times. The rest of the second party fell back, clutching their ears. The noise stopped and Durragon lifted his eyes. Nebeki had been flung beyond the barrier. His body lay twisted on the ground. The spines still trembled. They jerked upward. New spines crept from beneath the barrier and advanced across the ground toward the camp. Durragon had already started running, barely ahead of his troops. They backed away, stumbling over tent-pegs and ropes and each other. They ran over fallen Chasers and camp debris, leaping like antelopes.

In two minutes, one third of the camp was obliterated and the barrier stopped growing. Durragon lay where he had stumbled, barely three meters from the new-grown spines, his face flushed with terror. His aide lay crushed, eyes glazed, blood dripping from his mouth.

The general screamed until his throat ached, then stood and brushed off his clothes.

Reah hid behind a column, listening to the men talking. She recognized Belshezar's voice. The coat-rack waited motionless nearby, its workings making small noises. She raised a finger and it moved into the view of the men.

Breetod saw the movement from the corner of his eye and slowly turned his head. Sweat beaded on his forehead and fell into his eyes, making him blink. Belshezar pointed to the coat-rack. "There's a worker—it can tell us where everything is."

Reah waited until the men were under the archway, then nodded.

"Medical units will arrive soon to assist you," the coat-rack said. "Please stay where you are."

Ezeki dropped to his knees, lolling his head like a sick animal. He swallowed hard and looked up at the wonder of the city's interior. It was clean, warm, comforting. The floor under his knees and toes was gentle, faintly yielding. The air was filled with the sounds of the city's vitality, almost like music. The city may have been sick, but it was far from moribund.

Musa Salih brought out a *hijab*, an amulet, and pressed it

to each eye, swaying on unsteady legs. "They cut us too deep," he said. "We're weak."

Reah reached into her robes and brought out a blade she had removed from a dead garden tender.

Belshezar saw the worker spin around. He pointed and said he was going to investigate. Then Reah walked around the pillar. She was dressed in a red robe, knife hidden in one sleeve. Breetod drew his sword. Musa Salih smiled.

"What are you doing here?" Reah asked in a level voice.

"We were wounded in a fight," Ezeki said. "The city gave us refuge."

"You wounded yourselves," Reah said. "You sliced yourselves just to get in."

Belshezar frowned. "How can you still be here? You're healthy."

"I control the city now."

"Woman, your vanity is incredible," Musa Salih said in the old tongue. "Stand back and let men do their proper work. Trust you not in Allah?"

"What village are you from?" she asked in English.

"From the *Medain*, the cities north of here. You speak the old tongue?"

Reah didn't answer. "I want you all out of here. The city will bind your wounds, then it will put you on the perimeter and you can join your soldiers outside."

"We are suppliants," Musah Salih said, smiling toothily at her. "You cannot refuse us." He was still speaking the old tongue. At one time, she thought, he must have been a scholar.

"I don't refuse you. I treat you and release you like the wild animals you are."

"Nor can you refuse us food, drink, information. That is the code of our people."

"You consort with *Nasrany* and *Yudah* and ask me about the code of our people?"

"They are human like you and I," Musa said, finally using

English. "Were we not all exiled long ago, faithful and *káfir* alike? We all lacked something."

"Whatever we lacked, the cities can't help us find it. My word is final. Belshezar, show them the hospital rooms. The city watches closely. No miserable soldiers can—" She stopped herself and shook her head, then addressed the coat-rack. "You'll watch them and report to me when they're gone."

Belshezar started to walk toward her, but felt faint and faltered. "You're lying," he said. "You're still crazy. The city can't fix you."

"Makes no matter to me what you think," Reah said. She smiled grimly at the others. "Be wary. This city is full of ghosts. The sooner you leave it, the better for you." To the Chasers she said, "Dis polis chocka sperrit, compree?"

Then she turned and walked toward the heat shaft.

She didn't want them in the city at all. They could spoil her plans—the city wouldn't force them out until they were well, and they could perform much mischief before then. The confrontation had merely been postponed; until they were gone they were like vipers hidden in her bedclothes.

She returned to the top of the city and the control center. She commanded a map of the surrounding area to be projected on a wall screen. The area of Akkabar was shown covered by a broad river. "Architect," she said. The homunculus appeared on its plate. "This map is wrong. Prepare to make corrections."

"The architect has put all city memory on read-only status," the figure said. "No information can be altered except in an emergency."

She sighed. "This is an emergency, obviously. The city is dying. It needs much more water than it gets here. It's tapping the water table for miles around and the flow is weakening daily. But where two rivers meet, even in drought, water must exist a few dozen meters beneath the sand. There's enough for a dozen cities, if the geology you taught me is correct."

"Are you proposing the city should move?"

"I am."

"To what end?"

"To ensure long life and health for its components." She noticed the homunculus had changed color. She was now addressing the religious coordinator, dressed in blue.

"Why? Is it not time for an empty city to die?"

"No." She shivered with emotion. The city actually *wanted* to die.

"There is no purpose in going on."

"Yes, there is. I'm going to send city transports to all the villages for hundreds of kilometers around and have them bring back the sick children. This city can heal them."

"Children are exiled as much as adults."

"Are children filled with sin?"

"Yes. This city's creed is Baptist. Those—"

"Stop that! You're repeating the very contradiction that makes you sick. I am the leader. You will send out city parts to retrieve the sick children."

The homunculus suddenly fuzzed and wavered. Reah, with her fingers in the sockets, could feel something changing. Far below, in one of the hundreds of control drums, something died. She wondered what it was.

The architect's colors returned. "Yes?"

She sucked in her breath and mumbled a prayer to Allah. "Here is how you will do it."

And the city did not object.

Belshezar watched as the medical machines repaired his wounds. "I'd live here forever if I could," he said.

Ezeki, already bandaged, ate from a plate held by the worker the woman had left to watch over them. "They'll throw you out just like they did before."

"Why haven't they thrown her out?"

"As you say, maybe she's still crazy. But it seems to me there's method in her madness."

Musa Salih grumbled deep in his throat. "She's a woman. Women can't enter a man's tent when they are impure, much less a blessed city. This woman has the manners of one high-born, the wife of an important man. They get haughty when their men rank high."

"Perhaps the city made her that way," Ezeki said.

"She was ignorant when she came here," Belshezar said. "We taught her how to learn from the city. Now she shows her gratitude."

"When we go, we'll take her with us," Musa said. "She can tell us what she knows about the city."

"If we're forced to leave," Ezeki said. "If she can stay, why can't we?"

"Something's moving on the outside," Breetod said, looking through a window across the broad pavement surrounding the city. "Big machines are leaving!"

Durragon was roused from his tent by the new left-flank runner. "Sir! Dis we fight beas' fro' inna polis!"

He wrapped his sword belt around his waist and left his tent. The camp was in confusion. At regular intervals around the barrier, spines had dropped to form gates. Huge machines were pouring out. Most were transports—tractors with human-like torsos but no heads, spider-leg carriers and wheeled trucks with long, flexible carriages and suspensions. They maneuvered carefully through the camp, obviously intent not on destruction but on merely leaving. The spines erected behind them and the Chasers looked in dismay at the trails which had been gouged through the camp.

"Has anyone communicated with the men inside?" Durragon asked. The runner shook his head and shrugged. "Then try, damn it! Try to shout to them. Damned Chasers." The runner smiled and went to gather a chorus of men.

Durragon didn't get much sleep until morning. The Chasers marched from one side of the camp to the other, staying a respectable distance from the spines, shouting at the top of their lungs. When dawn was well along and they hadn't received any answer, the runner woke Durragon up and he groggily began to make other plans.

Ezeki lay on his back in a tub of healing fluid, half-dreaming about his home village. A network of green and chrome manipulators hung in wait over his body. Earlier they had massaged and applied unguents; in a few days the wounds would be healed.

And paradise would end. One way or another, the city—or the woman—would throw them out. Something had to be done before then.

The fracas with the disbanded Tomoye had taught Ezeki several things about organic cities. Diffuse and huge as they might seem from the outside, they were controlled by a small number of tank-like brains. The one they had captured had not been very cooperative. He opened his eyes and sighed.

"Bring Breetod to me, please," he told the worker. It rolled out of the room. A few minutes later the flank runner came in, sniffing at his hand and arm.

"They cleaned me up," he said. "I've never smelled this good before."

"How do you like it?" Ezeki asked.

The runner wrinkled his nose. "The smell is unfamiliar, and I can't tell as much about my health as I could before—" he sniffed his arm-pit and shook his head—"but I don't itch much, either. It's acceptable."

"This expolitan, Belshezar—has he told you much about the city yet?"

"He's more your kind than mine. He hasn't said a thing since he was bandaged. Musa would like to strangle the bitch."

"She looks like she can take care of herself. You might warn him. Besides, I think she's telling the truth. She runs the city now."

"Why do you believe her?"

"Does this city act like other cities?"

"No."

"There it is. Something's made it change."

"But she's just an old expolitan—"

"Not so old, maybe forty. Hard life. But she's smart now, for whatever reason, and I think she has most of the city under control, but not all; otherwise why would it let us in? She was right—we were faking. She obviously doesn't like having us here."

"So?"

"We'll meet today, before we get so perfumed and softened up we forget why we're here. Bring everyone to Belshezar's room—even the Chasers—and make sure the worker is *not* in attendance."

"Yes, but here the walls have ears for a fact."

"Then we'll speak Habiru dialect. Whether she hears and understands or not, we'll have a meeting."

"One other thing," Breetod said before leaving. "I went to a higher balcony and watched the machines that broke out last night. They scattered in all directions."

Ezeki settled back into the warm fluid again and waved his hand. "Go get the others."

When the despair came, Reah feared that the past was returning again. She sat quietly in the control center, trying to find a way out of the darkness. It all seemed hopeless. Where was the dividing line between the possible and the absurd?

She was furious. She clenched the soft edge of the seat and stared straight into the screen. She had been re-running the city's history, trying to understand. The idiocy of God-Does-Battle's first colonist was a hard stone in her throat. Understanding was no easier than forgiveness.

They had put the planet in a shadow from which it had never escaped. Reah thought she knew one of the reasons. The religions of her ancestors had been masculine religions, with masculine gods and prohibitions against the ways of women. Women were unclean, little better than livestock. Nature was a conspiracy of the unclean female against the hardpressed male.

Yet she had loved her husband once, and faithfully followed the codes of Islam. Her daughter's future, she had known, would not be as bright as a son's—

She was tense again. She looked at the screens and tried to unlock her neck muscles. Son or daughter, husband or tyrant, they were all equal now. "Better I had no memory," she murmured. The insect on her shoulder buzzed and she tapped its head.

"The men are holding a meeting," it said, relaying the coat-rack's voice. "This unit is not allowed to attend. I believe they are well enough that the city might consider putting them out soon."

"Keep watching," she said. They weren't going to foul her plans. Now that she controlled a city, albeit a disarranged one, it was time to correct the masculine blunders and set God-Does-Battle aright. And where else to begin, except with children?

But first the city had to be relocated.

She summoned the homunculus, now permanently dressed in the red of the architect.

"The city can move as soon as it's ready," she said.

"One transport has returned with information from the old alluvial plain," the figure said.

"I didn't send any transport there."

"This unit found it appropriate to check conditions before moving."

She smiled. The city was thinking for itself, at least occasionally. "What did it find?"

"Conditions are good. There is a deep flow of water and the soil is conducive to city maintenance."

"Now that the suppliants are well, isn't it time to put them out?"

"Tomorrow they will be escorted from the city," the architect said. "Not before."

Reah nodded. She knew her limits better now. There was no use arguing.

Durragon called the captured cylinder before him and stood in front of it—if it had a front—holding a finger to his lip and sucking on its tip. "You acknowledge my control over you?"

"This unit has been lifted from any established chain of command. Since it is this unit's duty to serve in a heirarchy, your orders will not be ignored."

The cylinder's voice was scratchy and haggard, as if from long disuse or internal wear. Durragon didn't like the cylinder's answer. There was something defiant about it, no matter how faint the tinge.

"No more riddles. Speak clearly. If I control you, then I control all the captured parts of Tomoye?"

"Yes."

"Do I control you?"

A pause, then, "Yes."

"Good." He wished Ezeki was there. The Habiru could split verbal hairs far better than he. "Do you know how other cities are put together? Where their nerve centers are?"

"No."

"Why not?"

"That was not my function."

"Could you point them out to us if we took you inside?"

"Yes."

"Do they look like you?"

Silence. He repeated the question.

"There is much variety, depending on the city. Some do."

"De polis!" a Chaser shouted. Durragon turned and looked up. The higher reaches of the city were disassembling. It was preparing to move. He put his hand on the cylinder's smooth surface. "You'll help us infiltrate the city, won't you?" He wanted to sound more masterful, but the change had caught him by surprise.

The cylinder didn't answer.

* * *

Reah watched the huge, spider-legged transports as they waited in the larger corridors and received rows of structural pieces. At other times, many of the transports served as bulkheads themselves, or as portions of buttresses and awesome support beams which crossed the entire city. Now the city was coming apart layer by layer, following a plan first put to use when they were erected a thousand years ago. Every part carried its own memory. Ancillary control units coordinated the motions. And throughout the city, the architect watched over everything.

She had played her part. In a few more hours the city would pour across the plain and through the hills, heading toward the old river bed and Akkabar.

She watched from a balcony overlooking one of the largest enclosed spaces within the city. A kilometer above the ground, the assembly hall spanned the central tower. Its floor was six hundred meters across. Light poured down from transepts windows where hall and tower joined. Stained transparencies shifted designs continually, automatically, turning the floor into a gigantic kaleidoscope, a garden of light-flowers which, by night, became a ghostly promenade for images from times long past. Reah had never found the nerve to walk across the assembly hall at night, for it was there that the city concentrated its dreams and recollections, resurrecting visions of men and women in simple, wonderful clothes, children running naked except for armbands and tiaras, strange animals conjured from the experiments of the city-builders.

Until now, Reah had never grasped the true size of the city. Her eyes were lost in the complexity of transports and parts gathering in rows on the assembly floor. As she watched, even the transepts began to come down, supported by new-spun cables and the cooperative limbs of lower sections. Hand-by-hand, slung from webs, walking and rolling and even flying, Resurrection spread itself out on the grasslands, moving its perimeter of spines and pushing back Durragon's army. But the time would come, Reah knew, when the spines themselves would disassemble, and she would have to rely on the uncoordinated mobile defenses to keep the men from breaking through.

The insect buzzed on her shoulder and she tapped its head.

"This unit cannot locate the wounded suppliants," the coat-rack said. "The architect has been informed they are missing, but all faculties are now concentrated on moving and outside defense."

Reah looked away from the assembly floor. "Bring me a quick corridor transport and join me here. We'll look for them ourselves."

Ezeki peered into chamber after chamber, trying to find something which by any stretch of conjecture would serve the purpose of a command center. The city had to have one—but where?

Belshezar came running after him. "Musa Salih says the city is taking itself apart," he said, out of breath. "I think it's getting ready to move."

"There's no control center down here. It must be up near the tower—and that's where she is, too."

"No, she isn't. The tower's already come down. There's nothing to do except leave, if we can."

Ezeki shook his head. "We can follow it, wait until it reassembles."

"It won't! Cities go to the mountains and die."

"Not if they have someone rational behind them."

"But the woman isn't rational. She's insane."

Ezeki took a last look into a small storage room and shrugged. "What good is coming here at all, then? She's won."

Belshezar grimaced. "No. I can take us to the upper levels, just below the tower. Most of the promenades are still standing. If we can find a control drum like the one Durragon captured, it may tell us more."

Musa Salih strolled into the entrance archway, smoking his crusted pipe. He watched with amusement while Ezeki tried to query a cube similar to the one which had followed the woman. "It doesn't talk," he told them as the device walked off on its interrupted business. "It must just be a relay, a messenger."

Musa pointed with his pipe-stem. "Gentlemen, Breetod is trying to throw a stone over the outer barrier, but it keeps shifting. He's very angry. He wants to get a message to Durragon. That'll keep him busy, but what are we going to do?"

"Follow me," Belshezar said. Musa glanced at Ezeki and they walked after him.

"One unit reports they are leaving the lower levels," the coat-rack said. "They seem to be looking for you."

"Good. Then we'll wait." She felt for the knife in her robes. The coat-rack suddenly trembled and halted. She turned to look at it. The insect buzzed off her shoulder. "What's wrong?" she asked.

"A failure—"

The floor buckled and jumped beneath them. A few meters from where they stood, in the broad vehicle corridor below the assembly hall, the walls gapped and groaned. A rumble echoed around them, followed by an ear-splitting squeal. The floor tilted and Reah fell on her hands and knees. The coat-rack rolled and toppled. As she began to slide, her hands struggled to get a grip on the floor. The cracks in the walls and ceiling grew. Fluids from ruptured city parts cascaded through the cracks, steaming and throwing up mists of alcohol.

Reah rolled over on her back and flattened out. As she watched, one whole section of a side tower separated and arced over, collapsing as it fell. The entire city seemed to be roaring. She blocked her ears with her hands, then put them on the floor again to keep from sliding. The end of the corridor was open to the air now. Across the gap she could see flying debris and a rising cloud, and beyond that remnants of the tower leaning against an outer ring of the city, swaying crumbling and falling.

The coat-rack flexed to right itself, then started rolling. At the last, it tried to flatten its arms and stop but it disappeared over the edge of the floor. For seconds the city was quiet. Reah lay with mouth open, a pain in her knees, her head vibrating with echoes of the scream.

Then the alarms went off. Automatic voices urged occupants of apartments to remain calm. The whole city was frantically murmuring and warning and relaying damage information. Reah crawled out of the way of a transport. It tried to block off the corridor but instead, with a grinding of treads, made the floor dip farther and sailed off into the pit.

After several minutes, the buttresses and supports far below made a titanic effort and what was left of the tower sorted itself into temporary equilibrium. Reah felt this as a shiver and a slow, elevator-like rise. Then the corridor was level and she stood experimentally, almost collapsing because of the trembling of her knees.

Reah could guess what had happened. Some of the weaker structures, unable to rely on totally dead parts, had collapsed and taken the side tower with them. Moving the city had been a calculated risk in the first place, and now the risk had come due. "How much?" she asked herself. "How much is lost?" Then, standing on the jagged rim of the floor, she began to weep.

Ezeki's arm hung broken by his side. He howled into the dust and gloom, cursing God, cursing his mother and father, cursing all who had helped him stay alive in the past—anyone who had contributed to the present horror. Breetod, Belshezar and the Chasers lay under head-high mounds of squirming, green-bleeding rubble. Musa Salih was nowhere to be seen. From all around, fine mists of choking fluid filled the air, and sounds of screaming matter tortured beyond structural endurance.

As the noise subsided to the distant buzzing of alarms, Ezeki sat on a fallen column with a shuddering breath. Then he took his hand away from his forearm and looked at the skin. The bones weren't protruding. If necessary, he could set it himself—not very well, perhaps, but enough to stay alive and heal.

And—if the whole city hadn't just died—perhaps he had an advantage now . . .

"Who's there?" someone called. "Is anyone alive?"

It was Musa Salih. "Here," Ezeki shouted. "El and Hell, I'm an old man and I don't want to see any more of this shitful life."

Salih appeared out of the gloom, wiping dust from his face and smiling broadly. "That was something, wasn't it?" he said. "Looks like the woman overstepped her bounds. This city is too old to move."

"I've broken my arm," Ezeki said.

"I think the hospital is still there. Here, walk with me." Hanging on to Salih's shoulder, Ezeki climbed over the low mounds of debris into the clean corridors of the intact lower levels. "What fell?" he groaned.

"I don't know. Everything is frantic. Workers running everywhere, going crazy. Voices, ghosts, Prophet's beard! It's a nightmare. From Paradise to—hey! I'm scratched on the hands and feet and you have a broken arm. What about Breetod and the others?"

"Dead," Ezeki said.

"City has to fix us up again. Let's go."

In the quiet, cool green rooms of the hospital, Ezeki lay on a soft bench and closed his eyes. The net of medical tools closed over him. Something burst above his face, a flash of pulsating green, and he fell asleep.

Musa watched without expression as his hands and feet were treated. Life was too ironic for words, so he said nothing and thought nothing. No matter what man attempted, Allah was the only victor. And what did Allah win? Nothing but the satisfaction of holding and throwing the die . . .

"Can the city recover?" she asked the homunculus. The screens and projectors were relaying information from the architect's remaining sensors. The apartment's information center couldn't compare with the control room in the now-dismantled central tower, but for the moment there was nothing else available. She felt half-blind.

"There is much damage, but mostly in areas already dead or dying. This may save time clearing dead units, in fact. Your worker was destroyed?"

"Yes. Only the flying thing is left."

"A new unit will be assigned to you. There were intruders killed in the fall. Two are alive. Medical units are tending to them. Pardon. Thinking interference—"

The homunculus faded and turned to purple, a color she hadn't seen before. "Evaluation of city net viability—"

Then to green.

"Construction coordinator. An emergency survey vehicle is being readied for the City Manager. The architect will act as interface. As of now, the functions of religious coordinator, central teaching authority, metabolism authority, ComNet authority have been terminated. City motion authority is in command."

Then back to red.

"The city manager will please follow a projected guide to the emergency vehicle." Reah nodded and looked around. A male figure emerged from the wall and motioned for her to follow.

Near the ground level, a vehicle mounted on treads, with a large cab and attendant workers stored in recesses in the outer skin, rolled up beside her and stopped. It bounced slowly on shock absorbers. It was smaller and lighter than most of the transports and obviously not made from the same organic material. She followed the projection up a short flight of steps into the cab and found a comfortable, form-fitting seat. On the arm-rests were finger-cups and three black retinal projectors hung just above the level of her eyes. She fitted her fingers, looked into the guide-lights and—

She was the moving city.

Durragon waited and watched expectantly. If the city was crumbling, perhaps the barricade would be breached and his soldiers could pour in. Victory was so close he could smell it. He smiled and patted his mount. "I'll command your brothers," he said to it quietly. "They can't ignore us any longer."

For the moment, nothing was happening. He examined supply requisitions with the chief of material for a few minutes in the early morning, then looked over fresh maps drawn up by a newly enlisted cartographer. The sharp-faced map-maker stood nervously by as Durragon ran his fingers over the inked lines.

"Sir," the young man began.

Durragon ignored him. "The maps are excellent," he said a few seconds later. "My army grows more sophisticated every day."

"Sir," the map-maker blurted, "I may speak out of turn, but I fear for your safety."

Durragon glanced up at him. "How?"

"The Chasers, sir—"

"Still aren't used to them, eh? I command with a strong hand."

"I know them well, sir. I lived with a tribe of them just three months ago. Your Chasers are not happy."

"Oh?" Durragon rolled the map up carefully.

"Your new flank runners talk behind your back." The map-maker was trembling now. "They'll kill me if they find out I've said anything . . ."

"We'll keep our little secrets," Durragon said nonchalantly. "What do they say?"

"That you refused to enter the city with the first rank

because you lost your courage. And you held back the second rank just long enough to keep them from getting in. They say you don't have enough nerve any more."

"Grumblings."

"I think more than that, sir."

"I'll take care of it. You attend to your own duties."

"Yes, sir." The map-maker took up his charts and left the tent. Durragon frowned at the swinging flap. The Chasers always grumbled, but he disliked dissent among his officers.

The new flank runners, Gericolt and Perja, sat around a fire and brewed olsherb tea in a battered metal pot. They didn't have as many friends as when they'd been common soldiers, and this irritated them. To assuage their feelings they added a little intoxicating froybom powder to the tea. Soon they were warm and relatively contented. As they lounged, a soldier in a worn cloth jerkin approached them, bowing profusely.

"Cutta," Gericolt ordered sharply. The Chaser stopped his obeisances.

"Dis em, in tent ob He, appree words ob de scribbler."

"Eabesdrop, dis you?" Perja asked, raising an eyebrow.

The Chaser nodded. Then he explained what he had heard and the effects of the froybom seemed to evaporate in the flank-runners' blood. "Dis we, kill dat talker," Perja said. Gericolt narrowed his eyes.

"Worry, ourselbes, por wat de Man'll do dis we."

Now they were thoroughly unhappy. Staring into the fire, trying to think how they could avoid punishment, they weren't the first to notice that the city had resumed dismantling itself. When other runners reported to them, Perja threw his ceramic cup onto the ground and stood, brushing dirt from his clothes.

Still anxious, he went to Durragon's tent and touched the General on the shoulder. Durragon turned around slowly, but the Chaser had noticed his jerk. Better to make noise when entering the tent from now on . . . unless . . .

"What?"

"De polis," Perja said. "At it all ober."

"Moob, de polis?" Durragon asked. Perja shook his head.

"Dis we, look close, nort side come doon an' show de bones ob undisside."

Durragon dressed quickly and went out to see if the barricade was expanding again. Where were all the city parts being stored? Soon enough the city would have to breach the spines and extend its bulk along the plain. Then, perhaps, their chance would come.

Perja left the tent, breathing heavily, and fingered his hidden pants-knife. Then he went to look for the map-maker.

Even in the jumbled thoughts of the move, the city was agonized. Reah felt the pain and guilt as if they were her own, as if she had been the one to order the exiling of humans a thousand years ago. For a moment she struggled to be free of the hurt, but then she gave in. It was time to learn what her city was like, all the way to its center . . .

Screaming. For days and nights, all around God-Does-Battle the air had pulsed with the despair of the cities, matching the wailing of the humans outside. Reah's mind whirled in the storm of ancient memories. Many of the cities had gone insane, shrinking within to dream only of the past, projecting ghosts to walk the halls and fill the rooms. These had died earliest of all. Their parts had either been scattered on the razor-ridge mountains, or left to wander rogue.

Other cities had died because of malfunctions in their central generation units, the devices which bred replacements for the parts which had worn out. Many cities had slowly crumbled away. Others, like Resurrection, had lasted longer and in fair health, until confusion and guilt had broken down any will to continue.

"Now there's a reason to go on," she thought. She tried to guide her thought from unit to unit, in the ragged remains of the city mind. "Now you've purged the programs and know that all humans are weak, that you were made in the image of their dreams, not in some false image of a pure

God. You cannot judge them; you are mortal clay, too, and weak."

The area that had been the religious coordinator was silent, but for a moment she thought she could feel a spark, almost of rage. Frightened, she continued to push her thoughts deeper.

"It is not your duty to judge."

What is the function? Like the voice of a young girl; startled, she recognized it was her own voice, from thirty years in the past.

"I give you a new reason to live: rescue the children. Bring them here, the sick and the lame, those who will grow strong only with your care and teaching. Teach them as best you can; for the moment those most in need must be treated first."

The voice of the architect, muffled and distant, answered her: *It is a commission, not unlike our original function.*

And a strident whisper—*But it is not our original commission!*

Reah stormed through the sudden strands of dissent as if she carried a sword, her face creasing with rage and disgust. Here was revenge, slashing away the dying, cluttered antihuman notions of the city; here was gratification, paying back the philosophies which had killed her husband and daughter, and kept her in bondage and insanity. "Remove this," she demanded, "take this away, leave this behind . . ."

And she came to the center of the city's being. She seemed to stand in a foggy glade. Golden sunlight poured from above, striking her outstretched hands. More like a plant than an animal, at this center the city accepted the bounty of soil and sun and gloried in the turning of nature. She reached out from the center.

"Like a tree," she said, "you are free to bear fruit and feed those who live in your shade. I free you from guilt, from the human functions, for those were improperly assigned to you. It is your duty only to revel in the light and the warmth, to work free of compulsion, to be what a more knowing nature would have made you, rather than what humanity made you. I free you all!"

As she pushed and probed, the city streamed from the high plains, leaving a ring of disrupted soil several kilometers wide, scattered with dead and dying parts.

Ezeki and Musa pushed aside their blanket and peered out of the recess in their appropriated transport. They watched the last of the barricades put out legs and join the river at its tail.

"Allah save us from sorcery," Musa said, rubbing his *hijab*. "I'd swear *Shaytan* has a grip on my eyes. This is unreal, and I am possessed."

"None of that," Ezeki said, smiling as he backed into the recess and let the blanket corner fall. "A thousand years ago, this was science, not magic. And by all my power, I'd have that time come again! By God or Allah, we deserve it, we've suffered enough!"

Durragon rode his mount to one side of the moving city, his Chasers walking nearby, a second river. The city crossed the plain and crawled through the low hills, then marshalled and passed through a cleft in the mountain, just as Reah had done two months before. Still no weaknesses showed.

Durragon fumed.

Then, while descending the slopes to the old river bed, he saw his chance. He brought the captured parts of Tomoye forward and spoke to the drum.

"Where is the city weakest?" he asked.

The drum hummed and said nothing.

"I think where the biggest structural supports march. They're slow. We can pass between them. Am I right?"

The drum rested on a cart, pushed along by four Chasers, who sweated in the hot sun. Durragon rode beside it, looking down. "That's an order, a command request," he said softly.

"You are correct," the drum said. Then it began to crack on its flat ends. Durragon watched helplessly as his Chasers brought up dirt and grass to caulk the splitting seams, but the fluid and tiny glittering nodules poured out and the unit died.

The Chasers looked at him, faces blank. He shrugged. "It's told us what we need to know."

He climbed up a ridge overlooking the pass and sat on a rock, chin in hand. How much of the city was he willing to sacrifice? He had to stop it someway . . .

"Start a fire on the opposite side of the valley and deflect the city into the rock pile south of here. That'll break up the organization and let us move in faster."

The runners spread out and his army began to move. As he resumed his mount, he saw a body lying in the tufted grass. He pointed and asked, "Who's that?"

The flank runners shrugged. He rode by the body. It was the map-maker. Suddenly apprehensive, he took the lead of the torchers and stayed well away from the mass of troops.

He wasn't afraid. There was too much to do. But he could feel a force rising against him, shifting his course of action just as he was going to shift the city. It was only natural, he told himself; now he was going to be tested.

Chasers rode the more limber city-parts to the mouth of the pass and waited. The torchers crossed to the opposite side and set the necessary fires.

"Stop, dig wells, feed the pumping systems!" Reah demanded. The city obeyed but they were still too high; the wells didn't bring up enough water. The fire caught the side ranks and destroyed them. Reah felt their end as a shrivelling in her extended awareness.

The city moved around the fire and flowed toward the rock piles. Reah saw Durragon's scheme and brought the city to a halt again.

"I release you from another obligation," she said. "It's necessary to kill human beings now—not as one steps on ants, but deliberately."

She felt the spark of rage glowing beneath her. At once she was aware of a new city mental space—a vast, dark realm, crossed by ordered textures of tradition. For a moment she sensed rebellion, but that subsided, and the spark vanished.

Still, it was best to try an alternative first. The city sent part of its mass into the rock-piles to engage the men waiting there. The Chasers attacked and the rest of the city withdrew, leaving expendable parts behind as bait. The Chaser army was divided.

She pushed Resurrection on to the old river bed. The smell of the sea, a dozen miles away, came to her through a thousand sensors. Much fainter, but sharply amplified, was the smell of fresh water. It was deep, and they'd have to dig near Akkabar.

She looked for the village and saw it. A few huts had risen among the ashes, and now she was dragging the invaders back. She would try to circle the town, protect it. She spread the city farther apart, knowing what she was risking. She was tiring, though. Chasers riding rogue parts were capturing and destroying structural members on both sides. Events seemed to swim in her memory. She struggled in the chair. Weakness used her veins as step-ladders to her mind. Then she felt her stomach heave and she lost contact with the city. Far beneath her, the spark grew.

Durragon rode away from the arsonists after ordering them to extinguish their torches. The grass fires burned away from them, carried by winds going north through the pass. That was good; the fires had served their purpose, and already too much of the city had been destroyed.

He told his runners to re-group the army and follow him in a charge on the city. His flank-runners shook their heads.

"Dis we, brayba do we be, do no' t'ink wisdom to dribe away de—"

"Those are my orders!" Durragon said. The runners continued to look at him darkly, almost insolently. He stared them down. Perja shrugged. "Ob de way, Man," the Chaser said. They jogged off.

Still no fear, but Durragon could feel sweat gathering on his forehead, not born of exertion.

The sky across the river bed was gold, and high above, an insect-wing blue of enchanting depth. In another hour night would be upon them. The city could entrench and they'd never get into it. He had to act now.

He rode toward the front of the flow as fast as the mount could carry him, passing Chasers. Some cheered, others watched silent. There were only a few bands at the very front of the city, and they were tired, smoke-smudged and disgusted. They shouted questions as he passed them.

There was no time for orders or explanations. He had to get to the front, to lead his troop in for the kill. He could feel the blood pumping in his neck and head. Best to lead, to fly into the face of danger even before his men . . . that was how he would stop the uprising. It wasn't overt, but he could feel it nonetheless: the lack of respect, the growing confusion in his men. He found an assistant runner trudging through the grass and almost rode his city part over the man, stopping short and kicking up clots of dirt. "Get all the guards down to the front," he ordered. "All the veterans, the advance guides . . . I want them all up here with me." *Around me*, he thought. "I'll wait for them before we move in." He felt for the secure hardness of his pistol.

The city was a mile away, bearing down inexorably. There were no more obvious weaknesses in its lines than there had been at the beginning of the day.

This was the confrontation, the last stand. If he failed at this, the Chasers would lose their near-mystical reverence for him (were losing it already) and they would suspect he didn't really care for them, not even as a God cares for his peon creations. They would suspect he only cared for the opportunities they gave him. He had wondered how long it would take them to realize. *No leader ever cares for the masses*, he thought. *It's a relationship of opportunity, not love*. His father had once worked him the same way, looking at him after the harvest with dark, suspecting eyes, in the candlelight after the meager dinner, unsure what this child was, but knowing there was work in it, help for his failing strength. And Durragon had felt a similar suspicion for the tired, seamy-faced patriarch, had dreamed at night of killing him, taking the family savings and going far away.

Now he was the father, and the children were restless. He had to get his most trusted men around him, or he could be killed in the charge, just as the map-maker had been killed.

Durragon had been born a Habiru. No Habiru, he thought, could ever really trust or respect a Chaser. They wasted their lives running in the wake of migrating cities, hoping to scavenge and caring for little else, praying to intractable monoliths that hardly knew they existed.

Now he was their leading edge, to split the monoliths and bring back rightful Paradise. But they were too stupid to even know knives must have a cutting edge.

The advance guides, guards and honored veterans were gathering around him in clumps of five or six or ten, and he rode among them, barking orders and arranging their ranks as buffers. He spotted Perja riding a mount like his own, no doubt captured in the raids of the past few hours. Ambition. The man was dangerous. Durragon didn't stop to let him have his opportunity.

The city was almost upon them. Some small bit of tactical judgement told him it was foolish, suicidal, but he shouted the command anyway. "Move in! Wedge your way through!" A hundred yards. His mount carried him smoothly and the wind between his teeth felt exhilarating. Then a giant structural column seemed to materialize, pushing through the smaller city parts, dividing his men. Perja rode beside him.

"Get back to the rear ranks!" Durragon shouted. Perja shook his head. Durragon turned away to see where his mount was running. In the corner of his eye, he saw something fly in, a kicked-up stone, a tuft of dirt and grass. He pulled out his pistol.

He slid off the mount, hitting the ground and knocking all

his breath out. He felt a pain, like a pulled muscle in his chest. He rolled over.

Perja stood above him, blocking out the sky. The Chaser put a foot on each of his arms. He couldn't find the gun or organize his thoughts. The Chaser brought out a thin woven wire. Durragon closed his eyes. A shadow passed over. Angel of Death.

He coughed and his eyes flew open. Perja was still there, but something black was above him. The Chaser was cringing, trying to hunker lower, but his head was snagged by an obstruction and he flew away, leaving Durragon on his back. The shadow passed. The wire fell into Durragon's hands.

The city had saved him. The Chaser must have thrown a knife and knocked him down, and now the city, like a jealous lover, wanting his command, had saved him. His chest ached. Where was the knife? The stars were visible. The self-defeating stars . . .

Things moved around him, silent as ghosts. Huge things. He could feel their feet tromping the ground. Legs rose into the air like pistons, giant insects, walking . . . what? Someone was shouting.

There was wet on his hand, wet dark against the starlit grey . . . what?

"I'm hurt!" He felt his lips with his fingers. They opened and closed in rhythm with the noises. They were his own. He got to his feet and reached out for a dark hulk moving swiftly by. His hand caught an edge and held, yanking him up, and something large and gentle gripped him to keep him from falling under the treads.

In the starlight, Resurrection circled Akkabar and began to rebuild.

By night, the city was dark and lifeless. Its pieces groaned as they settled, a mournful sound that raised the hair on Ezeki's neck. Musa cried aloud to Allah like a child.

For two days and nights the leaderless Chasers surrounded Resurrection and tried to get inside. The barriers, though greatly reduced, held. The Chasers' songs could be heard above the wind and city sounds:

> *"Dis we; purge and puriby, sin ob men*
> *And dog, and Debbils dribe out ob dark,*
> *Dis we, brayba mans oll . . ."*
>
> *"Der wa' an ald God, an' dis me broke de*
> *Pact ob dis awbul ald Shaytan call' Day-o,*
> *And dead, dey all lab, and cry por de pain*
> *Ob de paders and modders ob me-o . . ."*

Musa and Ezeki listened as the sun approached zenith on the third day. "I should have known better than to consort with infidels," Musa said, sitting on the back of the stilled transport with Ezeki. "They have weak minds." The vehicle was parked on a much reduced version of the parkway which had once surrounded the city.

"Weakened by history, I think," Ezeki said. "Doesn't part of you want to do what they're doing?"

Musa made a fist and shook it at the sky. "Yes, but I'm not a crazy man. I don't listen to the voice of *Shaytan* inside of me."

Ezeki gripped the Moslem's arm. "As of this moment, we have no past. We're exiled by our expolises and by Durragon. We should survive together. We share a God, at least in some respects. And what better place to survive than in the city?"

"You're crazier than the dogs outside," Musa said.

"Not at all. Each day, we'll prick our arms and go to the hospital and say, 'Look, we're still injured . . . take care of us!' "

Under the bright blue sky they laughed until they had to hold each other up. Then they shook arms, grasping each other at the half of the elbows, and declared themselves brothers by common insanity.

"Where's the woman?" Musa asked, suddenly sober. "Was she killed? Are we alone here?"

Ezeki shook his head. "We can check in the hospital. If she's not there, the city's still too big to find someone who doesn't want to be found."

They spent an hour searching through the changed floor-plan of the city's lower regions. The hospital had been moved closer to the central shaft; pieces of the buttresses springing from its outer walls were singed. Much of the city looked shabby now, but the basic functions were still being performed. Durragon's forces had reduced it, but not subdued it. They entered the hospital and looked at the small cubicles with their empty beds. In the last cubicle, they saw a figure stretched out on a table. It was bathed in green light and surrounded by a web of silvery wires and medical machinery. Three husky coat-rack type workers stood nearby, unmoving. Ezeki stepped into the doorway to get a better look.

"Is it her?" Musa asked.

Ezeki leaned forward, then walked quickly around the table as a worker advanced to stop him. His eyes widened as he was pulled away by a brass and copper-colored arm.

"No," he said "It's *him*."

Durragon, half-awake, with green limbs and silvery wires and stinging drops of fluid weaving above him, had thought he was dead for several days, whenever he thought much at all. He couldn't remember how many times he had been carried from bed to table and back. He thought he was a body, being preserved by funeral directors from the Habiru village, taking their revenge on him day after day . . .

Then he heard the voices. He turned his head, or tried to, and found himself held down firmly. He recognized the voices. It was no use trying to talk. If he was dead, then they were dead, too. Even in death, he could have an army . . .

Reah sat at the top of the highest tower, now barely two hundred meters above the river bed, tapping her fingers impatiently as a mobile medical worker checked her over.

"You are not sick," it said. "That is, you are not diseased or malfunctioning."

"Then why do I throw up? My stomach bloats like I've been eating green fruit."

The worker hummed for a moment. "You are not aware?"

"No. Aware of what?"

"It is the reason you have been allowed to stay in the city."

"What, in the name of Allah?"

"You are pregnant."

Reah laughed. "I'm too *old*!" she said, her voice sharp.

"Apparently that isn't true."

"It's ridiculous. Who—I haven't . . ." She shook her head.

"You have been pregnant since the day you came here, perhaps a few days even before that. We can give you several choices. Most citizens opt for natural childbirth, as that suits our beliefs. You may, however, have your pregnancy conducted outside the womb, with additional maternal conditioning to facilitate acceptance of the child. Also—"

"Quiet!" She shuddered. "No. I don't believe it."

The worker said nothing more. She stood and walked to the wall, looking over the scattered, disordered camps of the Chasers. She frowned. There had been something . . . but it wasn't clear. She remembered lying on the dirt, with a youthful, dirty face moving back and forth above her. She felt queasy again, but not from the abomination in her womb. She was sick remembering how, as a child, she had watched a grasshopper mating with another grasshopper which had been cut in half. The live grasshopper was unable to discriminate.

The man—or men—or boys—who raped her had had no more control than the insect. At that time, she had been a half-wit, an ugly and filthy harridan. But the very fact of her femaleness had driven men to mate with her, plant monsters inside her. She felt like screaming.

"I won't carry such a child," she said. "I want it dead."

The words seemed to burn her tongue.

"Removal can be arranged," the worker said. "But we will not terminate the child."

"I don't care. Just take it out of me."

"You must go to an equipped apartment, or to the hospital."

"Are there still men in the hospital?"

"Yes."

"Then take me to the apartment."

Durragon was out of his bed and walking slowly around. A worker attended him, supporting one elbow. Durragon hadn't spoken since coming awake. He had no idea how long he had slept, but he was suspicious now, and he didn't want to give anything away by asking questions, seeming weak.

He was inside the city! The thought both plagued and delighted him. Why had it taken him in? Just because he was injured? Did it matter? He was where he wanted to be. Whatever God or gods controlled his fate had seen fit to bless him with an unequalled opportunity.

He heard a footstep and turned his head to the doorway. Ezeki Iben Tav stood there. Musa Salih was behind him.

"General," Ezeki said, nodding slightly.

"Where is Breetod? The others?" If he had a loyal flank runner, perhaps he could regain control of the Chasers.

"They're dead," Ezeki said. "They were killed when the city tried to move."

"But I was dead, and the city brought me back to life."

"You were not dead," the worker said. "You had a chest wound and a fractured skull. This city cannot resurrect the dead."

"The city no doubt has a different definition of death than we are used to," Ezeki said. "You may have been dead, General, in one way or another." The old man was standing stiff, his fists clenched.

"Whatever, the plan had worked. We're inside."

"Not for long. We'll be thrown out again."

"Tell me everything that's happened," Durragon said. "Brief me."

Ezeki hesitated, then began a disjointed, muddled description. His mind seemed elsewhere. Durragon frowned and tried to draw him out on several points. Musa added details.

"How were you wounded?" Ezeki asked when he was finished.

Durragon shook his head. "That isn't important. Now that we control the city, we'll change everything."

"We don't control the city," Musa said. "A woman does. A madwoman."

"The city manager is not insane," the worker said.

"The city isn't too bright, either," Musa commented, showing his teeth.

"You haven't . . . reasoned with her? Days, weeks in the middle of our goal, and you haven't taken advantage of your position?"

"We were waiting for you," Ezeki said softly. "We're not going to stay in the city any longer than it wishes. And I suspect neither will she."

"We'll find ways."

Ezeki sighed and looked away. "You are the General."

Durragon sensed something unpleasant in the old man's tone. "You couldn't hold this city if it was a starving dog and you had a bag of meat! You're a half-lettered pedant. What do you know about command?"

"Nothing," Ezeki said, surprised at the outburst. Good, Durragon thought. If I can surprise them, I can still control them.

"So!" Durragon laughed and straightened, wincing at the stretched skin on his ribs. "We'll have to get along as best we can."

"Yes, General," Musa said.

"I need rest. I must get well soon."

They nodded and left the cubicle. Ezeki looked like he was close to tears. "He'll have me killed when we get outside," he said.

"No, he won't. He's no better than we are now." Musa's eyes narrowed. "He lost the Chasers. Something happened out there; someone tried to kill him—not the city. He bungled his command!"

An hour earlier, Reah had opened her eyes to the kaleidoscopic flow of the ceiling, moaned, and rolled over in bed. She hadn't changed her position since. She felt like one of the damned. The operation itself hadn't been painful, but she was torn into a multitude of dissenting, condemning parts. Suddenly she jerked up in bed, screaming, "Where's the child? What have you done with it?"

There were no workers in the apartment and the louvres on the nearby desk screen didn't open. The panels above the bed which concealed medical equipment hadn't closed all the way, and she heard a faint ticking behind them. She tried to pry them open and broke a fingernail. She rose to her knees on the bed and pounded on the doors.

"Answer me!"

The ticking stopped. She backed away, shuffling across the bedclothes, which were trying to rearrange themselves beneath her knees. "Where is everything?" She felt close to panic. Had she pushed the city too far? Had it finally just given up and died?

The apartment door slid open and a worker entered.

"Do you need help?" it asked, holding up one brassy limb.

She stammered, then closed her mouth and shook her head. "It was a dream," she said. "I dreamed I had a child."

"You did," the worker said.

She nodded slowly, then sat in the desk chair. "What are you going to do with it?"

"It will be brought to term."

"And then?"

"You have renounced all claim to the child."

"Yes," she said. "What would I do with such a thing? A monster. An abomination." Her voice rose. "Why let it live?"

The worker didn't answer. Such a question was beyond its

capacity to understand, Reah thought. It could edit out her words when they made no sense, just as it would edit out a burp, or a stammer. "What do I care, anyway?" she asked.

"It's done with." She pointed to the screen. "This apartment isn't complete. Find me something more suitable."

"Of course," the worker said, and went out the door, motioning for her to follow.

It had been a week since the journey. Ezeki had spent the time learning how to use the apartment screens. Though the service was erratic, he was spellbound. He could learn more in one week than he had learned in all his past years. Musa saw very little of him.

Durragon had left the hospital and wandered through the city. The beauty was staggering. He wanted the city very badly. It had always been difficult for him to appreciate something until he knew he owned it completely. Now, with the opportunity to do so many things, he did nothing but walk and take a speculative inventory. His plans grew.

From the rebuilt control center, Reah followed their movement—watched Musa sitting in a courtyard, sunning himself; watched Ezeki through the receiver in his screen; but most carefully of all, watched Durragon as he paced and explored.

She did not show herself. She stayed in the reduced central tower performing her own inventory, assessing the city's new limitations and damage. How many children could she accommodate now? What did she care? She couldn't accept her own child—why ask for thousands not her own? All her life she had been compassionate, even when oppressed. Now she found it difficult to care.

But the children would be coming whatever she thought or felt, and having started the project, she couldn't bring herself to give up. With a worker beside her chair, and the equipment waiting at her fingertips, she half-heartedly began to arrange things. Apartments had to be cleaned out, but so many workers had been lost in the move. She felt a flash of anger again.

"Why can't you throw him out?" she asked for the tenth time.

"He is not completely healed."

"He's the one who almost destroyed us!"

The voice of the homunculus was flat and expressionless. "The city still has functions to fulfill."

How Reah hated! The tears would not come, however. She wasn't even sure what she hated any more—was it Durragon, or that terrifying spark she felt whenever she assumed the complete mantle of the city? That spark which in turn, seemed to hate her . . .

With evening, she took her walk, stiff-legged and slow, around the upper promenade. The worker followed her.

She watched the Chasers.

She thought of Abram Iben Khaldun, ages dead, and of her daughter. What would the new child be like? Where did the city keep it? Slowly, her anger turned away from her insides—still fertile, like seeds in a dead, dry fruit—and even away from the thoughtless scum who had raped her.

She could not hate the helpless and defenseless, not even the ignorant and crude. All together, they were common victims. They were products of an evil that went beyond understanding, of a philosophy that had wormed into the brilliance of the city-dwellers and designers. But she could not even hate them. Perhaps they had suffered most of all.

Whom did she hate? She stopped and felt the pressure build behind her face as if she were a pot coming to a boil. She lifted her hands. "Allaaa-a-ah!" she wailed. "Help me! You despise me, you torture me, help me-e-e!"

She was on her knees, lifting her hands. The tears poured down her face. That was weak, very weak; that was giving in to the madness again . . . to the insects buzzing, the bells ringing, the filth and scavenging. But she couldn't stop. Her thin body shook. Her colorful robes formed a wrinkled circle around her, the contours changing with her spasms.

She looked up, beseeching. "Allah, all my life I have

served you, never cursed you—not until I became mad and entered this city—all my life I have been a good Moslem woman, obedient and faithful. Not once did I dream of being more than I was, yet you visited grief upon me time and again until I broke. What are you testing me for?" She had an image of a club of males—djinn and prophets and men risen to Paradise—around a shadowy, masculine Allah, with Mohammed at their fore, in a city of jeweled minarets and stone walls and gold walls and gates of pearl . . . all looking down on her, mildly amused. They had risen above life, and how the suffering of those still in the material realm seemed like the scuttling of ants to them. She was an object of pitying amusement. She would never attain such heights. She was a woman, barely possessed of a soul, bound to Earth, her tides determined by the motions of a moon so far away it was beyond consideration. Her blood flowed and ebbed, she was unclean, she bore the gate of creation, she was an object of desire and disgust. She was not even most desirable. For children, go to a woman. For pleasure, go to a young boy. For delight, go to a melon! Such had been the dirty rhymes thrown at her when she had been a child, by boys and even other girls, blaspheming as all children will do when not supervised. They hardly knew what the words meant. She had always wondered what men did with a melon, until finally she had learned that merely eating a melon was considered better, more desirable than consorting with a woman. That was the ultimate refinement, in discernment.

And yet in her deepest despair she still turned to Allah. "Allah," she murmured, head buried in her arms, bowing over. "Allah." The insects buzzed.

And . . . what was it? She seemed to hear a song. She turned . . . and her past fell away, as if she had all her life been falling down a long tunnel, and only now had emerged in sunlight. She felt herself lifted up and fitted to something, not like man to woman but . . . she searched through her more recent education—like a molecule fitting to another molecule. She was very small, but valued, and the thing she fitted against, so well, was huge and beyond knowledge, but loving. She removed her clothes and stood naked, surrounded by the sprawl of fabric. Her breasts were high, her stomach was flat, her hair was smooth and red-gold, and honey hung between her thighs. Then that was gone, too, and she was like a thin leaf of gold, wavering in an electric wind.

"What am I doing here?" she asked, and the larger molecule seemed to quiver with a vast, benevolent laughter.

You are not quite ready after all

"No," she said. "I'm not."

And she wafted down, neither sad nor despondent at the sudden release. She found herself fully clothed, walking with purpose and energy down a corridor of trees. She was laughing at each trunk, each spray of leaves. They had been carried by the city and lovingly protected from fire and Chasers, to be planted here, that she might walk among them. They were all parts of the city. And she was a part too, for the city had a soul. Distorted as it was, it lived and desired. Now she had to fulfill those desires and teach it how to survive, as a mother would teach her child.

Durragon stood fifty meters away, hidden by a stand of trees. Musa and Ezeki stood beside him. "That's the madwoman," he said. They nodded. "How does she control the city?"

"We don't know," Ezeki said. "We've only seen her a couple of times."

"She walks like she's drunk. Look how she reaches out and touches the trees. What's inside the tower?"

Reah entered a half-circle archway and a wide door closed behind her. Ezeki sighed and held out his hands. "We have only seen this place just now."

"You've been wasting time," Durragon said. "We have to talk to her, reason with her if that's possible. She looks harmless. A crazy old woman. If the city can do without her—if we can control it the same way she does—if she does—" He cocked an eye at the two men—"then we can do without her, too."

Musa looked down at his feet. He was tired of fighting and killing. The old Habiru must be tired as well, he thought. Yet Durragon was able to lead them around like gullible Chasers.

The children were coming, just a day or two away. She wondered how the parents had felt—if there had been parents. Had the machines just snatched them away, or taken only those who were sick beyond help, or abandoned? Perhaps the villagers had been asleep and saw nothing, or perhaps they had regarded the machines as appointed angels. She sat in the chair, watching through the city's far-seeing eyes. Her legs ached, and her breasts no longer seemed as high, or her hair as bright and silken—but that had been a vision. What remained was more important. The purpose, the energy. She closed her eyes to rest them. Outside it would be growing dark. She could return to her apartment, clean herself, lie down and rest, perhaps get up after a few hours and watch the stars, then use the screen, tap the city's memory less directly.

She got out of her chair stiffly. The screens and equipment dimmed and shut down behind her as she walked to the door. There were fewer workers now; none followed her. To feel more secure, she would post one in her apartment.

The air was cool and scented with the fragrance of pine. The sky above was a rich royal blue, streamered with flame-red clouds. Stars were appearing, and a scimitar moon. She looked ahead.

Three men stood in front of her. She stopped, hands by her side, puzzled. Durragon stepped forward and smiled.

"It's time to meet," he said.

"I see."

"We have to talk about what we can do for this city."

"There isn't much time now," she said cautiously, "the children will be coming in a day or two. I have to get things ready for them."

Durragon's smile faded slightly. "Children?" he said, with the merest flex of a question.

"Probably thousands of them."

"I don't see what you mean—"

"The city is here to take care of all the children it can. The sick ones, those who have no chance outside. I am directing it." She looked at the two others and gauged them by their expressions. *They aren't with him any more,* she thought. "I can use your help. It'll be difficult doing it by myself."

"There isn't enough space now, or facilities."

"Nonsense." She returned her shrewd gaze to his face. "You're a leader. At least, you were for a time. You can help."

"I—"

She pushed her verbal advantage home. She was ahead of him; he was weakening. "Or you can leave."

"No," he said, grinning. "I can't do that."

"Then come with me." She walked past him. They stumbled out of her way and Durragon spun around, his face flushed. He was frowning and his fists kept opening and closing. "Come," she repeated, looking back at them. "I'll show you all you need to know." She continued walking. She trusted them—or Durragon, at least—about as much as she trusted a scorpion. But even with her back turned, she felt no fear. She was in control.

Durragon held Ezeki and Musa back when they tried to follow. "Later," he called out. "We'll go with you later."

Ezeki gave him a puzzled glance. "Let her go," Durragon growled. "We'll see what's in the tower."

But the door wouldn't open for them.

In the apartment, with the door closed and a worker posted, she rested and felt some of her self-confidence slip away. They had caught her by surprise, had come so *close* . . . And she had behaved like a fool. What had she seen in the expressions of the old man and the Moslem? Had she seen enough to expect them to stand up for her against Durragon? She shook her head and tears started up in her closed eyes. She was so weak, and what she had felt earlier had been a moment of girlish stupidity, weakness . . . exaltation. Molecules fitting together! Youth and beauty forever! Bitterness and death, more likely.

She swallowed back a clot of phlegm and tried to feel for the joining again, the ecstasy. It wasn't there now. How could she be sure it had ever been there? Would it protect her from Durragon? If she was wrong, and the old man and the Moslem weren't sympathetic to her, then in time there was nothing on her side. Nothing except a still-huge mass of contradictions, neurosis and fear . . . the city. Resurrection.

Could she get the two apart from Durragon, talk to them? It wasn't likely.

"Think of the young ones," she said out loud, but the confusion remained.

While Durragon slept, Musa met Ezeki on a parapet looking over the central shaft, several floors below the Apostate's quarters. They sat and drank their health with the city's wine, which left their heads clear. "I'd like something with more persuasion to it right now," the old man said, lifting his glass and peering through the amber fluid.

"In the Earth days, my people would not drink anything . . . ah . . . persuasive. Nor would the more orthodox Moslems on God-Does-Battle. So I am chastened by Resurrection."

"What are we going to do?" Ezeki asked.

"He'll kill her soon," Musa said.

"We've been with him for five years. I don't know any other way."

"The city shows us another way."

Ezeki shook his head despondently. "I'd leave him. I really would. But what can we do with a city like this? Get healed, then thrown out?"

"We're healed now."

"Then we'll be thrown out any time. But if he kills her, takes over . . . perhaps we can stay. The city let her stay."

"Yes, but why?" Musa asked.

Ezeki shook his head. "Perplexing."

"She wants to help children, crippled children. Did you see the way she looked at us? Perhaps we could work for *her*, instead of him."

"Crippled children! Sick kids! She's a dreamer," Ezeki said. "I was a dreamer, once. Now I'm just an old fool with pretensions to learning. And the city doesn't even leave me my pride. It shows me how ignorant I am."

"We could kill him, now," Musa whispered. "In his sleep. She would reward us."

Ezeki stared steadily at the Moslem. "We're crazy, as crazy as she is."

"Then perhaps it's best the whole foresaken planet should go crazy again. Sanity hasn't been much good for us, has it?"

Ezeki started to get to his feet, then hesitated. Musa rose all the way. "Now?" the old man asked. The Moslem nodded. "If we get thrown outside, the Chasers will probably kill us."

"What will we use?"

Musa pulled out a crudely made folding knife. "I clean my fingernails with it," he said, grinning wickedly.

They went to Durragon's apartment. When they got there he was gone.

The general had come awake and found himself alone, unable to sleep. As the two men searched frantically for him below, he stood by the tower door, deep in thought. He felt good now, almost as if he could will things just by thinking. The woman was strong, but he was stronger. And he had made up his mind. "I will get in there," he said, "and I will control the city, just as she does."

He stared hard at the door, trying half seriously to make his strength manifest. When the door opened, he jumped back, the hair on his neck prickling. The old woman stood there. "Neither of us can sleep," she said. "Can insomniacs ever be enemies?"

"We've both been planning," he said. "Maybe we can

plan together.'' There was something disturbing about her, a placid acceptance he had never seen before. His words might not have even been heard, but for her turning inward and motioning him to follow with a crooked finger. Durragon stared at the control center.

The charts, the throne, the ranked screens and odd machinery . . . it was terrifying, and more beautiful than anything he had ever seen. It was powerful. It was the navel of the world.

''Why let cripples into the city?'' Durragon asked. ''They won't know what to do with themselves. The city should belong to those who can best use it.''

Her expression was almost apologetic.

''I have a plan,'' he continued. ''I thought you'd . . . like to hear it. We can rebuild the planet, make it like it was. We have to find the place where the city grows new parts—''

''No,'' Reah said. ''We'll start a new way. Someday, perhaps we won't even need cities. We'll use the fragments of the old world to help lay foundations for the new.''

Just like that, her words made him seem like a savage, a child again. She was babbling, he decided. His ears hurt him and he tried not to listen—but she went on. She took him around the room, showing him things and telling him their names, using words he didn't understand, magic words, powerful words. Her control was daunting, but she was no better and no smarter than he. That was obvious. If she was gone, he could take control as easily as she had. She was mad! A city filled with cripples. It was obscene.

He watched her closely, waiting.

''I've been listening to the city for days now,'' she said. ''For a while, it kept me here because I was—'' The briefest of pauses. ''I was ill. But now I'm well, as well as I can hope to be, and it still lets me stay. Perhaps it's made a decision. Perhaps it needs me. And if it needs me, it needs us . . .''

He came closer. He pulled a wire out of his pocket. He had wrapped the ends in tough bedsheet fabric, rolls of it, and spliced the pieces together to form handles. It would be like the death Perja had planned for him.

She had her back to him. A worker rolled in through the door. Behind the worker, eyes wide, walked Musa and Ezeki.

Durragon stepped forward, wrapped the wire around her neck, applied his knee to her upper neck, pulled back her chin, and felt the snap. He loosed the wire and backed away. The body fell to the floor.

The worker rushed past him. It brought out a net, like strands of hair made from silver, and laid it over the woman's head. No, that wouldn't do—Durragon kicked at the worker

And almost broke his foot. It seemed rooted to the floor.

Musa stood and stared, slack-jawed, but Ezeki shook his head wildly and grabbed the Moslem's knife from his hands. "Damn YOU!" he screamed. Durragon half-turned.

Reah, vision dimming, felt the net around her and was again in the vast space with the textures of tradition. But this time the spark was a sun, rising under her, and its rage was beyond all measure.

Then there was an enormous time.

It was the middle of the month Sivan, a calm, dry day in the village of Akkabar. The smooth walls of the city's inner circle surrounded the town. Near the main school, a stream of water passed from the wall—not under it, but through a surface slick as glass—and meandered out one side of the main gate. There were four gates in the inner wall, but none of them lead into the city. Instead, broad tunnels let the citizens pass to the outside.

Ezeki Iben Tav sat at the front of the main classroom in the school near the river. He had just finished a lesson in history and the students were writing on slate tablets. They were beautiful children, and more of them came every day. The dormitories the villagers had built were now almost full of children, yet still transports delivered the sick and retarded and lame to the outer barricades. The city took them in, healed them, and weeks later, at night released them in Akkabar. They were healthy and bright, just the sort of children bereaved parents might be willing to adopt. The supply of parents was small, but with such children, what matter if each parent adopted a hundred, a thousand? The city provided. Fruit grew along the inner walls, and other foods—grain, fodder for cattle—rose out of the ground with little tending now that the water supply was assured.

Musa came to the classroom and clapped his hands. It was time for the pupils' physical training. Musa taught them games and how to fight properly; the Chasers occasionally returned to Resurrection and skirmishes had taken place.

The older boys and girls stayed behind for a few moments to socialize. Ezeki looked out the open front of the classroom at the village then stepped into the sunlight, away from the reed awning, and shaded his eyes. A slender tower rose on the city's northern side.

He had only two regrets. There had been so little time for him to sample the knowledge the city contained. He would always be haunted by the memory, and by knowing he could never return. His second regret was that the children, bright as they were, emerged from the city haunted not only by the beauty they could not have, but by peculiar notions impressed on them. In time they seemed to come around. Ezeki was a good teacher and a good teacher of teachers. For their health and bounty it was a small price to pay.

The children told stories. In the city they had often encountered a figure they called, simply, Spirit-Woman. She came and went, neither smiling nor frowning, and a star glowed in her forehead. She might have led the star or been led by it, no one could tell.

They had occasionally seen another child, alive and not a ghost, but segregated from them, never allowed to play. The city had told the children, in the rare times it spoke, that the young one was Christ reborn, waiting to cleanse their sins in due time. That disturbed Ezeki. He could imagine the city cradling a stray infant but why was it allowed to stay?

Of all the mysteries and memories, one haunted him most. The city's final screams, the day he and Musa and Durragon's corpse had been thrown out into Akkabar . . . the entire sky, burned with flaming brands, could not have screamed so heart-rendingly. After all, it had been betrayal stacked upon betrayal—the attack on the woman, then the murder of Durragon. No holy city could stand such a thing. They were lucky it had carried out the woman's plan.

Was she still in the city, or her spirit, controlling it? The questions piled up and he smiled as he always did, then shook his head. Where was she now?

Between the textured spaces, Reah felt her children enter and leave. There was one child who stayed, but she was never allowed to see him clearly. This disturbed her. She was constrained by the glowing spark, now reflected all around like a million bright searchlights in the fog. She was not alive, and she was not dead. While she sensed the presence of the huge molecule, she could not fit into it. Somehow, lacking everything, she was content. Long ago, her mother had told her that Paradise was not for women.

But while she did not command, neither did she serve. She wandered, thought when it was possible and appropriate, but usually just waited.

It was all a game, lapses of indefinite time between the fittings of huge molecules. Soon enough, others would do what she had done, or the cities would die and wither away like ants under a spyglass beam. Either way she would be freer than she had ever been before.

Still, she swam in a kind of pride. She had made important moves in the game. When she felt the pride, the molecular connection loomed up, seemed to query, Not ready yet, eh?

No, not yet . . .

The cities became fewer and fewer. Strength of will failed, environments changed; where they weakened, often enough Expolitans and Chasers moved in to finish them off. Centuries of bewilderment and self-accusation had hardened into anger and hatred.

As the numbers of cities dwindled, some reached out to the others, using communications links long abandoned. Dialogues were exchanged, shy, halting at first, then more extensive. Information passed from city to city, and queer stories were told, for in some cities marvelous things had happened.

The cities continued to die. Finally, as if tired of the pain of links suddenly silent, or the worse pain of links growing more feeble every day, the city talk stopped.

The few still alive were silent, like stars in a dying universe, waiting for dust and defilement.

BOOK THREE
3562 A.D.

The Revenant

WHATEVER else they took away from him, they could not touch the fact that he was a fine architect. He had created enough monuments that long after the petty disputes and clashes of personality were forgotten, his name would still—

For the merest moment, he was amazed that such a trivial line of thought could have been preserved in the simulacrum. Then he had a dizzying spiral of recursive wonders—that he could be thinking about the miracle of such trivialities, and *thinking* about thinking.

Best to concentrate on the last memory—Danice, long black hair, hugging him before the process, saying good-bye forever to a man she would see the next day, after the block had memorized him; very strange for her—

In a rush, he spilled from the block, arms flying, legs tangling in each other. With a sigh, the block delivered a neatly folded stack of clothes and then paled, crusted over, and died.

Robert Kahn blinked. He lay naked in a heap of dirt and debris. Sticks and leaves clung to his moist skin. He smelled mustiness and decay. Nobody had come to meet him. The expected hum of the living city of Fraternity was an empty, echoing wind.

The great architect, come to inspect his work after two centuries and offer advice, suggest revisions if necessary, was alone.

He stood and brushed the dirt and leaves off, then looked at the clothes beside him. He should have arrived dressed. Instead, as if trying its best, the block had tossed out his apparel separately. His vision blurred and he rubbed his eyes. He was a little weak. He shouldn't have been. The block should have re-created him fresh and strong.

He wasn't frightened yet. He felt blunted, as if coming out of a drug haze. But fear wasn't far away. Like the wings on a new butterfly, his emotions were spreading out, stiffening.

The block—cornerstone of the great Aquinas Gate archway—was a wreck. How it had produced him at all was a wonder. The walls around it were grey and cracked, dry-looking. The pipes lacing back and forth through the arch, integrated into the overall floral design, were empty of fluid.

Outside the Aquinas gate was a broad plaza covered with mounds of dirt and pitted with holes as if people had been digging for buried treasure. Evidence of fire was clear in scorched walls, piles of blackened ash. He glanced up at the ceiling within the city, beyond the arch. The vault was still there, great upside-down beehive-like shafts of basalt hollowing to form the dome a hundred meters above the floor. But everything was grey, not vibrant green and sky blue and violet.

A huge part of the city—perhaps all of it—was dead. As far as he could see down the walkway to the main heat shaft, a kilometer away, the walls and buttresses and pipes were lackluster.

He walked out onto the plaza, avoiding the pits, until he reached a spreading field filled with large chunks of broken silicate. He stepped out of the city's shadow and looked back. The sun was brighter than he remembered—brighter and hotter. Around the city there was nothing but a plain of dry grass, isolated scrub trees, and a crude dirt road.

He squinted at the city's towers. The lines had changed. It

was obviously the city of Fraternity, and from this direction he could make out—with some difficulty—the abstracted portrait of Saint Thomas Aquinas in the central tower, but—

Like a sand castle in the rain, the outline had eroded. Up and down the heights, marks of burning and decay and vandalism vied with collapsed supports and walls for first place in the game of destruction.

The whole city was dead.

He was still naked. He had to return to the city for the clothes—and to retrieve the record. His work on the one hundred and fifty-three cities of God-Does-Battle had at times been so frustrating and arduous that he had decided to leave a secret network of city recorders, in case something should go wrong and he be blamed. But he had never considered anything like this . . .

How long had it been? More than two centuries—perhaps much more. He stepped back into the shadow and re-entered the corpse of Fraternity.

Arthur Sam Daniel wasn't surprised to see the oddly dressed stranger traveling the road past his small farm. Just the day before, a large, dark man carrying a talking head under his arm had gone in the same direction. Arthur's grandmother had often told him about "trods," or spirit roads. It was common knowledge that God-Does-Battle was a haunted world; times were changing, and apparently the trods were shifting. Arthur sat on the wooden bench under the mulcet tree, ten meters from the road and the stranger and twenty or so from the house, wondering if he had time to run back before it got him.

It stopped by the fencepost. Arthur could see that it wasn't sweating, despite the heat. It spoke a few words. Though the stranger's language sounded familiar, he couldn't quite understand. After another attempt, the stranger shook its head.

"Are you human?" Arthur asked loudly, poised to leave the bench and run if need be. "Or maybe a spirit?"

Of course, it could also be a city part. New Canaan had been plagued with mimics for almost a generation.

The stranger looked puzzled, then smiled. It said something in what Arthur recognized as Hebrew, but the Daniel families hadn't spoken Hebrew since leaving Bethel-Japhet during the Break Wars. The Daniels had been Catholic then, but had learned Hebrew in the Expolis Ibreem to be neighborly.

It was truly hot—the hottest summer in Arthur's forty-five years. Even if the stranger didn't sweat, it might be thirsty. Arthur brushed off his pants legs nervously and stood to face it. "Well, whatever you are, the least I can do is offer a drink of water. Come on in." He gestured for the stranger to follow him between the withered thorn bushes to the house. Hospitality was one of the few pleasures left to Arthur these days. The stranger shaded his eyes to look, then complied.

"Nan!" Arthur called to his daughter from the front porch. He looked over his shoulder; the stranger was a few steps behind. "We have a guest."

"Who's that?" A woman's voice inquired from inside.

"I don't know," Arthur said. "I've decided you're human," he said to the stranger, opening the door. "But my decisions don't mean much around here. I wasn't sure because of those clothes, you know." The stranger wore a fancier outfit than any that the Canaan Founders could produce, that was for sure. Arthur especially admired the boots that seemed to flow right down from the pants, and the way there were no buttons or zippers visible. "You spoke a bit of Hebrew there, but I've forgotten mine since I was a kid." Nan met them in the front room, rubbing her hands on black coveralls.

"Who is he?" she asked suspiciously.

"Doesn't speak like us," Arthur said.

"Why did you invite him in? What if he's a city part or something? He could be dangerous."

The stranger glanced around the front room, a worried look on his face. The structure of the house was primitive but sound—a strong wood frame with glazed brick walls—but litter and filth speckled the front room and adjoining kitchen.

The fireplace was almost choked with ashes, and the pot hanging over it on black cast-iron rods was caked with remains of old meals. The floor, except for well-worn trails, was centimeters deep in dust. Arthur and his daughter had not cleaned since the dust storms three months before.

"Haven't been keeping it as well as we should," Nan said guiltily. She was thirty years old, at least, going premature grey, with a thin face weighed down by lines of worry. Arthur was balding, with long fringes of hair around his crown. He wore coveralls much like Nan's.

"No need, just ourselves alone here," he said.

"I see," Kahn said, and Arthur understood him. The accent wasn't quite right, but at least they could talk. Arthur smiled.

"You been away a long time?"

"I'm not actually back yet," Kahn said. "Sorry, I'm certainly not here to speak in riddles. By the way, do you understand me?"

"Pretty well now. Just forgot for a minute there?"

Nan clearly didn't like the stranger in her house. She backed away and held her hands clasped in front of her.

"I'm a quick study at languages. Yours is a bit like English, with a touch of evolution clocked in. There's a machine in my head which lets me extrapolate rapidly, memorize, compute." At least, there was something in the simulacrum which imitated the original machine he had had implanted decades ago. Strictly speaking, he was all machine now.

"In your head?" Nan asked. "How? You from the polises?"

The stranger didn't answer. The woman's tone was distinctly unfriendly. "What happened here?" he asked, holding out his arms.

"Dust ruined the crops two years running," Arthur said. My wife left with my other daughter to find work with the Canaan Founders, didn't come back."

"No, I mean, why aren't you living in the cities—the polises?"

That stumped Arthur for a moment. Then he looked the stranger's clothes over more closely, seeing how truly unique they were. "Maybe you should tell us where you're from, first. Then I'll tell you what I know. Who are you?"

"My name is Kahn," the stranger said. "Robert Kahn."

"That's a peculiar name—not peculiar, not like no one could have it," Arthur said, "but more like nobody wants to have it."

"Why?"

Arthur and Nan exchanged glances. "Go get us some water," he told her. "That's the name of the man who built the polises. You don't look that ignorant. You should know about him."

"I did build the cities," the stranger said.

Arthur smiled tolerantly. He had the man pegged now. He had met someone like him when he was conscripted twenty-four years ago—a fellow who had tried to get out of service by acting crazy. "Don't tell the Canaan Founders that. They have a bone to pick with you." He chuckled. "You got us in this mess, long time ago. Just watch your tongue around them. Us, we haven't got anything against you—we're tolerant enough."

"I take it something went wrong."

"You're not playing the fool for me, are you?"

"Not at all," the stranger said, face perfectly serious. "I'm here to look over my work, check up on things. Looks like a great many things have gone wrong, and I've returned a lot later than I should have. Does anyone live in the cities—the polises?"

Arthur didn't answer. He pulled up a chair for the stranger and shouted at Nan to hurry up with the water. She came into the room hauling a full bucket, with two dirty tin cups in one hand.

"How long has it been?" the stranger asked.

"You think I'm so ignorant I don't know what year it is?" Arthur shot back, getting angry now. "I'm no fool, and you're no spook, you can't get away with baiting me that way!"

"Father's a very intelligent man," Nan said quietly, putting the bucket on the table and handing out the glasses. "We've been through rough times. We're not tidy here, but we're not simple."

"I'm not teasing or baiting you or anything, sir. I honestly don't know how long it's been since you lived in the polises."

"I didn't ever live there. Nobody for fifty generations has lived there. It's been nearly eleven hundred years."

"What's the date—the Christian date?"

"No such thing now. I don't know."

"Apollo year?"

"Don't know that either."

Kahn ignored the dirt on the cup and swallowed a cold draught of water. It was a nervous gesture more than anything else—the simulacrum needed a minimum of water and no other kind of sustenance.

"Inside pumps don't work, so we raise water from the well," Arthur said, tapping his bony fingers on the wood table top.

"The water's fine," Kahn said. Eleven hundred years!

"It's hot today, no denying it." Nan wiped sweat from her forehead and poured more water into their cups.

Jeshua Tubal Iben Daod put down Thinner's head in the shade of a withered mulcet tree. "Just plant me here somewhere and I'll replace this poor bush," the head said, grimacing. "A headfruit tree."

Jeshua had carried Thinner for three weeks, covering at least eight hundred kilometers. The head kept him company. Your jokes are getting worse," Jeshua said, sitting down against a rock.

"It's the heat."

Jeshua lay back in the grass and rubbed his back in it. His clothes were covered with dirt and grass stains, but none of the dirt was his own. For over a century he had known how to shut off the artificial sweat and excretory systems in his body, making him cleaner than either a real human or a pure machine. Getting used to not being human had taken him some time.

"Come on," Thinner said. "Don't sulk. What would we be doing right now in the city, anyway—"

"I don't sulk," Jeshua said darkly. "And if we were in Mandala, I'd be studying *kaballah*, meditating, fixing whatever could be fixed."

"Which wasn't much, the past few years. I'm amazed it lasted as long as it did."

"We tried," Jeshua admitted. They had had this conversation at least two dozen times already. It was like making the first four or five moves in a game of chess, each opponent knowing the exact piece and square the other would use, so familiar the board could be set up that way, and the real game begun. For Jeshua and Thinner, the real game was figuring out where they were going, and what they were going to do when they got there.

"So we did everything we could. It was a lost cause," Thinner said.

"Not according to my studies."

The head made a sound like a sigh. " 'The vessel of the Holy One Blessed Be He has broken and scattered its drops of worthy oil into the nether reaches . . . One part in Mandala, another in each city, and now the parts must gather themselves together again.' "

"You're memorizing me," Jeshua said, smiling.

"It's about the only thing I *can* memorize any more."

"I feel it inside," Jeshua said, looking across the grey-brown grassland and the waves of heat. "Don't you?"

"Some of the words strike home," Thinner said. "But wishes don't bring rain." The head rolled over. "Prop me up again," he said stoically. "I just find it ridiculous that two city parts would sit around discussing human religion."

"We go where we must."

"I'd much prefer Resurrection."

"If we go to Resurrection, our cause will be lost there, too. All the cities are dead or dying."

"Not Resurrection, not yet," Thinner said. "That's *my* faith."

"The regathering will occur at the Bifrost. If we go there first, we don't waste time, take chances."

"We don't even know what the Bifrost is. Or how to get there, exactly. Communications haven't been the best for some time . . . we don't even know if it still exists!"

"It must. And I think the signals came from Throne."

"Fine, but do we know where Throne has moved? No. In Resurrection, there could be information—a library. You could study in the library, pin down your prophesies more precisely."

"And you could find spare parts—perhaps another body," Jeshua said.

"That has occurred to me once or twice. I'm not sure I can last long enough to get to the Bifrost. Or you. Look at your skin."

Jeshua pulled a flap of skin together on his arm and fastened it. It was getting worse now, opening and showing the green capillaries and silver-white bones whenever he wasn't vigilant.

"I admit I'd like to have some means of walking around without being carried. I wouldn't even mind being a remote again. I'm tired of being a cripple."

Jeshua held his fingers in an inverted pyramid, elbows on his knees. "It is the suffering of the—"

"Birth pangs of the age of the messiah," Thinner said. Jeshua looked at him mournfully.

"The texts are very clear."

"I've never found them so. You've been at them for fifty years—Rab City Part Jeshua, combing out hidden secrets from the books like fleas from a beggar!"

"We're machines," Jeshua said, his expression showing he was about to return bait for bait. "Machines don't suffer."

"Tube waste," Thinner said. "We mimic. We were made to play the roles. Let *them* decide if we're faking it." By *them* he meant humans. "We're as real as they are." The pair had been avoiding humans since leaving Mandala. In Mandala, of course, there had been no humans at all. They had grown used to living alone, and life in the city had inevitably rubbed in an aversion to humans. Even Jeshua, who had grown from a small child believing he was human and living with them, felt vaguely misanthropic.

He had been alive for more years than he cared to remember now, never aging, learning how to use his body all over again. He could still eat human food if he wished, and be sustained that way. Thinner could not. Jeshua had to periodically peel off the tip of a finger (which was getting worn, too, and dropping away at awkward moments) to give Thinner some of the nourishment his body had processed. Above the metal and colloid, blue and green chemicals, cables and valves and sensors, was the sandy flush of skin and the dark, thick hair. Despite the years, the image of Jeshua's exterior still haunted him with humanity, and in that way he would always be human, not a city part.

Thinner's body surrogates had never quite taken. With the breakdown of the last—a wheeled water-sprinkler which had tended the city's gardens—Thinner had resigned himself to being bodiless. Jeshua didn't mind carrying the head around. He had long since come to regard Thinner as his only friend, and, like him, one of the last living parts of Mandala.

He stood up and brushed off his clothes. Thinking of Mandala was depressing. He reached down with his broad, rugged hands, but Thinner objected.

"Just a moment. We don't talk as much when we walk, and I'd like to get this settled now."

Jeshua shrugged. "All right. But we're just bickering to give us an excuse to keep moving. I don't think either of us wants to decide. We don't know where Resurrection is now, and what if one is gone, or the other, and we make the wrong choice? We might find out how things really are."

Thinner's jaw moved as if he were swallowing. "We're very naive out here. Sooner or later, if we keep moving, as ignorant as we are, we're going to be caught, killed, put on display—whatever. We're freaks. I am an obvious freak, but you're no less one. If we got to Resurrection, not only might we get the information we need, but we might be able to ride a transport part to the Bifrost."

Jeshua considered. There was nothing in the texts forbidding such a sidetrip—just the risk of encountering humans. If they find out what we are—"

"Don't," Thinner said. Wherever they had been, even the dead cities had been scourged—burned, used for the dumping of trash, destroyed when possible. With the death of Mandala through its own madness and decay, they had had to face a sobering fact.

Most of the cities—dying for lack of the citizens they had once exiled—were no longer able to defend themselves.

The time for humanity's vindication was at hand.

Kahn finished his explanation. Arthur stared at the opposite wall, the cords in his throat working.

"If you really are from a polis—"

"From Fraternity," Kahn repeated.

"—Then I'm not sure you should stay in this house."

Arthur got up from his chair and stood by the table. "We're supposed to report rogue parts."

"I'm not a part."

"You're a ghost," Nan said. "Someone who should be dead by now."

"Whether or not I'm dead, somewhere else, has no bearing on my existence here," Kahn said. "I'm not a ghost." He reached out and gripped Nan's arm, making her jump in her seat. "Feel. I'm as solid as you are."

"You claim you're like a picture, then," Nan said, slowly pulling her arm from his fingers. "Except . . . round."

"More than that, even. I think and act and feel just like the original. To myself, I am Kahn. But my time here is short. I only have about thirty days." He looked between Arthur and Nan. "Certainly not enough time to try to convince everyone."

Arthur stacked the cups and carried them into the kitchen, dropping them into a dry washtub. "Crazy people say they're Robert Kahn."

Kahn looked up.

"They say it all the time. Especially if they are crazy for being beat up. That sort of thing." He refused to face Kahn. "You don't sweat in the heat—maybe you're sick. Where you get clothes like that, I don't know, but I don't travel much, either. Maybe you're crazy and from a place I've never been."

"I don't do magic tricks," Kahn said. "I'm not claiming to be a god, or a ghost."

"I'd believe a ghost," Nan said.

"When I was stored in the block's memory, there was a universal program in the cities. They have to let me inside. Take me to a city that's still alive—"

"There aren't any here," Arthur said. "They're dead and the Chasers and Founders tried to burn them. We fought city parts." He pointed to a heavy-bore rifle sitting alone in a gunrack next to the fireplace. "I was conscripted. Twenty-four years ago, they gave me that, and took six years out of my life because they were afraid of polises taking all of us over. Then I came home to my family, got back to farming—that's been eighteen years." He paced across the creaking floor. "Back then, the Founders were just soldiers and hotheads. Now they're bankers, merchants, farmers, engineers."

"You mentioned Chasers. What are they?"

"Hunh!" Nan said, incredulous.

"They used to worship polises, chase after them. Didn't respect them—peculiar type of worship. They'd just as soon burn a polis down if they could, and when the polises got weak, they burned them, sure enough. Now the Founders hire Chasers as soldiers, police."

Kahn shook his head. "It'll take years just to catch up on the history."

"History! History is dead people and crooked Founders and no laws any more—"

"Founders have laws, Father," Nan said patiently. "They're a government like any other."

"A touch more harsh," Arthur said sharply. "They're expolitans like all the rest of us, but they don't like that word now. No more talk of exiling, of polises. The old government just accepted the fact we weren't worthy, lived with it, made good laws. Then the Synedrium converted itself into the Syndine to handle bigger problems, more land and people, and the Syndine couldn't keep people from getting angry. You can't sit around thinking you're weak and sinful all the time. A thousand years is enough. So the Founders said we weren't weak, we're better than the polises! Tear them down, wipe out their memory, start over!"

Kahn nodded. "Why did the cities kick everybody out?"

"Because we're sinners," Arthur said. "Some of us still believe that. Founders can't kick it out of us. So now they make their own guilt. I fought side by side with them, watched them die, and I still don't like them. Arrogance. Mine, theirs." Arthur was growing more and more agitated. "They take whatever they want, now. No guilt. That's where my wife and daughter are—other daughter. I told you about them." Arthur's face was dark and deeply lined with sun, hard work, worry.

"Why aren't you one of them, if you fought for them?" Kahn asked.

"I'm an independent sort. They want complete cooperation. Bunch of young, skinny men and women run things now, chase the old out—more guilt in the old." He made a wry face. "Not my sort at all. If you join and don't cooperate, you're in even worse trouble than if you just mind your own business."

"Why do they leave you alone?"

"They don't, not entirely. I don't have much they want, though, now they have two of my family. Nan is the only one who stayed with me. The land here isn't worth much, but they'll come and take that when they please."

"When did the farm start to go bad?"

"Four years ago. Weather heated up, not as bad as now, but enough to wither the corn. Founders offered seed for other crops, tents to cover them during the heat, if you became a Founder and handed over your land, tenant farmer sort of thing. I didn't go along. Jorissa—that's my wife—she said I was a fool. I suppose I was. Everything burned off. Couldn't get the seed or tents yourself unless you joined."

"Is that when the sun started getting brighter?"

"That's when it started getting noticeable. But this is all talk about us, and we haven't settled anything about you, yet."

Nan nodded her agreement.

"I can't convince you," Kahn said. "My clothes are some evidence. Feel the fabric." He removed his coat and offered it to the woman. She looked it over carefully, then passed it to Arthur. "Father does as much knitting here as I do," she said dourly. "Some things the Founders did weren't too bad. Women are better off in some places."

"Syndine did that during the Reform," Arthur said. He turned a sleeve inside out. "No seams. Fabric stretches two ways. Doesn't feel like fabric. So you could be from someplace far away—or from a polis. They had clothes like this in the polises."

"Yes, but I'm not a city part."

"We're no judges," Nan said. "We're not that educated, we don't know what to make of you. You have to go to the Founders."

"I wouldn't recommend that, daughter," Arthur said. "They'll think he's a city part for sure."

"If the Founders know more, I'll have to go to them. Have you heard any people talking about the star being a variable?"

"Star?" Arthur asked.

"The sun, he means, Father," Nan said.

"Not that I know."

"Do you know what a variable is?"

Arthur hesitated, then shook his head, looking levelly at Kahn.

"A variable is a star that gets brighter or dimmer periodically. If it's a long-term variable, it's hard to determine the period, or even to tell if the star is stable over millennia. If it truly is hotter now than it was just four years ago—or in my time—" He stopped. If the star was a long-term variable, his problem was far worse—and it was already monumental. "Are there any cities still alive?"

"Yes," Arthur said slowly. "Resurrection, it's called."

"Can I get there?"

"It isn't too far, maybe a hundred kilometers. Across the border. The Founders don't touch Expolis Ibreem proper, it has its own government—last of the Syndine states. Too powerful. So the polis stands."

"If I could go there—"

Arthur struck an attitude of listening, then shook his head firmly. "No, dammit!"

Nan went to the window and peered out.

"I hear them goddamn scooters again," Arthur said. He stood behind her and pulled asidc a ragged blind. Kahn could hear voices and a weak putt-putting.

"Who is it?"

"Founders, six of them, a tall, curly-haired spindly fellow in the lead. I know his type. I know his goddamn type. You stay in here; whether you're crazy or what you say you are, you shouldn't mess with them. And if they get in, say you're visiting from Ibreem, hiking on a sabbat march. And your name isn't Kahn—it's Cohen, Azrael Iben Cohen, something like that. They have treaties with Ibreem, can't mess with religious people."

"Be quiet!" Nan warned, opening the door for her father and shutting it behind him.

Arthur stood on the porch, hands buried in his torn pockets, expression grim.

The tall leader dismounted his gas engine tricycle and strolled up to the steps, looking down at a pad of paper. "Arthur Sam Daniel, son of Julius Sam Daniel, son of Giorgio Sam Daniel?"

"You know all that," Arthur said. "Wife tells you all that, all you want to know."

"We're here to account for your crops, take census, that's all. No trouble, now friend."

"No crops, just me and my daughter. Easy enough."

Three of the six were women, wearing the grey and black that Founders wore almost without exception, smiling and talking with each other as the leader looked mildly at Arthur. "The Canaan Founders just have your best interests in mind. You living alone now?"

"I told you, just my daughter and I. You don't need more facts than that."

"We've been told a stranger came to your house earlier today. I thought he'd like to meet us and be welcomed to New Canaan West."

"He'd rather not," Arthur said, throat bobbing.

"Now," the leader began, his voice rising faintly, "don't you think it's more polite to let your guest answer for himself?"

Kahn stood, but Nan vigorously gestured for him to stay put and resumed peering through the curtains.

"We like to keep track of visitors, give them information that will help them get around New Canaan West. Mind telling us where your friend is from?"

"I don't see any need—"

The tall man walked up the steps and put his hand firmly on Arthur's shoulder. "You're making me very suspicious, neighbor." He smiled, showing snaggled teeth and a gold crown. "We need to see your visitor."

Kahn stood again and ignored Nan's gestures. He opened the front door. "Can I ease your day?" he asked, hoping his language was up to the confrontation.

"Perhaps," the leader said. "I'm Frederik Bani Hassan. We need to know your origin, destination and intentions."

"No trouble at all. I'm hiking from Ibreem."

"Long hike. Your family and name?"

"Azrael Iben Cohen."

"Lots of Cohens in Ibreem," the leader said. "But you weren't born there. Where were you born?"

Kahn blinked, then said casually, "Here, originally. In New Canaan."

"No, I don't think so," the leader said. "They don't have clothes like that in Ibreem—or here, for that matter. I think you'd better come with us."

Kahn nodded and followed the leader to his motorbike. Arthur said nothing, but his fists were clenched tightly.

The bike sputtered off. Arthur stayed on the porch for several minutes, watching the trail of dust. Then he walked back into the house and stood in the filthy kitchen, looking around, his lips trembling. "We've been living here like dust in a snail shell. They aren't going to let us stay much longer. They want the land. They want everything we have."

"Now, Father—"

"They do," he said quietly. "Poor, crazy man."

Jeshua's footsteps echoed in the empty halls. They had spent more than a week in the dead city, exploring, trying to find something useful to them. All they found was decay and defilement.

"They destroyed it," Thinner said as he was lifted around to see the crumbling walls of the third level gardens. "It let its guard down and they destroyed it."

"It was probably dead when they came in," Jeshua said. "I went through Fraternity once, before I met you. It was a quiet place. They'd built it for seminarians and it was less fancy than some of the polises. It had a huge collection of books—real books."

"I hope they didn't burn the books, too," Jeshua said.

The silence settled over them. Thinner made a noise like a sigh. "You looked around the upper levels?"

"Yes," Jeshua said, frowning. "I took you with me."

"I'm growing forgetful," Thinner said. "No spare parts?"

"Nothing."

"No, of course not. Then we move on."

As they left Fraternity, an early evening drizzle settled on them. They turned west.

Thinner talked of the days in Mandala before Jeshua's return. Jeshua had heard it many times before, but the sound of the head's voice was soothing, rising above the hiss of rain on the hot, dry dirt and grass. A thin ground-fog crept around his legs and he walked between thin, skeletal trees, tall and shadowed, the head clutched in his arm.

Four men on horseback saw him that way. The horses reared in terror and the men, quite agreeing, gave them their reins, hanging on as they galloped into the foothills.

It was late evening and two moons were up above the mountains behind them when Jeshua stopped. The land was cooling now and a thick, moist breeze was falling out of the hills. The rain had stopped and the ground was dry again.

They spent the night in a copse of withered mulcet trees. Jeshua laid Thinner delicately on a prepared bed of dry grass and leaves, making sure his mouth was pointing up. Then he sat with his back against a trunk, thinking. Thinner was getting more and more forgetful each day. Jeshua wondered if his nutrients weren't enough for the head—if Thinner needed something only the internal working of a full body could produce. He hoped they would make it to Resurrection before the head gave out completely. Jeshua did have much in the world to lose, little more in fact than his existence—which he wasn't too concerned with—and his companion.

He wished he could sleep. Thinner lay with his eyes open, in a kind of stupor, but Jeshua had long since abandoned the human habit.

He was quite aware, then, when a crowd of men on horseback surrounded the copse and began to close in.

* * *

Kahn tried to shout above the noise of the motor tricycles, leaning forward toward the ear of the thin curly-haired man. "I need to talk to people in your city . . ."

The Founder shook his head.

"It's very important," Kahn said. "I need to talk with meteorologists—with weather men, with astronomers—with land managers."

"You're not talking to anybody," the Founder shouted back over his shoulder.

Kahn wriggled his wrists reflexively to loosen the bonds tied to the rear cushion of the trike.

The town of New Canaan was busy, prosperous-looking, and—to Kahn—painfully primitive. He was removed to a two-story stone and concrete building, square and ugly, and taken into custody by a burly officer in a loose-fitting black uniform.

"We have reason to believe you're a mimic," the officer said, walking around Kahn and tapping him lightly with a thin wooden dowel. "We've had problems with mimics in the past. We still find them now and then. You know how we tell if you're a mimic?"

Kahn shook his head.

"We cut you open."

The room was small. Through a tiny barred window, Kahn could hear the grind of internal combustion engines and the hiss of steam vehicles.

"I'm not a city part," Kahn said. "I have to speak to—"

"You don't know anything about us, do you? Like most mimics. Ignorant. Locked up in cities, never bothering about us, here in the dirt and flies."

"I come from Fraternity, but I'm not a city part."

The officer pursed his lips and raised his eyebrows. "You came from a city. That's good enough for us." He leaned forward and lowered his voice. "Whatever you are, we don't need you. We have laws here, and I think you should be glad. If I had my way, we'd dismantle you right now. Find out what you work. Not that you'd care, I suppose. Mimics don't feel pain, don't eat, don't sleep." The constable shook his head. "But then, you're probably lying. You probably came from Ibreem, crept out of the city there. Hide your tracks. Well, we're a democracy. We have treaties with Ibreem, we can't just go in and clean them out. The borders aren't nearly as tight as they should be." He motioned with his hand.

Kahn was taken by two guards to a concrete pit. He walked down a flight of wooden steps into the cell and iron bars were lowered over. He barely had room to squat. "If you shit, maybe we let you loose," one guard said. "Maybe not. Mimics can shit, too, they say."

He settled in to make himself as comfortable as possible. After a few minutes, he pinched himself on the inside of his left arm, then tried to indent the skin with his fingernail. What would they find if they cut him? His knowledge of simulacra was slight, ironically. Except for the brain, he had heard, the interior structure was pretty amorphous. Not at all like a city-part.

Could they disable him? He wasn't sure.

No one had considered the possibility a simulacrum would have to face such circumstances.

He didn't think he could sleep, though he could close his eyes. He certainly couldn't shit. There was no way he could convince his captors he was human.

After an hour, he shut his eyes and began running numbers and architectural images across the darkness. Soon he had a Romanesque cathedral mapped out. Then he began to change the types of stone, working out strength of materials problems and redesigning accordingly.

To his surprise, something like sleep cam along shortly after—dreamless, dark, not very comfortable, but much better than useless thought.

He was stirred out of the darkness by the squeal of the bars being raised. "Inside, hunker down," said a guard. It was dark and the guard carried a dim electric lantern. A large shadow descended into the pit with him, brushed up against his legs—he curled them tighter—and settled into silence.

The guard's light pointed down into the pit and Kahn saw it briefly touch on his companion's chest. The light moved a few centimeters, then stopped. The guard took a deep breath, flicked the light off and locked the bars.

Whoever his companion was, it carried a head under its arm, and the head had blinked at him.

Kahn didn't sleep or meditate for the rest of the night. Dawn threw a vague orange glow into the cell, outlining the figure.

It was human-like, and it did indeed carry a head, but the head's eyes were closed. As the glow brightened, coming through a skylight above the cell, Kahn saw that the large figure was a man, terribly wounded. Shafts of arrows stuck out all over him, most broken off. There were bullet holes in his ragged shirt, and brown and green stains around the holes. His free arm appeared to have been sliced open.

Beneath the flap of skin was not muscle, but glassy green tubes and a purple, foam-like filler. Beneath the filler was metallic bone. The figure was not human—he was a city part, a mimic.

No wonder he had been suspected, Kahn thought. The mimics must bc everywhere.

"Hello," Kahn said. The mimic opened his eyes.

"Hello."

"From which city?"

The mimic didn't answer for a long moment. "Mandala," he said finally. The voice was deep, quite convincingly human.

"I come from Fraternity," Kahn said. The mimic nodded and looked at Kahn's clothes, and finally at the shoes. The shoes had been undone in a search for weapons and no longer sealed against the pant legs.

"Fraternity made you?"

"No," Kahn said. "I'm not a city part."

"Then you're human."

"Not exactly." It was difficult treating the mimic as something other than a human; the cities had never specifically been instructed to make humans. For some of Kahn's clients, that ability would have been blasphemous. But Kahn suspected that city programming still operated in the mimic. "I am the builder," he said. "My word is *qellipoth*. It is a practical word, not a theoretical word."

The mimic jerked as if kicked. "I am Jeshua. This is Thinner." He held up the head. "Builder . . . I am . . ."

"Be quiet," Kahn said softly. "I have questions."

"Builder, I am shocked . . . doubly shocked. I feel the power of your words . . . but I have been studying *kaballah*, too. For a long time, a century, Builder." Jeshua's eyes filled with tears. He reached out to touch Kahn's foot. "Are you here to rescue the sparks?" he asked. "Is it time for the regathering?"

The mimic's humanity ran deep. His independence was surprising. A normal city part would have come completely under his control upon hearing that sequence of words. And it knew *kaballah*! Kahn had only briefly studied the mystical teachings under the spotty tutelage of George Pearson, God-Does-Battle's financial minister. Kahn had considered it his duty to know more about his heritage, for in past centuries his family had been Jewish.

"I don't know about the regathering," he said. "I'm not a messiah, I'm not a kabbalist. I'm the builder."

Jeshua sagged and his eyelids lowered as if in fatigue. "I feel the compulsion," he said again. "Only the builder would know those words. But I don't know how I know . . . I am very confused."

"I programmed a code and command into all city parts long before you were made," Kahn said.

"You were human. How could you live so long?"

"I have questions, too," Kahn said. "I hope you can answer my questions, and I'll try to answer yours. But first, we have to get out of here. I don't think I'm going to see any higher authority."

"Why are you in jail?"

"They think I'm a city part."

Jeshua moved the head into his lap. "They destroy cities, city parts," he said. "They're human."

"There's a place where humans are more tolerant, Expolis Ibreem. If we can find our way there . . ."

Jeshua reached up with a hand at least half again as wide as Kahn's and tested the bars overhead. "They're too strong for me to bend them. Besides, I'm damaged." He looked down at Thinner, who still had his eyes closed.

"Is the head alive?" Kahn asked. He felt like an artist who had once painted a simple picture, and come back years later to find it growing more and more bizarre.

"I think so," Jeshua said. "Thinner. Wake up. Open your eyes." The head opened his eyes. "We're with the Builder."

"I heard," the head said hoarsely. "Now I know why you study *kaballah*. He planted the seed. Let me see him." Jeshua turned the head and lifted it. "Welcome, Builder. Your coming is a mystery to us."

"Then we're even. You're a mystery to me."

"Jeshua, the walls are concrete and the bolts holding the bars are set maybe only a few centimeters deep. You can't break out in your condition, but maybe you can spread a little pouch fluid on the concrete."

Jeshua considered that for a moment, then set the head down gently on the dirty floor. "*Peah,*" Thinner said. "Smells like a sewer in here."

Kahn's eyes widened as Jeshua pulled up his dirty white tunic. The mimic was fully equipped with genitals, body hair, anal opening. Jeshua touched several spots on his belly and pulled aside a flap of skin.

"Think you're hungry," Thinner said.

Jeshua pulled out a milky pouch from his abdomen. "I'll have to cut it, there's no opening here."

"Let me bite it," Thinner offered. Jeshua held the head to the pouch. Despite his own lack of viscera, Kahn felt strange and looked away.

"Now I won't be able to eat," Jeshua said. "We'll have to reach Resurrection soon, get a city-fed meal, get fixed." Almost sorrowfully, he said, "I'm a real wreck now, aren't I?"

"You're still better off than I am," Thinner said, his task finished. "Wipe my mouth. I don't want to blister."

"You can eat human food and city fluids, too?" Kahn asked.

"The builder didn't provide for our construction?" Thinner asked. Jeshua cupped his hands and clear, steaming fluid poured into them. He dabbed the fluid on the concrete around the bolts, then dipped his hands in the water bucket in one corner. The concrete sizzled and became a greyish mud. The bars groaned and settled a centimeter or so.

"I didn't know cities could make parts like you," Kahn admitted. "My creations exceed my expectations."

"Builder is a proud father," Thinner said, his voice muffled. He had fallen over again. Jeshua was re-sealing his belly skin. Kahn reached over and righted the head.

"Not so proud," Kahn said. "What will that acid do to your insides?"

Jeshua smiled. "Not much leaks. I just have to remember not to get hungry. Shouldn't be too hard—I've only started eating human-type food again in the last few weeks."

"Can we get out now?" Thinner asked.

"I think I can wrench up this end," Jeshua said.

"And after that?"

"We should probably wait for guards," Kahn said. "When they come to get us—surprise them."

"I'll stand between their guns and you, Builder," Jeshua said. "I'm already injured—a few more bullets won't hurt."

"You're amazing," Kahn said. "I would never have guessed city parts could take so much abuse."

"That's why the Holy One, blessed be He, put us

here—using your master plan," Jeshua said. "We are to absorb the pain of the messianic age."

"My friend has gone a bit deep into that stuff." Thinner said. "From what I've heard, he has only you to blame."

Kahn grinned at the rebuke. "I don't think my code is wholly responsible. You both seem to be true individuals. If I didn't know, I'd say you were human."

"No," Jeshua said. "We are not that."

"Well, technically speaking, neither am I, and I think I can take a few bullets as well as you." He wasn't positive about that—especially not where his head was concerned—but he felt it was time to assert himself, show a little courage. He felt almost ashamed in the face of his latter-day creations.

A guard opened the door at the end of the cell corridor. Kahn held his finger to his lips. Three pairs of boots clacked on the pavement and he looked up to see men leaning over the pit, shadows against the dim blue skylight.

"All city parts?"

"We think so. Haven't cut them open yet—but one is hurt, and he isn't human. The other's just a head, no body, and one is dressed in clothes like he came out of a polis."

"Open up, then."

The guard bent down and inserted a key into the lock. The hinges slipped in their corroded seats, making the bars fall against the outer frame with a clang. The guard inserted his lever to pry the bars up, but they had jammed.

Jeshua braced his feet on the floor of the pit and reached up with both hands. Heaving suddenly, he pushed the bars away from the frame. The guard was knocked backward and Jeshua stood, using the bars to pin the other two against the corridor wall. Kahn grabbed the head and climbed out of the pit. Jeshua plucked the keys out of the bars and they ran to the opposite end. With the second door open, they found themselves in an exercise yard adjacent to the old Synedrium judgement chambers. Jeshua kicked a flimsy panel door open and they came to a flight of stairs opening onto a street. They were in the delivery alley in back of the jail. The alarm hadn't gone off yet; the Founder police weren't as efficient as Kahn expected.

They were in Canaantown proper, running through the early scooter and foot traffic, when the jail bells rang.

Arthur sat on the front porch of the house waiting for the first cool winds of evening, chin in his hands and knees braced against a broken board. The stars were twinkling furiously as the land gave up its warmth. To the west, heat lightning flashed silently between clouds pushed high during the late afternoon. The tall anvil-head billows looked like faces in the brief purple and green illuminations.

The house was empty. His daughter was in Canaantown, visiting Jorissa. Nan's visits with her mother grew longer each time. This visit, he suspected, would be the longest of all. He doubted she would return.

He didn't want to feel betrayed. There was nothing here for Nan, after all; little enough for himself. The farm was a memory and a deed to a tract of dead land, soon to be appropriated by the Founders. He was an old man withering under the sun, doing nothing, promising nothing. It was best she leave.

But the betrayal was real and it hurt him nonetheless. It was a hard time, pushing people to do hard things. Soon, he suspected, he would either die or he would leave, and at age fifty-five, he doubted it was time for him to die.

For the moment, however, he felt like doing nothing more than sitting on the porch, wondering how long it would take for God-Does-Battle to bake and blow away.

The lightning was coming closer. Some of the flashes were almost directly overhead, still silent, but bright enough to pick out the trees, front fence and road like full double moonlight. In a vivid purple flash that left an image swimming in his eyes, he saw two figures standing by the fence.

They were on the trod, both of them this time. The one

who called himself Kahn and the big fellow with the head in his arms. Arthur was too tired to care.

"So come on up," he shouted into the hot dark. "I feel half crazy, half a ghost myself. Come on!" He waved them to approach.

The dim lantern light coming through the front window picked them out about five meters in front of the porch. The big fellow was frightening, sure enough, more like a giant corpse than a man, and carrying a head just like Arthur had seen him before. Except for dirt, Kahn was no different from two days before.

"We need your help," Kahn said, coming closer. "Where's your daughter?"

"In town."

"We need to know the way to Resurrection. This is Jeshua." He pointed and the giant nodded at Arthur.

"Aren't you going to introduce me to the head?"

"My name is Thinner," the head said. Arthur tensed and moved up one step.

"If I can get to Resurrection, I can at least begin to put things right," Kahn said. "With the problems you've faced, you must understand how urgent this is."

"My problems are my problems. They've been with me for a long time, and I don't think you can do anything about them. Did they take you to jail?"

Kahn nodded. "I met Jeshua and Thinner there."

"City parts, aren't they?"

"Yes."

"And you aren't."

"He is the builder," Jeshua said.

"So I've heard. You have to go to Ibreem to find the polis. That's across the border west of here, maybe fifty, sixty kilometers. Just go west."

"I think we need more specific directions. Which roads—landmarks—"

"I've never been there," Arthur said. "I've just heard

stories. Oh, I've been to the border. Take any road west. How did you get away from them?"

"With Jeshua's help," Kahn said. "Just west, then?" He pointed.

"No, more that way," Arthur said, correcting him. "The wind blows from there mostly, nowadays. Used to blow from the east."

"Thank you for your hospitality, and for trying to help me," Kahn said. "I won't forget your decency."

Arthur looked away. "Great deal of good it's done me. But I appreciate your saying so."

The giant city part had been looking at him steadily, brow knit as if in thought. As Kahn turned to leave, Jeshua said, "Is your name Daniel?"

"It is. Arthur Sam Daniel."

Jeshua smiled. "I knew your—great grandfather, great—great grandfather? A man named Sam Daniel the Catholic."

"I've heard of him," Arthur said. "He was supposed to be the great man in our family. But that was maybe a hundred years ago."

"The age of wonders is at hand," Jeshua said. "Your ancestor was an honorable man, and someday I would like to know what happened to him."

They walked off into the dark, until only the vague starlight outlined them. Arthur was shaking on the porch as if he were cold, but the air was still tepid.

He stood, brushed off his pants, and cupped his hands over his mouth. "Wait a moment!" Under his breath, he muttered "Crazy bastards, crazy stupid asses," and he ran into the house. "Just a moment!"

He came out with a canvas bag filled with all the canned food and clothes he thought worth taking. If Nan returned, he had scratched a note on the kitchen table top. There was enough left to make it worthwhile for her to come back, but if she didn't . . . then she would never know.

He felt like a child running away from home, but the feeling exhilarated him. He had never done anything this crazy before.

"I'd like to come with you," he said as he met them next to the road.

They traveled by night—not as safe as it might seem, since most travelers moved by night and spent at least the heat of day under shelter if possible. Still, they were careful, and they did not encounter more Canaan Founders.

Neither Kahn nor Jeshua tired as they walked, but for Arthur's sake they paused every few hours. Their first stop was within sight of Fraternity, and they sat on a fallen log while the heat mist washed around their legs.

"If there's anything you people or parts or whatever you are can do that I don't know about—fly, disappear, fight like demons, anything like that—don't wait to tell me," Arthur said. "Let me know so I can figure a way to take advantage of it."

Kahn smiled. "Nothing magical. The food is for you alone, since I don't need to eat and Jeshua can't just now. The water we can share, but you'll need much more than we do. When you get tired, tell us."

"I'll have to slow down now and then," Jeshua said. "I'm a little worried about Thinner." The head was silent most of the time, eyes closed as if asleep. "I can't feed him much now."

"My grandfather used to tell me about capturing city parts and using them like horses or cars. But they're mostly gone now. I was just wondering how much like a city part you are." Arthur looked at Kahn.

"Not very much, actually. The technology of the block was more advanced than the technology I had to use in the cities. I didn't really have much to do with the block, so I can't say I know how I work . . . not clearly, anyway."

Arthur's eyes narrowed. "Makes sense, I suppose. I don't know much about how I run, either. Be a bit perverse if we did, like looking in a mirror too hard."

"I'm quite aware of how I work," Jeshua said. "But then, I've had many years to learn such things, and excellent libraries."

Arthur nodded as if he were engaging in a perfectly normal conversation. "I still don't believe all this, you know," he said matter-of-factly.

"About the only way you'll be convinced is to see us in action," Kahn said. He stood.

"That could do it," Arthur said.

A single moon illuminated the misty path as they walked around one quarter of Fraternity. On the outskirts of the city, Kahn bent down to pick up a shard of silicate. "I've been wondering what these were for. I remember installing a minor city defense like this, but not so extensive."

"Used to be cities would bristle all around to keep people out," Arthur said.

"I put in the defense by request," Kahn said, dropping the fragment. "They asked for it. Wanted it in case the world was invaded by pagans."

They crossed part of the perimeter on solid paving. The city walls were dry and grey-white where the moonlight hit them, like translucent bones.

"I designed Fraternity for contemplation," Kahn said. "A cross of two intersecting cylinders, topped by a Hofstadter figure—the central tower, there." He pointed. The moon was just passing behind the tower. The upper promenades and portions of the crossed cylinders had collapsed, leaving the tower in prominent relief. "Did all the cities die like this, in one piece?"

"Not that I heard about," Kahn said.

"Most broke apart and moved," Jeshua said. "They died that way, scattered. Only a few cities die in one piece. Mandala did. The city just quit functioning, sections at a time, and finally all of it . . . except for Thinner and I."

"They were only supposed to move parts around when the cities were being remodeled. That was a novelty—walls that could walk by themselves. We could do it, so we did.'' He laughed sharply.

''You said something about a Hof—Hofshtad figure?'' Arthur frowned. ''I know what a cylinder is, that's like a well is a cylinder's hole, but—''

''The tower was designed to represent three portraits when viewed from three different angles. Fraternity's tower carried portraits of Christ, Aquinas and George Pearson.''

''Who was Pearson . . . and Aquinas?'' Arthur asked.

''Aquinas was a philosopher on old Earth. Pearson was the man who negotiated for the purchase of God-Does-Battle.'' Kahn remembered the monumental arguments they had had. Pearson had appointed himself shepherd to all the Jews, Christians and Moslems on God-Does-Battle; at the time of Kahn's memorization in the block, Pearson had become a recluse living in the Asian Jewish city of Thule.

''Who can we see from this angle?'' Arthur asked. Kahn turned and followed his gaze.

''That's Pearson,'' he said. ''He's as responsible for this as I am, in his way.''

Arthur felt briefly dizzy. It was more than just walking while craning his neck—it was as if, for a second, he had indeed looked into a mirror too closely—the mirror of God-Does-Battle's history, with a crumbled, monumental face staring back, eyes filled with moonlight, smiling benevolently.

They were less than a kilometer from the border, staying close to the road but not traveling on it, when they stumbled onto a camp. A man in brown canvas shorts and sleeveless shirt, wearing a broad-brimmed round hat, was giving instructions in a melodic tenor voice. Four others—a woman about the same age, two adolescent boys—and a young girl—were loading the truck and taking down a large tent.

Arthur, Jeshua and Kahn watched from the cover of some brittle bushes.

"They're from Ibreem," Arthur whispered. "Sounds like their visitor's pass is running out, so they're going to cross the border tonight."

The man was talking about Resurrection.

"They act as if they live there," Arthur said. "I've heard about an enclave surrounded by the city. Maybe that's what he means."

"He sounds like he's a teacher," Jeshua said. "I recognize that tone."

"Wife and students?" Kahn asked.

"One's his son, I think," Arthur said. "Ibreemites have different ideas about polises than Founders. They try to live with them—not interfere. They're a Syndine state."

"So?" Kahn asked.

"Maybe we can get a ride with them. Jeshua should hide the head—we don't want to be too shocking. We could certainly fit on the back of the truck."

Kahn agreed. They stepped forward into the lantern light. The girl was startled and dropped her burden of metal tent poles with a clatter.

"Don't tell them everything all at once," Arthur said. "I still have my doubts about you—so give it slowly, or not at all. We're just travelers, pilgrims."

The man stood between them and the camp, holding out his hands in a gesture that could have been welcome but for his wide eyes and flaring nostrils.

"We need a ride, if you have room," Arthur said. "My friends and I are going to Resurrection."

"What's your business?" the man asked.

"We're pilgrims," Arthur said. "We need to visit Resurrection. I've never been there."

The man looked at Kahn's clothes and Jeshua's wounds, some of which had started healing over. "It looks like you've had a rough journey so far."

"That we have," Arthur said.

"Excuse us for bothering you," Kahn said, stepping forward. "We're from New Canaan West. I desperately need to get to Resurrection."

"You're fugitives," the man said cautiously. The four others had grouped themselves near the truck.

"He isn't," Kahn said, indicating Arthur. "We are. But not for crimes."

"The big fellow—what is he?"

Kahn motioned for Jeshua to step closer to the lantern light. "If I'm guessing right, he can get into the city—the polis. He can be repaired there."

"City doesn't take in sick people any more. That stopped a long time ago. There are hospitals in the enclave . . ."

"He's a city-part," Arthur said. "A mimic. They're trying to kill him here."

"What has he done?"

"Nothing," Kahn said. "He was trying to get to Resurrection and he had to cross New Canaan West."

"Names?" the man asked.

"Mine is Arthur Sam Daniel, my family used to live in Ibreem. This is Jeshua, and this is Azrael Iben Cohen."

"My name is Hale Ascoria. I'm a teacher. My wife, Lod, and son David. My students, Sanisha and Coort. Your country gave us a four-day pass, and now we're going home." He glanced over his shoulder at the group, then took off his hat and fanned his face slowly. "New Canaan isn't known for thieves, not now, anyway. You say you're pilgrims . . . how can I be sure you're not police?"

"Jeshua, show him your arm," Kahn said. The mimic stepped forward a few paces and peeled back his skin. Ascoria squinted to see more detail in the dim light.

"Mandala," Jeshua said. "Originally I came from Ibreem, too, when I thought I was a human being. I grew up there as a child."

"How old are you?"

"About a hundred and forty years."

"We have an obligation to deliver city-parts to Resurrection. This is our pact. But I've never seen a mimic as old as you say you are. Most are from Fraternity.'' He looked at Kahn. ''We came here to study Fraternity. We're from Expolis Geshom originally, but we moved to the Resurrection enclave ten years ago.'' He took a deep breath. ''If I'm taking a chance, God help your immortal souls. Join us, pilgrims.''

The truck was gas-powered, smelly and noisy but rugged enough to travel the rutted roads. The students rode in the front seat with Ascoria; his wife and son sat behind the truck bed panel, and Kahn, Jeshua and Arthur squatted near the tailgate. Tent and provisions separated the groups. Jeshua kept Thinner in the bag, looking into it now and then. The big mimic's face was impassive, but Kahn could sense that the head wasn't doing very well.

The border was sparsely patrolled these days, Ascoria explained. Friction between Ibreem and New Canaan was slight, and with the heat, patrols were kept to a minimum. They passed through a wire gate with an empty sentry booth and were in Ibreem.

They had started out in the early morning. Within an hour, they were driving across the old alluvial plain. Resurrection gleamed in the post-dawn light. The sun was already as bright as an electric torch.

A few kilometers out on the plain, the dirt path turned into an oiled road. The truck bounced less vigorously, and Kahn was able to concentrate on the city ahead. It was much smaller than he remembered, as if great chunks had been removed and the walls had closed up after them. There was no central tower, but a circle of smaller towers, with one larger than the rest on the north side. It looked for all the world like an overgrown sports amphitheater.

The oiled road circled the city about thirty meters from the outer walls. The walls rose smooth and silver-green at least a hundred meters above the plain, topped by translucent spikes like the bristles around Fraternity, but fresh and formidable-looking. Except for the obvious reduction and redesign, the city looked healthy.

"Here's the gate," Ascoria called back. He turned the truck's wheel and drove them up to a smooth tunnel entrance. A man-made fence had been constructed, touching the outer wall but not fixed to it. Two guards sat under a wooden canopy, drooping with the heat. Lod dug in the glove compartment for identification.

Kahn listened closely.

"I have pilgrims and a city part—a mimic," Ascoria said. We brought them in from Ibreem."

"Fugitives?"

"Only the mimic."

The guards circled to the back of the truck to look them over. One asked if they had any identification. Arthur produced a thin leather pouch with a scored metal card.

"And you?" the guard asked Kahn.

"I'm a pilgrim. I've lost my identification."

"Then we can only give you a two-day pass." The guard returned to the cab on Ascoria's side. "We have no warrants from the Founder for fugitives, parts or otherwise, but then, they never tell us, do they? If you'll vouch for them, put them up until their visit is done—deliver the part—we'll let you through. You know the procedures?"

Ascoria nodded resolutely. The guard waved him on and the truck drove through a smooth-walled tunnel.

The enclave was a separate city contained within Resurrection. It was made of mud-brick, wood, plaster and concrete. Ascoria drove cautiously through clean, narrow streets overhung by third floor balconies.

Kahn noticed the skilled carpentry and design. Raingutters wound around buildings, sometimes jumping the short gaps between and becoming part of the ornament. The plaster was expertly textured and studded with river stones and bits of glass.

Resurrection had been on the river plain for a hundred

years, Ascoria explained. It had left its home in the highlands, resisting marauders, and rebuilt itself where underground water was plentiful. "It took in sick children, and once it even treated sick adults. That was before it moved. A woman named Reah entered the city in the highlands and guided it here. She was Moslem, or at least came from a Moslem town. That's where we'll drop off the part—at Reah's Temple, on the west side. She was killed after the city settled here, but by that time she had ordered city transport parts to go out and gather all sick and crippled children. The city took them in long after she died, for about seventy-five years, and let them out in the enclave when they were cured. Then, about twenty-five years ago, the city stopped taking anybody in. That was when a city called Throne came down to the river plain, about ten kilometers from here."

"Throne disappeared overnight," Lod said. "Some believe it walked, others say it was sucked underground."

"By that time, all the children who had come to the enclave had made a fine place to live. Many stayed, grew up here, established hospitals. Now pilgrims come from all around to worship, especially at Reah's Temple, and to be treated. We have the finest doctors on God-Does-Battle."

"Never heard any of this in New Canaan," Arthur said.

"The Founders think we're fools," Lod said bitterly.

Kahn listened silently, looking at the brown and white buildings, the crowds of pilgrims and citizens—the white robes of the one discernible from the more tailored pants and coats and dresses of the other. There were gas engine cars and horse-carts. On the west side of the enclave was Reah's Temple, a cubic structure decorated by columns and simple bas-relief carvings. Pilgrims sat under broad awnings, napping or kneeling in prayer, waiting for the heat to die down. Next to the building was a pillar about twenty meters high, topped by a bronze statue of a woman in a straight dress.

"Do they worship her?" Arthur asked.

"No, no!" Ascoria said. "To the Habirus, she's a prophet, and the Moslems believe she's a saint, as do the Christians.

The Moslems—some, anyway—use the pillar as a substitute for Mecca."

"Don't they know where Mecca is?" Kahn asked.

"No, how could they?" Ascoria asked.

"The pole star is the Earth's sun," Kahn said. "Or at least, it is by now."

"What?" Ascoria asked, incredulous.

"They haven't forgotten . . ." Kahn hesitated. Arthur shook his head slowly. "That's what some of us think in New Canaan," he finished. "Old records."

"Moslems have accepted that Mecca's direction is lost," Ascoria said. "It would be pretty hard to change their minds now."

"This is where the Break Wars are healed," Lod said. Sanisha, the young girl student, nodded agreement. "We show the Canaan Founders that humans and cities can live together, if not intermingled."

Arthur stared up at the city's towers. Their shadows fell across the enclave, then climbed the wall on the other side. "Where's Reah now? I mean, her body."

"She was killed inside. We don't know what happened to her body," Ascoria said. "But we know she's dead. The first teachers saw her die. Most of the children are citizens here now, doctors, priests, rabs, mullahs and muezzins in the Moslem quarter. Some of them claim to have seen Reah in the city." He smiled indulgently.

They stopped near the temple and Lod offered a prayer of thanksgiving. A broad space separated the inner wall and the outermost buildings on the enclave. Pilgrim's vehicles parked in the gap, with horse-drawn carts placed under wooden sheds. Streams of water flowed under the wall, one passing through a conduit directly beneath the temple. The wall itself produced fruit and vegetables at shoulder-level, a vertical garden which the pilgrims harvested for their meals. In the beginning, Lod explained, the food from the walls had sustained the entire enclave—children and teachers—but now it was not enough, and was reserved for pilgrims. The citizens were fed by food grown and purchased outside the city and—in emergencies—on shaded rooftop gardens. Most families had gardens.

Most of the hostels in the enclave were full now, so white tents were pitched in the inner perimeter. Families sat in front of the tents, shaded by broad awnings or the city's shadow. The atmosphere was that of a holiday gathering, restrained by the heat.

"It's beautiful," Arthur said.

Ascoria parked the truck at a small brick guard house near the wall, connected by a covered walkway with Reah's Temple. He motioned for Kahn and Jeshua to follow. Jeshua picked up the bag and walked behind them.

"You and your friend can stay with my family and students tonight," Ascoria said. "We're already sharing our home with pilgrims, but if you're gregarious, there should be enough space." He turned to Jeshua. "Are you ready to be delivered to the city—willing I mean?"

Jeshua nodded.

"It's quite simple, really. Approach the wall by the cubicle. The guard there will let you through—once he sees you're a city part." Ascoria pointed at Jeshua's arm. Jeshua reached down and opened the seam.

"Will you join us later?" he asked Kahn.

Kahn nodded, then glanced at Ascoria. The teacher's smile had frozen. Jeshua walked to the cubicle and waited for the guard to step out. The guard nervously looked him over, then passed him through.

As Jeshua stepped up to the wall, a circular patch grew milky and parted. He stepped inside. The gap sealed behind him. Ascoria and the guard watched intently, mouths slightly open. Then the moment passed.

"We give to the city what is the city's," Ascoria said, trembling with awe. "Now it's done. Come, we'll go to the house."

The house was a school for more advanced students, located near the edge of the enclave. Kahn estimated the city enclosed an area of about half a hectare, in which about a hundred thousand citizens lived, and a third again as many pilgrims. Housing was dear, and Ascoria's house climbed four stories, each story crammed with people—pilgrims, students, more of his family.

"Let's stay on the ground floor," Kahn suggested to Arthur.

They ate lunch, then napped or pretended to nap through the scorching afternoon. As dusk turned the sky above the enclavc to dark blue and grey-green, lights came on along the roadways. Arthur and Kahn helped distribute the evening meal, then sat down and ate, Kahn nibbling with convincing hunger, Arthur with unfeigned ravenousness. The guests on the first floor glanced at Kahn's odd clothes, but the mix of the crowd was broad enough that he didn't draw too much attention. The night was hot and still. As they ate, Lod and Sanisha led a group of male students in singing prayers, and Ascoria led a group of female students in reciting them back. Arthur felt like joining in, but he didn't know the words. Kahn watched with his usual unreadable expression, dark eyes seeming to fill their sockets in the dim electric light.

Outside, clouds were moving across the stars. Kahn and Arthur found blankets and matting in one corner of the ground floor and lay down with twenty or twenty-five others. As the evening prayers were said, the rain began to fall. Lod rigged a funnel and a large glass jug outside the front door, under the roof's main drain.

Ascoria kneeled beside Arthur and Kahn. "You know, I'm very curious about you," he said to Kahn. Lod was turning off the lights by unscrewing the bulbs. The air was humid and big drops were pattering on the street outside, clearly audible through the wood door and window shutters. "I'm a teacher, and I like asking questions. But I don't believe you want anyone to ask questions of you—not yet."

Kahn looked down at the floor, embarrassed. It was a rare emotion for him, but he didn't know what to say to the man.

"The city part seemed to know you," Ascoria continued.

"I look at you, and I shiver. Nobody else reacts that way." He pointed with his face at the people lying, waiting for sleep, all around. "I don't know why, but you're different. Not a pilgrim."

"Let's go to sleep," Arthur said, looking at the two from the corner of his eye. "We're just pilgrims."

Ascoria stood. "What the mimic said . . . I have this feeling . . ." He cut himself off. "But I'm imposing on guests."

"It's a wonderful community you have here," Arthur said.

"It is indeed," Kahn affirmed, swallowing.

"We wish it would stay that way, but the heat is becoming too great, I fear. The weak want to leave. They say we're cursed again, that we'll never have peace on God-Does-Battle. Will we?" He gazed directly at Kahn, his eyes intense.

"I don't know," Kahn said truthfully enough.

"Of course not," Ascoria said. "It's not one's lot to know what the future . . . what we face. Good night."

Arthur nodded and rolled over.

When the others on the first floor were asleep, Kahn went to Arthur and shook him gently. "We have to go now," he said, then held his finger to his lips. "They'll wake up in a couple of hours."

The streets were almost dry, and the air was filled with mist. Most of the street lamps were dimmed, singing a dull orange. Kahn led Arthur through the streets.

They came to the perimeter space and walked between the pilgrim tents, past the cubicle and the guard. The guard was asleep, his face beaded with sweat. The entire enclave was like a place in a fairy tale, enchanted with heat, sleeping in the minimum comfort of early night, waiting for the cool of midnight to get up again and work. Kahn walked up to the wall, but Arthur stood back a few meters. "Come on," Kahn said. "You can enter with me."

"Come where?"

Kahn laid his hand on the surface. "I'm the builder," he

said to the wall. "I'm the true architect, and my word is *qellipoth*. It is a practical word, not a theoretical word."

The wall flowed aside, forming a smaller version of the smooth tunnel which led into the enclave. Arthur shook his head. "Why?" He was suddenly panic-stricken; he had never actually believed the man.

"I may need your help," Kahn said. "You wouldn't want to miss this chance, would you?"

Arthur's throat bobbed. "No."

"There isn't much time."

More than anything else, Arthur wanted to follow. If someone had opened a gateway to paradise, he couldn't have been more interested. But he was terrified. He felt like a boy listening to Old Woman tales in New Canaan. He walked up to the tunnel, legs shaking. Kahn stepped through, and Arthur followed.

The city seemed to breathe. Cool air blew steadily through the corridors, carrying a green smell and a flowery smell that was neither sharp nor cloying—in fact, that was almost unnoticeable until Arthur stopped and lifted his head to sniff. Kahn looked back. "Faster," he said. "These are service-ways. There's nothing down here for us."

Kahn led him down a hall to a blank wall. The floor lifted, the ceiling parted, and they were on an elevator, rising through a translucent shaft. Things hissed and sighed around them. Through the walls, Arthur could see fluids moving, vague white circles pulsing. His fear was subsiding. His hands still shook, but with excitement now.

"It *is* beautiful, isn't it?" Kahn asked, as if needing reassurance. Arthur nodded.

Above, another ceiling parted, and they rose into a broad plaza. The floor beneath them sealed up. Kahn motioned him on. The architect was walking faster, almost running. They came to a heat shaft and Kahn whistled. From above, a leaf-shaped flying thing three meters across spiraled down and stopped a few centimeters from the shaft floor. Kahn took a seat on the vehicle and Arthur climbed in alongside.

"City manager's chambers," he said.

The leaf-vehicle responded by rising slowly, then accelerating until they were pushed back into their seats. Arthur gripped the armrests tightly, wanting to scream but embarrassed by his fear. Kahn seemed to take the ride so calmly—what was there to worry about?

Kahn looked across at him and smiled, giving him a reassuring pat on the arm. "Just a few seconds," he said. Arthur kept his eyes on his knees.

The vehicle began to slow, moving toward the side of the shaft. Balconies and hallways leading off into green-lit depths flashed by. They rose above the lip of the shaft and the vehicle sidled over, then landed with a hum and several internal clicks. Kahn helped Arthur out.

They were on top of the tallest tower, above most of the clouds. The starlight was bright and clear, and this high the air was cool and dry. The smell of greenery was stronger. Looking to the opposite side of the shaft, Arthur saw a flat expanse of grass. Inlays of light in the sward seemed to send up beams which curved, then diffused, illuminating the area softly but clearly. On the other side, they were at the edge of a walkway. Glowing stripes of light streamed down the walkway, beckoning them through a forest of tall pines and aspen.

"This way, please," a voice instructed.

"Who is that?" Arthur asked Kahn.

"We are the aide of Matthew," the voice replied. The accent was hard to cut through, but it wasn't too thick to understand.

"What is the 'aide of Matthew' function?" Kahn asked.

"We are under the command of Matthew out of Reah."

"Where is the architect?"

"You are the builder."

"Where is the agency I left in my place?" Kahn restated.

"That function has been subsumed. Matthew has reorganized all city functions."

They followed the bands of light down the path. Through the trees, at the edge of the tower, they could see a bright warm glow surrounding a building. The building was about ten meters tall and just as wide, cylindrical, with a numeral 2 painted on one side. Beneath the 2 was a small omega.

"I don't recognize any of this," Kahn said. "Everything's been rearranged. The city's about a third as large as it should be, even taking the enclave into account."

"This way, please," the voice instructed. The bands of light led up to the edge of the building, beneath the omega. A circular door slid aside. Kahn looked into the darkened interior. "This is the city manager's chamber?"

"It is a reconstructed portion," the voice said.

"Where's the rest? This is too small."

"Matthew no longer needs the chamber for his work. Its function has been subsumed."

Kahn stepped inside and the room lighted up. Arthur followed slowly after. In the middle of a blank room was a large chair mounted on a dais. The arms of the chair were covered with silvery nodes and dimples. A woman was sitting in the chair, motionless. She had long pepper-grey hair and a restful expression. Her robes shimmered like a rainbow. Her eyes appeared to be fixed on them, but as Kahn moved, he saw she was staring at the door, not them, with a vague smile. Arthur stayed by the door, hands clasped behind his back, returning the woman's gaze.

The entire figure was translucent, like an image from the city's guide or teacher projectors.

"She isn't real, is she?" Arthur asked.

"No."

Kahn walked completely around the chair. The chair, at least, was familiar and unchanged. The emptiness of the rest of the chamber disturbed him. Once, the city manager's control center would have been filled with screens, displays, and communications equipment, all used to coordinate the city.

When he came back within the line of the woman's gaze, he noticed that a bead of light had appeared in her forehead. It grew brighter as he watched. The figure stood and filled with light like a vessel fills with water. She vanished. The air smelled faintly of roses.

Arthur gave a shuddering sigh. "I'm—"

"Sh," Kahn said. He sat in the chair and put his fingers into the dimples, then looked into retinal projectors arrayed on the edge of an armrest.

He seemed to fall into emptiness, with a vague glow far beneath. The emptiness became filled with a presence.

You are the builder?

"Yes," he answered.

You have been here before, not to this city, but to God-Does-Battle.

"Yes, thirteen hundred years ago."

No . . . But the voice trailed off. It was a woman's voice, but not immediately recognizable as such. Kahn could detect more familiar overtones—the combined voices of the old city, smoothly blended, indistinguishable. *You are here again.*

"Yes. I only have three weeks left."

What will you do?

"There is an emergency."

The voice seemed to ripple. *An em/em/er/ergency.*

He was flooded with sudden information. The increased brightness of the sun was charted for him, but then, irrationally, compared with the decline of the living cities. Some attempt was made to explain the sun's behavior with the rising into space of the souls of dead cities. "No, that is wrong," he said.

These are the views of Matthew.

"Who is Matthew?"

Our son/son/son we are not allowed to see.

"Where is he?"

The information seemed to grow fainter until he was simply sitting in the chair. He pulled his fingers out of the dimples and turned away from the armrest projectors. Then he removed the packet from the lining of his coat.

"I'm going to be a little longer, Arthur."

"I'll just sit," Arthur said.

Kahn found a slot in the arm and inserted the packet. He replaced his fingers and turned to the projectors.

To his surprise, the packet's first stream of information did not concern the early years of the cities. It had been updated, reset, and that meant someone on God-Does-Battle had tampered with the recorders—machines only he was supposed to know about.

What had the mingled city-voice said a few moments ago—?

The record took up his full attention. It would have taken weeks to play the packet back at a speed slow enough to allow him to absorb everything, so he selected for highlights. In doing that, he only caught snatches of a voice-over.

"Cities have been chosen for—"

A kind of evacuation procedure, outlined in some detail, but with no mention of the final goal—which, he assumed, must be the Bifrost.

One of the cities, Throne, had been on a harbor at the time of the record, about nine hundred years ago. It had stood just north of the river plain where Resurrection now rested. According to the Ascorias, Throne had long since walked and disappeared—but in the record, Throne was in position, healthy enough, and sported three new structures—needle-thin spires which rose above the towers and nearly met at an apex. His suspicions were confirmed when he caught the word "Bifrost" in the accelerated garble.

Another city—Eulalia, which at one time had been occupied by Pentecostals—appeared in the record. Again, three spires rose above the city. Again, the city was on the shores of a natural harbor, where large numbers of people could be brought in by boat. (More evacuation plans—as if the record had been used as a kind of notebook. He scanned for source annotations and the record showed, "Transmission from Eulalia 2765/3/3".)

The record then switched to words only, and he had to slow to pick up what was being said. The voice was familiar, even though using brevity code and distorted by the record's occasional lack of fidelity.

"City reacting badly. Comnet rebels. RelAuth blocks. Bifrost allowed, no object my presence, but no agreem on exiles. Aband Eul, on to—"

Thule, the third city, was even farther south, on the continent of Brisbane near the south pole. The record showed fields of ice and snow, bleak volcanic scarps, pale, rugged landscapes. Kahn had built Thule for the Asian Jews. That was the city where George Pearson had finally gone to live after his disputes with the Judaeo-Christian Councils. Again, three spires rose above the crystal towers.

The record was blank in many places now. Suddenly, it slowed and the voice took over, not using brevity code, tinged with anger and despair.

"Thule was the last city to exile its citizens. Under Pearson's last years as mayor, it became a city of heretics. The councils had exiled Pearson for his heresy—Gnostic leanings, I gather, since the city is now Gnostic—so Pearson retaliated by opening Thule to everyone the council rejected. In the last few years, the councils were eating themselves alive, and what the cities did later was only a kind of imitation. Heresy was everywhere. Only the Moslems kept their calm, and they were a minority here. Thule accepted them all—neo-Nestorians, Arians, rabid mystics, Manicheans of course. Now, Thule is the last hope, something I am not very happy about. All other cities fight me when I announce I'm bringing exiles back, but Thule is calm, quiet . . ."

Kahn had designed Thule with substantial differences. Its source material had been more insectoid than botanical, and its programming—at the request of the Asian Jews—had been made more flexible, to allow for whatever changes of creed the inhabitants might undergo. Kahn had never been happy about the result. He had considered Thule a particularly volatile product, not exactly dangerous, but sufficiently unstable to make him uneasy. Apparently Pearson had taken advantage of that instability.

Distracted by his own musings, he stopped the record and rewound it to catch what he had missed. But abruptly the record faded and stopped. There was a blank of several seconds, then the mechanical recording returned with the early centuries of the cities.

At the moment, he was more interested in the voice than in the details of city history. He wound back further and replayed the tense, angry words, then searched for annotations. He found a numeric code click and had it translated and displayed for him. "Transmission from Thule," the code label read, "2766/1/5."

The speaker had moved from Eulalia to Thule after failing to accomplish his tasks in both Throne and Eulalia.

There was logically only one person who knew about the recorders, one person who could get into the cities after the Exiling.

The original Robert Kahn had returned to God-Does-Battle nine hundred years ago—four hundred years after the simulacrum was memorized—to set things right. He had constructed the Bifrosts in three cities, and failed in at least two. And he had left a sketchy, idiosyncratic record by transmitting to all the secret recorders that could still receive. Nine centuries ago, most of the cities had been intact.

He pulled his fingers out of the cups and closed his eyes. Someone was calling for him. In the seconds that it took to re-orient to externals, he heard footsteps, words exchanged, then a high-pitched, crackling voice. He was numbed for an instant by the thought of opening his eyes and staring at himself still trying to save God-Does-Battle . . .

Arthur was calling his name and had stepped to one side of the doorway.

In the half-circle stood an old man, his skin as brown as

wood, naked except for a pair of white boxer shorts. He carried a translucent, jade-colored cane in one hand, leaning on it and repeating, above Arthur's voice, "Who the hell are you two? How did you get into my city?"

"I'm Robert Kahn."

The old man smiled grimly and shook his head. "No, I don't think you are."

Kahn stepped down from the chair. "Are you human?"

The old man said nothing.

"I am the builder," Kahn said. "My word is—"

"That nonsense is useless on me. I'm not a city part and I can't be controlled by formulas. I can see how you got in here, sham that you are. But who is this?" He pointed to Arthur.

"His name is Arthur Sam Daniel."

"And the mimics came with you, too, I suppose. Well, that isn't my jurisdiction. Mother takes care of that." His emphasis on the word "Mother" was slightly acid. He reached up to scratch his chest. "Pardon my appearance," he said, his voice low and ragged. "I haven't seen living people this close for twenty-five years. But you aren't exactly alive, are you?"

"I'm a simulacrum."

"I've been expecting one. You look like him. And the city, of course, must obey your orders, let you in. A lot has changed since you last came. You know that?"

"I can see."

"Why are you here now?"

Kahn saw no reason to withold information. "I was supposed to return a long time ago. I wanted to look over the work, see that everything was functioning properly."

The old man laughed a single, tight-lipped bark.

"Perhaps I could have done something," Kahn continued, uncomfortable in the old man's steady glare. "There have been problems, I can see."

"The greatest of all understatements, surely. I've spent my

entire life trying to undo your sabotage. Do you know who I am?''

''I think so.''

''Matthew. Would-be son of Reah.''

''I see.''

There was a moment of silence. Despite his defiance, Matthew seemed more than a little nervous. ''Now that I'm here,'' Kahn said, ''perhaps we—''

''None of this makes any sense!'' Matthew cried out. ''You have no right to keep popping up. No right at all.'' He seemed to deflate, his chest sinking, shoulders inclined, head bowed.

''Do you operate this city, or have any control over it?'' Kahn asked.

The old man nodded.

''Then you can help me. We must organize all the cities still alive, re-program them, build more cities. I'll certainly need help. Some functions have been changed here—''

''I've dismantled them,'' Matthew said, straightening. He flicked his rod at Kahn. ''Resurrection's mind has been reorganized. I control everything by my voice and presence. Except for what Reah watches over, of course. And I've even made some inroads there in the last twenty-five years.''

''Where is Reah?'' Arthur asked. Matthew looked down on him with mingled contempt and anxiety.

''She's long dead. Stored in the city. As I suppose I'll be when I die. These were her chambers. Stand back from her chair . . . you have no right to sit there.''

''How long have you been here?'' Kahn asked.

''A century. Every year of it, trying to put right what you destroyed. Your little time-bombs in the city minds.''

''Listen, Matthew—''

''I stopped letting people in twenty-five years ago,'' Matthew stepped forward one stride. ''For seventy-five years there was no peace, only children, schools, hospitals, ignorance and confusion. No peace. Now I'm used to being alone. Not that any of them ever saw me clearly. I stayed away after

I grew older. You know, I sympathize with you, hating the people on this planet.'' Kahn flinched. ''They're not easy to love. But you didn't have to sabotage!''

''I didn't sabotage anything,'' Kahn said, holding back his anger as best he could. ''I never hated the people.''

''How appropriate.'' Matthew turned away from him. ''You came back nine hundred years ago and tried to make up for your sins. You failed. And now you send a ghost, to look over a world filled with other kinds of ghosts . . . the ghosts of dead dreams. Do you have any feeling for how they felt, the exiles? After the cities cast them out? How they felt they were the sinners, and longed to be allowed back in? For a thousand years, there was no progress, only guilt. But it was your cities that were unworthy. I've been raised in one. I know. Great, overgrown dreaming monstrosities. Beautiful monstrosities. The only way to put my people right is to let the cities die natural deaths, not to rebuild. And you won't take my people away from me! You tried even before I was born, and you failed. Don't try again.'' He started to walk out the door.

''I need more information,'' Kahn said. They followed him outside and along the path. ''Facilities to find out what happened.''

''Not available,'' Matthew muttered.

''Then they'll have to be made available,'' Kahn said, seething.

''Oh?'' Matthew smiled back over his shoulder. ''I can tell you whatever you need to know.''

''I doubt it,'' Kahn said. Then he and Arthur stopped. The old man had disappeared. They stood on the lighted path. One by one, the lights went out. Only the starlight above remained for them to see by.

''Is he real?'' Arthur asked softly in the dark.

''Yes,'' Kahn said.

''He certainly isn't very cooperative.'' Arthur sniffed.

''I'm not sure we should expect him to cooperate. We're moving in on his game.''

"What'll we do?"

"You forget, I designed this city. I may know it even better than Matthew does." Kahn's tone was defiant. "Take hold of my hand."

They walked down the path slowly, their eyes gradually acclimatizing until they could see the edge of the shaft. A flier waited for them, its guidance lights glowing faintly.

"Looks like only our floor is dark," Kahn said. "I don't think Matthew is going to find quarters for us very soon. You'd better find a place for us to stay. The flier should be able to tell you where to look. If not, come back up and I'll meet you here."

Arthur started to protest, but Kahn seated him firmly in the flier and stepped out. The flier began its leaf-motion drop.

"I don't know anything about polises!" Arthur shouted as he descended.

"You're under my protection," Kahn said. "Besides, I doubt the city could hurt you even if you weren't."

Kahn turned away from the shaft and followed the path a little way into the forest. Then he stopped and sat on a grass hummock. He reflexively rubbed his face with his hands. He regretted sending Arthur off so abruptly, but he needed time to be alone, to think over what he had learned from the packet.

He was obviously no superhuman; the simulacrum could get confused, grow brain-weary if not tired, experience near-despair. For nearly two and a half weeks, he had faced up to failure after failure—and now, facing another, he wished his body could tremble, feel squeamish, mirror in some way his emotions. But his hands were steady and of course he had no stomach per se; he was alone, he couldn't even refer to himself.

He shut his eyes and allowed a few moments of wandering thought. In his organic body he had never been much for abstractions; the religions of God-Does-Battle had always seemed weak because of their reliance on abstractions, and supernatural ones at that. Pearson's lessons in *kaballah* had fascinated him in a perverse way, but had never taken hold;

that they should flower in Jeshua was ironic, to say the least. In the simulacrum, however, he found abstractions remarkably easy to deal with. Not distracted by mortal flesh, when he closed his eyes he became like the city mind speeding through its ComNet, unencumbered, fluid. Had he known this years before, he might have had simulacra made to help him with the theoretical side of architectural planning . . . especially in the area of social design. He might have foreseen the problems on God-Does-Battle.

The exhaustion crept up on him suddenly and all his thoughts came to a standstill. For a moment, he felt like a body without a mind, as if some logical process had slipped and disengaged everything except the most basic awareness.

Some dim, whispering third level speculated the simulacrum was failing ahead of time; it didn't worry him. He sat on the hummock, still as the trees in the breezeless night air, his eyes closed, and simply listened to the distant sounds of Resurrection.

"Okay," he said after a half hour had passed. He opened his eyes. The forest was still dark, which was just as well. He was going to mentally recall some of the packet material, slow it down. The simulacrum's abilities were clearer to him now. He hadn't been using them to anywhere near their full extent.

First, Throne. There was absolutely no mention of what the Bifrost was, or even what it looked like within the city; the original Kahn's transmissions must have been spur-of-the-moment. So he could not tell what the Bifrosts did. But Throne, according to legend, was gone.

He focused on Thule, Pearson's final home (did he live to see the exiling?), home of heretics and heresies, insect city in a network of largely botanical cities.

The abstraction that came to his mind this time, from the tapes and from his own memory, was fear. It was cool, separated from his anatomy, almost metaphysical.

He would have to go to Thule, and he didn't relish the thought at all.

Arthur sat in the most beautiful room he had ever seen in his life, dejected. For the first hour, he had looked at the shelves of sculptures and examined the intricately decorated wall, tracing the abstract floral patterns and geometrics with his fingers. The way the figures fit together, yet were all the same shape, amazed him. When he grew tired of being amazed, he hefted each sculpture, running his thumb over the smooth, silvery metal. They flowed like a closely bound fountain of water, yet came apart into cubes and pyramids, and into other figures—crosses, many-sided things he didn't know the names for—which couldn't be put back together again. No matter how he tried, the puzzle eluded him. He finally put the pieces back on the shelf.

The floor was soft to his feet, like grass, but even here there were designs, and the designs changed completely at least four times in the hour. His eyes grew tired, trying to fathom the process. When his mouth was dry, he asked for something to drink—as the pipe-joint guide had instructed him—and cups of fluid appeared on the table in the center of the room. He sampled each in turn, found a variety of fruit juices and something that tasted like wine, and downed the wine. Several glasses of the stuff had no effect on him. Disgusted, he sat in a rounded nook, leaned back in the formfit chair, looked at the pearly ceiling—that sort of thing was popular in Resurrection—and thought of New Canaan West, the dying farm, the heat. His daughters and wife. The Founders. What would they think, seeing him here now, where none of them had ever been? He smiled and patted the chair arms with his hands, then slammed them. They yielded just enough to absorb the blow.

"I'm bored," he said well into the second hour.

"What do you wish to entertain you?" the pipe-joint city part asked.

"What are my choices? The hell with that—I want to see Kahn again."

"We have dances, dramas, diversions, Or you may join the education net."

"Sure. Anything." It was a prison, no matter how beautiful it was, or how temporary. Kahn or somebody had tricked him; the door wouldn't open. He was trapped. He fought off a momentary touch of panic. He didn't know anything about cities. What if it should start to move? He had never seen one move. How would it transport a room? Break it down, or shrink it up, with him inside?

"Forget that," he ordered himself.

"Forget what, sir?" the city part asked.

"Nothing."

He stood up from the chair and walked to the table. "I'm hungry." The part asked what he would like, and after going through the whole routine, another variety appeared on the table. Arthur looked underneath, but the top was no more than a centimeter thick. Another thing he couldn't puzzle out.

He picked at a bowl of fruit and slices of something like cheese, but creamier than he was used to. As he bit into an apple, he felt someone was watching him. He turned.

In the center of the room stood a woman. She was dressed in a long green gown and her hair was pepper-grey, thick and wiry. He could see through her. There was a star shining in her forehead. It was the woman who had sat in the chair at the top of the tower . . . it was Reah.

He put the apple down. This time, he was sure she was staring at him. Her mouth moved, as if to ask a question, but no sound came out. He backed away. She raised an arm, fingers spread, smiling. He was terrified. Ascoria had said she was dead, but this wasn't just some magic trick or projection. She was *looking* at him, following him with her eyes!

"Who is that?" he asked, pushing the words across a dust-dry tongue.

"Who is who?" the part asked.

"There," he pointed.

The woman shook her head and held her finger to her lips. Except for being translucent and silent, she was every bit as alive as he was. She mouthed a word carefully, and he thought he could tell what it was:

Welcome.

"Thank you," he said. The room wasn't built for hiding in. He could see her from the nook, and he wasn't about to turn his back on her—so he had to stand his ground, make the best of things.

Where? She pointed with a skinny finger. *Where from?*

"New Canaan," he said hesitantly. "Outside Expolis Ibreem, not too far from here. Where they don't like cities or what come out of them."

She nodded, then turned and faded. Before she vanished completely, she walked toward a wall—and passed right through it.

"Jesus, Jesus," Arthur said softly. He picked up the fruit again, then looked at it long and hard. Perhaps it was best not to eat anything. His grandmother had told him about eating fruit from trees that grew on spirit paths, and how it might make you a spirit yourself. He hadn't considered that possibility before. There were a lot of dangerous things he probably didn't know about. The panic rose again. He clutched himself with his arms and sat on a small chair near the table, water rising in his eyes, his stomach churning.

He decided to lie down. Almost immediately, he fell asleep. On the edge of dreams, he felt a loving touch somewhere inside his head. Then, as it had done for seventy-five years, the city's education net went to work.

Arthur felt only vague dreams, one of them quite peculiar. He saw Jeshua, and next to Jeshua, another figure with carrot-red hair, rather like the head the mimic had carried. But the head had a body now, and from its brow came the fierce light of a star.

Jeshua and Thinner were carried through the racks of replacement parts on a cart. The chamber was large and dark. Jeshua could see row after row of mimic human and animal bodies, like a mortuary—like the chamber he had visited on his first day in Mandala. The bodies were attached to the racks, held upright, and fed through tubes. Most were in bad shape—or, at least no better condition than he and Thinner. If these were the mimics that had haunted New Canaan, they had had a very rough time.

The cart stopped beside a city-part that looked like it had been constructed out of old steel pipes, with straight arms and legs and rounded joints and a small sphere mounted on a thin neck. It bent over him.

"Where are you from?" it asked.

"Mandala."

"And the head?"

"The same."

"What was your mission?"

"We were built to go out among humans," Jeshua said. "And to suffer the pain of the age."

"How long ago?"

"A hundred and forty years, approximately."

"You're a labelled city part—though the label has been effaced. Not a logical sequence of planning. Would you like to be made whole again?"

He hadn't thought about death since he'd found out he wasn't human. Now he was being given a choice. The possibility of an end was very real, almost attractive.

Still, it wasn't entirely his decision. There was action to be fulfilled. "Yes," he said.

"Your repair will begin in a few seconds. There will be some disorientation, and then—"

A moment like a tiny death, entering into the ComNet, swimming. Moving around some still point, above a red, glowing sea of thought, calm and warm . . . looking for Thinner, but not a sign of his presence. Where was he? Then, rising from some unseen position, a woman with pepper-grey hair and a star shining in her forehead. Jeshua recognized her immediately. His exultation was enormous. It was She who mingled with the *Qellipoth*, the Bride of God who sacrificed herself by going downward into misery to watch over the captive souls of the material realm, those scattered sparks of holy fire, sacred drops of oil, which had fallen into worldliness with the breaking of the *Sefiroth*, the manifold vessels of the Holy One, blessed be He. She seemed to stand over him.

She addressed his thoughts, poking at them. Suddenly he wasn't sure that he had ever properly mastered the complexities of *Kaballah*. Her judgement was stern, critical, yet sympathetic to his folly . . . perhaps because she recognized her own place in his thoughts, in the scheme.

He opened his eyes. Thinner was standing over him, holding his chin with a strong, healthy hand.

"Better?" Thinner asked.

Jeshua nodded. The pain—ignored, but always present—was now truly gone. The awareness of damage to parts without pain was also gone.

"You had enough left that was functioning, the city decided to patch you up," Thinner said. "Me, they just put on the best body they could find. Takes much less time." He removed Jeshua's straps.

"I have seen her," Jeshua said, still slightly groggy.

"Who?"

"The bride of God, who gave herself to the false world that we might all be redeemed. I saw the *Shekhinah*."

Thinner nodded, neither agreeing nor disagreeing. Jeshua closed his eyes and swallowed, trying to remember the exultation.

Kahn had returned to the stripped control chamber and skimmed through the rest of the packet. The recorders in other cities had continued to transmit information to one another long after most intercity communications had stopped. The picture slowly and painfully evolving in his mind was quite broad-based; the disaster had been manifold, horrifying in its completeness.

The exiling had been carried out quickly everywhere but in Thule, and apparently without mercy or discrimination. Everyone—man, woman, child—had been forced to go from comfort and civilization to virtual anarchy.

He cursed the people and organizations beyond God-Does-Battle who could have stepped in and brought things back under control, and didn't; he cursed them, but he understood why. The entire planet had been in chaos. Fleets of thousands of ships would have been required to land sufficient troops and social engineers to bring back order. Kahn suspected —since he felt more than just a twinge of it in himself—that the ruling figures had regarded the situation as fitting and just. Jews, Christians and Moslems had not been looked upon with good will on Earth and elsewhere for some time.

But all that was long past. He could not avoid the fact that he was responsible, in part, for the biggest disaster in the history of organized religion. There was no one left to share the blame; generations by the score had come and gone.

He put the packet into his coat lining and took two steps away from the chair.

"Is it enough?"

He looked back over his shoulder. Matthew was watching from the other side of the chamber, sitting on a raised portion of the floor. "Not nearly enough," Kahn said.

"But it's all there. I've read your packets . . . two of them, anyway."

"You found the recorder in Resurrection."

Matthew nodded. "And in Throne. They even touch on what I've done, briefly. And on what you did."

"What happened to Throne?"

"I guided it to the river plain, then dismantled it. I put it to good use."

"What sort of use?"

Matthew's face hardened and his lines seemed to deepen. "You might as well be a ghost. I've been fighting you and what you did. You resisted every time through your city programming, your Bifrosts—"

"What are the Bifrosts?"

"You can't guess? That's just as well. The best thing is for you to leave. I'm the one to fix what you've torn apart." He held out thin, trembling hands.

"You don't know how," Kahn said. "Have you communicated with the—with other worlds, our people out there?" Kahn pointed up, uncertain how sophisticated Matthew really was.

"I tried once. The city fought me for months, but I finally convinced it to make a transceiver. It wasted its energy on a huge system, and I sent a signal out to the stars. Nothing came back. Nothing. We have been wrapped in our own box of dark, velvet sin. They have isolated us, and that is as it should be. Now we have the freedom to choose where we will go."

"Who's this 'we'?" Kahn asked. "You and who else?"

"I am alone now."

"Then who are you, to think you can save God-Does-Battle without help—"

"I am Matthew, son of Reah! My mother was Moslem, raped by pagans, killed by an apostate Jew-Christian! I am more qualified than anyone to save these people, for I am all of them, born of hate and conflict and despair!" He lowered his voice. "My own mother chose to abort me rather than bring me into the world she knew. This city saved me, raised me as the new Christ." He smiled. "Which I most emphatically am not. So I've taken up where my mother left off, guided Resurrection, helped it reorder itself. And I've destroyed what you started nine centuries ago."

"The Bifrosts?"

"Yes. In Throne, in Eulalia."

"And in Thule?"

"Thule is safe enough, left alone."

Kahn held out his hands. "Listen, I'm not your enemy, and I'm no more Satan than you are Christ. If you help, we can solve our problems together."

"In the final analysis, you probably have more power than I do," Matthew said. "You can go places I can't. You don't need my help. I wouldn't give it to you if you did."

"At the very least, let me look over your transceiver. Help from outside—"

"There is nobody out there. I destroyed the transceiver when I saw it was useless."

"Damn you, Matthew, your people may die if we don't do something!"

"Perhaps that's only fitting. Let God's will be done. Go away, ghost. Vanish. Your companion is safe in a very comfortable room. Take him with you. Leave the mimics if you wish; I may be able to use them."

Matthew stood and walked slowly toward the door, leaning on his stick. "I'm old," he said, as if answering an unasked question, "because I chose to grow old. You have no such grace in you."

When Kahn reached the door, the old man had disappeared again. "Ghost, ghost, I'm not the only ghost on this planet," he muttered.

Arthur was flying above the river plain. He saw Resurrection, and he saw beneath the ground, into tunnels radiating out from the city, going for hundreds of kilometers. The tunnels were filled . . .

But not with people. Not this time.

They were mimics. Thousands of them emerged from Resurrection, going out into the countryside, coming out of the ground, raising their arms to the hot, bright sun. They fanned out across New Canaan, were caught by Founders and tortured, dismantled.

Behind him he could feel the woman, the warmth from the star in her forehead. She was guiding him in his flight, guiding his dream—

He started awake at the sound of the apartment door sliding open.

"Arthur?"

"Yes, I'm here."

Kahn entered, followed by Jeshua and somebody familiar—the red-headed figure from the dream.

"We're leaving now," Kahn said.

"Oh." Arthur struggled up from the couch and stood on wobbly legs. "Where?"

"Matthew doesn't want us here, isn't going to cooperate. But I know where the Bifrosts are."

"More than one?" Jeshua asked. Kahn nodded.

"How do we get there? More walking?"

"No," Kahn said. "We have transportation."

"Oh." Arthur rubbed his eyes. "Is that the head?" he asked, looking at Thinner.

"That I was," Thinner said.

"Oh."

They stood silent for a few awkward seconds.

"I've been dreaming—" Arthur started, but Kahn interrupted.

"We'll go to the heat shaft. There's a city transport waiting there, unless Matthew has interfered again."

Thinner was regarding Arthur fixedly, which made him uncomfortable. There was something familiar in the stare. "I'm ready," Arthur said quickly. "I'd never get used to all this." He motioned at the apartment.

In the heat shaft, a large white object like a smooth clay dove hovered, hatch open for them to enter. In basic form it resembled an airplane Arthur had seen the Founders flying, but much sleeker.

As they boarded the craft, Jeshua looked down on Kahn with an unfamiliar, almost queasy reverence. It was built in to him that he should obey the builder, even at the widest limit of his freedom; yet if it had been different, he would have obeyed anyway. He could feel the forces of regathering and redemption working within Kahn, within the *Shekhinah* which surrounded them. He sat awkwardly in a seat barely large enough to hold him, felt supple restraint close around his chest and legs, watched the others being gently wrapped in white bands. They sat in a circle near the center of the craft, beneath a transparent portal as wide as the cabin.

Thinner closed his eyes and laid his hand on Jeshua's.

Kahn took his seat at a console beneath a forward-facing blister.

The craft rose slowly, and sections of the walls around them became transparent. Their seats seemed suspended in a cage of wide, flat white bars.

Above the city, looking out across the enclave and the smaller towers, Kahn told the craft, "We are going to Eulalia."

"Where's that?" Arthur asked quietly.

"It's a city south of us," Thinner said. "Used to be inhabited by Pentecostals."

"Ever been there?" Arthur felt awkward sitting next to the mimics, without Kahn mediating.

"No," Jeshua said, smiling as if at some secret joke. "It's across the sea. Last we heard, it was surrounded by Pentecostal expolises. They were being very zealous, wouldn't allow the city to move. They built concrete barricades all around, higher than the city parts could climb."

"How long ago was that?"

"Fifty years."

"Oh." He leaned his head back and looked up at the blue sky. A cloud was floating past in the morning light. Suddenly, the cloud shifted and disappeared.

The craft accelerated above the river plain, banked, and headed south.

Kahn felt like his entire thorax was filled with expanding lead. He couldn't call the sensation dread, or fear—it had too much of something else, directed toward Arthur and the city parts. They were such pure symbols of his failure.

Matthew watched Kahn's commandeered aircraft vanish to a pale point in the brightening sky. He sat beneath a tent looking south from a broad portico. Another aircraft waited just beyond the edge of the portico, but Matthew was in no hurry. He knew where Kahn's final destination lay. And he knew about Reah's capabilities; he had opposed her long enough, in silent warfare, not to be surprised by anything she did.

She had controlled city part repairs. At one time, she had overseen the education net for the children brought in from outside. And she had controlled the medical facilities.

He was reminded of her control with every creak and twinge of his aging body, with every failure of memory and intellect. She was dead; she was immortal, not human. And she had allowed her son to grow old. It was the only way she could guarantee eventually wresting his part of the city away from him. When he died, he would have been on her home territory . . .

But now, Reah was no longer in the city mind.

She had joined the false Kahn on his journey.

He let the hot morning wind blow across his skin and shaded his eyes against the blowtorch glare of the sun, bright even through the tent fabrics.

Arthur looked down on the flat expanse of water. They had crossed over into night again, and two moons cast twin arcs of wave-textured light across the sea.

He had given up worrying. The marvels were coming so thick and fast that he simply planted an almost animal trust in Kahn.

Kahn remained in the blister beside the emergency operations console. Charts were projected into his eyes and he checked their course every few minutes, a gesture of nerves. At least he didn't grow tired. While Arthur slept and the mimics talked softly, he ordered the craft higher, until the atmosphere was as black as space and the horizon was a purple line of sunrise. When the sun appeared, he darkened the windows.

Four hours from Resurrection, they flew over land again. Up from dazzling yellow sand beaches rose sharp-spined mountains covered with thick foliage. Inland, the mountains merged into tablelands and valleys. A wide fjord cut from the sea into the tablelands, and in a natural bowl-shaped valley adjacent to the fjord was Eulalia. Three needle-thin spires rose from the Pentecostal city, just as Kahn had seen in the record. The craft dropped steadily, improving his view.

Within its concrete barrier, Eulalia was dead. Close-up, the spires were pitted, rusted, ready to collapse. The city itself was little more than a shell. Still, he had to look to be sure. The craft descended a dilapidated heat shaft.

Many structural parts and virtually all detail parts—walls, floors—lay in ruins, the decay far more advanced than in Fraternity. The heat shaft broadened and they saw collapsed promenades leaning outward at crazy angles, buttresses fallen in rows like soldiers fainted in parade-ground heat. And at the very center, the city had been hollowed, burned out, by some kind of explosion.

He was satisfied that the Bifrost no longer existed in Eulalia. The destruction was so complete that he decided not to investigate any further.

He carefully maneuvered the craft back up the shaft, then slowed as something caught his eye. There were bodies scattered across a tilted and cracked promenade. He brought the craft as close to the leaning surface as he dared.

"Jeshua," he said. "What are those?"

Jeshua looked out his window, which gave a better view. "Dead city parts," he said. "Mimics and others . . . servants, all kinds."

"What are mimics doing in Eulalia?"

Arthur frowned. "Matthew sent them," he said finally.

"How do you know?" Kahn asked.

"I can see them leaving Resurrection, in my memory. I don't know how . . . I was having dreams in the city . . ."

"Why would he send them?" Kahn asked, but he could guess. To destroy the Bifrost. No more than twenty-five years ago, Eulalia had been alive and whole, or so the record showed.

He flew out of the city and did a quick tour of the surrounding valley floor. The Pentecostal villages had moved or been forced to move. Their vigil over Eulalia had ended.

"We're going south," he said. Matthew had indicated Thule was still intact. Now he was curious as to why Thule had survived Matthew's crusade.

As the craft gained altitude, Kahn lapsed into that speculative frame which was the closest thing to sleep. He lost track of the hours.

Arthur became hungry and the craft fed him. The craft also took care of Jeshua's and Thinner's needs.

They flew low over desert, sometimes passing villages and clusters of nomads. Here, the season was cooler, closer to whatever winter the bright sun allowed, and the desert was at least tolerable. In the summer, it would not be. Arthur wondered where the people would go then, whether they would leave at all or just die, clinging to tradition and hope.

He looked across the cabin at the mimics. He couldn't shake the notion that there was something familiar about Thinner—something he had seen in his dreams. Gestures, eyes. Arthur shrank back into his seat. His fear was returning. He felt his humanity acutely, going to the restroom every hour or so, while the others needed no such facilities. He felt like curling up into a ball, sleeping. In time, he did sleep again, but fitfully.

When he awoke, Kahn said they were still flying south, over the Sea of Galilee. Before God-Does-Battle had been purchased, the Sea of Galilee had been called Cold's Sea, after a geographer aboard the first colony ship. When the new owners had moved in, they had stretched Earth's Middle East and Bible lands around the planet like a sheet of rubber.

Kahn spotted icebergs floating like overlarge whitecaps far below, then stretches of pack ice beneath the clouds. God-Does-Battle's south polar region was extensively frozen over, with deep fingers of white reaching across the four continents of the southern hemisphere; but the ice was less dominant than it had been thirteen hundred years ago. The oceans were expanding. Soon—perhaps in months—the alluvial plain around Resurrection would be flooded.

The displays showed hundreds of kilometers of pack ice, then an edge of solid white which denoted the continent of Brisbane. Pearson's colonizers had left these names alone—Brisbane, Asgard, Scott and Amundsen. By rights, Kahn thought, the Bifrost—whatever it was—should have been built on Asgard, but that continent was much farther south, buried deep under two kilometers of ice, still scarcely touched by the sun. Thule, the only arctic city, had been built on Brisbane. It must have been difficult for the original Kahn to settle on Thule, isolated as it was; obviously, he had had little choice.

Kahn spotted the triplet spires in the sunset. The aircraft began its descent. At five thousand meters, rough air shook it. Stabilizers took hold and their course smoothed. Thule grew on the darkening land, glittering in the pale yellow glow like a palace made of glass and ice.

Thule had been ruled by Jemmu Yoshimura, president of the Asian Jews, a tough little rabbi with scarcely any Japanese blood, but descended from a famous family. Except for the spires, Thule hadn't changed much and was apparently still alive. Its twelve outer towers flashed with the changing angles of their approach. The central temple—part of which supported the easternmost spire—was as intricate and fascinating as when Kahn had finished it, a cold radiolarian sculpted in city parts.

The sunset reflected from it bathed his face and the cabin. A flat plain of snow surrounded the city, laced with roads leading to a harbor which no longer existed. Outlying areas of the city had stopped functioning, obviously, but for a kilometer around the snow was a thin layer of white and not a thick blanket; Thule's environmental envelope still tempered the cold and storms.

The craft banked and Kahn looked down from an altitude of three thousand meters.

The snow and ice were covered with black specks.

"Entering city environment," the craft said softly.

"Double back and take us lower, slower," Kahn ordered.

They flew in a broad, unhurried circle over the snow within Thule's environment.

The specks were bodies. Some were mimics contorted and in pieces, surrounded by sprays of city part fluid. The battlefield—for so it seemed—stretched right up to the now-familiar circle of silicate spines. Under the envelope, the bodies lay where they had fallen, frozen but kept free of covering snow.

"Transmit my voice," Kahn said. "I am the builder . . ." He repeated the phrase twice.

Then a voice replied from the city, low-pitched and almost musical, seductively pleasant. "Welcome, Pontifex."

Kahn raised an eyebrow. "I am not the pope," he said. "Respond in an appropriate manner."

"You are a builder of bridges, so you are Pontifex. You are also Archon," Thule's voice said.

Kahn leaned back and looked at his passengers. "What the hell is it talking about? Jeshua, you seem to be up on such things . . ."

"Pontifex means bridge-builder, I believe. Archon is a kind of demiurge."

"Oh? And what is a demiurge?"

"The creator of the shadow world, standing between true Godhead and humanity."

"I see." Ghostic doctrine, he thought. He didn't relish facing a city so full of strange conceits.

The aircraft slowed even more, spilling its air with a faint hiss, and drifted onto a glittering, sky-blue landing deck. Broad light-absorbing banners hung limp from stanchions at one end of the field. They fluttered briefly with the wash from the craft's passage.

The door opened. The air was not as cold as Arthur expected, but it was cold enough. Kahn walked past them and stood in the doorway. If it was possible for a simulacrum to have premonitions, he was having one now, and it told him to leave, to put as many kilometers between them and Thule as he could.

He stepped down the ramp. The air was perfectly still under the city's weather umbrella, silent.

The platform was deserted.

"Warm the air, please," Kahn said, his voice echoing from the distant walls. In a few seconds, the air became more comfortable. "Something's responding," he said to the others.

"You are the builder," Jeshua said. "Shouldn't the city obey your orders?"

"Resurrection did," Kahn admitted.

"Is Thule any different?" Arthur asked.

"Yes," Kahn said. "We'll have to be careful."

Thinner nodded, looking around with a watchful but calm expression.

From across the plaza, they heard a sound like wind whistling through a narrow opening. Then a light appeared, resolving as it approached into a framework pyramid made of bars of crystal. Within the framework was a smaller, solid pyramid, seemingly made from gold, but giving off a warm light. Kahn didn't recognize it—no city part had had such a design in his plans, even in Thule. It was possible Pearson had added such parts later.

The inner pyramid reversed itself in the frame, and the same rich voice came out of it. "Welcome, Builder. Thule has awaited your return. Your companions are also welcome."

"What agency do you represent?" Kahn asked.

"I am the religious coordinator."

"May I address the architect?"

"The agency left in your place is no longer functioning," the pyramid said.

"Who built you?"

"I am from the reign of Pearson."

"Do you know what I'm doing here?" Kahn asked.

"You are here to attend the Bifrost."

"And who am I?"

"You are an image of the Archon, Kahn."

"Where is Kahn?"

"Standing before me."

"And the original?"

"Transformed."

Kahn stood silent for a moment, wondering how he should approach the situation. "Where is the Bifrost?"

"In the central amphitheater."

"Is it still functioning?"

"It is intact, but only you can make it function."

"I see." He didn't, however. He was more confused than ever. "Please take us there."

"Certainly." The pyramid floated slowly over the platform. "If you will follow . . ."

They walked across the plaza, under the pale blue-green arches and down a corridor whose walls and ceiling seemed made of ice crystals woven in geometric patterns. They came to the promenade surrounding a heatshaft and the pyramid halted.

"This will be your transportation to the lower regions," it said. The heat shaft vehicle resembled a giant snowflake, glittering in the cold white light reflected from the vent a hundred meters above.

"When we arrive," Kahn said, "I would like to have four terminals waiting, and open access to the ComNet."

"All things can be arranged," the pyramid said in a pleasant tone.

Matthew stood on the snow-covered plain north of Thule. His aircraft and four pipe-joint city parts waited behind him, one part clutching a portable environment pack. He walked to the edge of a cluster of stiff, rime-covered bodies and looked down on them, frowning slightly.

Every other city had allowed his city parts to enter . . . Thule had rejected them. With one hand, he brushed away the frost, then backed up quickly. The body was human, skin desiccated but intact, lips drawn back in a mocking sneer.

Resurrection's mimics were mingled with the centuries-old bodies of Thule's inhabitants. He bent down over the corpse, gingerly pulled back a stiff white coat—they had all worn clothes much too thin to keep them alive, even in the comparatively mild city environment zone—and saw a silver star of David on a lapel.

Matthew wandered from body to body, examining humans, mimics, city parts. The mimics and city parts were all badly mangled, pierced by shards of crystal. When he had sent Resurrection's mimics out of the city, through tunnels dug beneath the river plain, he had expected few difficulties. But even when Eulalia and Throne had let his mimics inside, they had resisted his attempts to dismantle the Bifrosts. They had resisted Kahn, and they had resisted him. He had had to destroy Eulalia, finally, but Throne had come to the river plain, as if attracted by Resurrection's healthy example, and with his overwhelming army of city parts he had killed the city from inside, dismantled it, carried it underground. He had used the materials to build the army of city parts and mimics which he sent to Thule.

Thule had never even let them inside. When they had tried to break through the city's barriers, the battle had been incredibly short. The few that had survived returned with stories of legions of parts designed specifically to destroy.

With its Byzantine city mind, it could do almost anything. It had let Kahn in—the original Kahn—and then somehow thwarted him. And now it had swallowed the simulacrum.

But Matthew couldn't afford to trust Thule to be as efficient this time. He didn't like to think of what he would have to do if the simulacrum succeeded—he hadn't enjoyed destroying Eulalia. There were few enough cities left as it was, and perhaps in time he could think of a use for Thule.

He walked back to the aircraft and sat on the door ramp. "Come here." He motioned to the nearest city part. It approached. "Bring down the flier, just in case."

Another ramp opened in the side of the craft and a bee-shaped flier floated out. It had been modified slightly; now a black cylinder stood upright in the middle of the passenger section. On top of the cylinder was a silvery cube with three delicate antennae, measuring about ten centimeters on a side. By Kahn's technological standards, no doubt it was very crude, but Matthew had long since abandoned self-conscious comparisons. He was the son of a peasant; the best he could hope for was that his methods be effective, not elegant.

Either way, Kahn would not drain his planet of people. There was nothing out there for them to go to, nothing they would understand. God-Does-Battle was their home, for better or worse, so God had decreed ages ago. And Matthew would do anything to carry out God's will.

A crystal framework pyramid—the same or different was hard to tell—met them at the bottom of the shaft. "Pontifex, the Bifrost is in an amphitheater on his level. We have also arranged for terminals in an adjacent library to have ComNet access. But we expect you would liked to see the Bifrost first."

Kahn agreed, and the pyramid led them into the amphitheater. It had been designed to hold sixty thousand citizens, but the circular stage set up in the middle of the grass-covered field played to empty seats.

They walked across the well-kept, lustrous green grass. The stage was not made of city parts; for that reason, Kahn suspected it had been constructed later, perhaps nine hundred years ago. Their angle of approach—from the rear—didn't give them a good view of the Bifrost, if indeed it was located on the stage. Two white, wing-shaped arches stood in their line of sight. He wondered how it was all connected with the spires. Perhaps there were no physical connections—and at any rate, how could he even speculate?

It seemed that the original Kahn's planning had included psychology. The stage was very like an evangelist's proscenium, decorated in rather angelic fashion.

They rounded the stage.

Between the arches rose a rectangular spacc of such intense

blackness that it looked like a hole. Around the base of the stage was a half-circle of steps. Everything had been arranged so that hundreds of thousands of people could enter each hour, walk up the steps—and, Kahn presumed, into the blackness.

From this perspective, it looked very much like an advanced matter transmission system.

"Is that the Bifrost?" Arthur asked.

"I'm not sure."

"That is the Bifrost," the pyramid said warmly.

"Is it operating?" Kahn asked.

"This unit does not know. The Bifrost has been in this mode ever since the transformation of the primal Archon."

"It's never been tested?"

"No."

"Where are the terminals?"

"This way." The pyramid moved toward an aisle and Kahn followed. Jeshua and Arthur were close behind, but Thinner held back, staring at the black rectangle.

"Were many records left by . . . the Archon?" Kahn asked, deciding the simplest expression of a confused situation would have to do.

"There are records," the pyramid said.

"Don't you know what the Bifrost is? Not even now?" Arthur asked.

"I'm not the same Kahn who built it. Why should I know? He had four hundred years on me." At the end of the aisle, they passed through a broad gate. Thinner followed several dozen meters behind, feeling the walls with his hands, stopping occasionally to stroke a pillar or buttress.

The terminals were in an antechamber. The walls had been festooned with multi-colored crystal flowers, intricate circular designs with mystical symbols etched in glass and city material. The result was eye-spinning and garish, not at all like the original Thule.

Kahn pulled a chair out from one terminal and sat. "Feel free to use the others," he said to Arthur and Jeshua. Jeshua followed suit, but Arthur remained standing.

Kahn spread his hands over the dimples in front of his terminal screen. "Records of Robert Kahn, please."

A homunculus formed on the plate. It was a black and yellow locust standing on its hind legs, wearing a formal black suit and round black cap. "Those records are separate from the city ComNet," it said. It cocked its head at him inquiringly. "Any questions I may answer?"

He wanted to ask if the original Kahn was still alive, but the words stuck in his throat. "Where are those records kept?"

"In the Archon's chambers."

"Where are the chambers?"

"I will find out. Do you have any other questions?"

The homunculus should have known immediately. Either Thule was not completely integrated or it was hiding things. And he was worried by other aspects of the homunculus—its use of a personal pronoun, its peculiar form and animation, quite unlike the service figures in other cities. What it represented in Thule's scheme of things, he couldn't tell.

"I need a record of solar flux in the last five, six hundred years."

"I believe the Pontifex has notes on that subject, but there are no records in the ComNet." The homunculus' tone of voice was faintly taunting now.

"Are there any city records?"

"No."

"What does the ComNet . . ." Kahn took a deep breath and bent closer to the little figure. "Then I'd like city history, starting with the return of the original Kahn."

"Coming up."

Kahn and Jeshua fit their fingers into the cups and stared into the projectors. Arthur leaned against a pillar, tapping one foot nervously. He looked around for Thinner. The mimic hadn't followed them into the antechamber.

Arthur walked to the door, then down a short corridor. Thinner wasn't in the amphitheater, and he wasn't in the corridor. Arthur returned to the antechamber, saw that Jeshua and Kahn were absorbed in whatever the terminals were showing them, then went in search of Thinner.

He was tired and not a little afraid, but the rebodied mimic had puzzled him since they'd left Resurrection. Weren't the city parts supposed to follow Kahn's orders? Thinner obviously wasn't doing that.

Trying to memorize his path, Arthur made his way to the main promenade, then walked in the pale light to a spiral ramp leading to higher levels. He spotted the mimic on the ramp.

Arthur followed him. The mimic didn't seem much more familiar with Thule than Arthur was. It was easy enough to tail him; Thinner stopped every few meters to feel the walls, stroking them or just touching with his fingers.

Up elevators, moving stairways and more spiral ramps around a ventilator shaft, Thinner stopped five floors above the amphitheater level, his face expressionless. The way he touched the city's surfaces, he seemed to be reading, following some hidden pattern.

Then, inadvertently, Arthur lagged behind too much and the mimic spotted him across the ramp. He froze. Thinner stared at him for a few seconds, then turned away and kept walking. Arthur waited a discreet interval, unsure how the mimic felt about being followed, then hurried to catch up.

"Do you know what I'm looking for?" Thinner called back.

"No," Arthur answered.

"The terminals won't tell Kahn anything he really needs to know. They're stalling. So I'm looking for ComNet entry terminals—not just terminals with read-only capability."

"Why?"

"A safeguard. What do you remember about Thule?"

That was a strange question, but he answered without thinking. "A Gnostic city now, but before the Exiling Gnosticism was only part of its . . ." He stopped, startled by the flow of words—and not just words, but images, understanding. "Part of its heretical programs. George Pearson apostasized ten years before the Exiling became the mayor of Thule.'' His thoughts raced ahead. ''The city didn't accept the judgement of all other cities during the Exiling. But two months later, for reasons of its own, first it kicked out all Jews. Gnosticism is antagonistic toward Jews and their God. Then everybody else. They all died in the cold.''

''Where did you learn all that?''

''In Resurrection, I think.''

''Given history lessons, just like a child. How does it make you feel?''

''Confused,'' Arthur said, walking in step with Thinner. And stronger . . . and deeply afraid. There was a part of himself he hadn't earned, somehow, not truly himself, but the memory of cities. He felt violated, but not just violated . . . pleased, shamefully proud of the knowledge he hadn't earned.

The sensation of understanding his own words, of being somehow a larger person—as if he had been given an atlas to his past, a magic mirror—was incredible, inexpressible.

Thinner stopped abruptly, then turned. ''There are entry terminals in a room at the end of this corridor.''

''You know that just by touching the walls?''

''All cities have a nerve system. I can read the impulses. They tell me things not even Kahn knows. Thule is very unhealthy now. Even a heretic city would be warped by what it did. It watched its citizens freeze to death in the snow. And it exiled them not under compulsion, but because it chose to. It's dangerous here.''

''Does it know you're listening?''

''Its ComNet isn't aware throughout the entire city. It's contracted, withdrawn. But it might know.''

At the end of the corridor was a broad, high-domed room, lit as if by skylights, though they were deep within Thule. Arranged around the room were larger versions of the terminals in the antechamber. Some had been broken and scattered, others tossed haphazardly. Thinner righted one and tested it by pushing several buttons.

The screen's louvres opened. Thinner bent over the terminal, bringing his face close to the dimples. The mimic's forehead glowed.

"Thinner died before you came to Resurrection," the mimic said, its voice faint. "Kahn's chambers are on this floor. Take the corridor in the opposite direction, to the end. I will prevent the city from harming you, if I can." The mimic pressed its hand into the dimples on the console.

Arthur stepped back, then slapped his hands to his ears. There was a high-pitched noise, almost beyond the range of his hearing. Then all was silent. Arthur lay on his back beside the terminal. The mimic's body had fallen forward, bending its head so that it seemed to rest on the console, disconnected. The eyes were open, blank. At last he understood. Thinner had never made the journey with them. The head had been used.

Arthur got to his feet, turned slowly, and ran.

There was a commotion among the pipe-joint city parts Matthew had brought with him. He looked up from the patterns he had been scrawling in the snow.

Thule's silicate spines were lowering. He stood and gestured at the flier with one hand. "Go." It would hover above the city until it was needed. If it was needed. He still had hope, but it was fading rapidly.

He walked across the field of snow until he came to the edge of the spines. Then he entered Thule's boundaries, with nothing to stop him. Reah had entered the city mind using a mimic's body, her personality confined in the blank mind of the damaged city-part. Matthew marveled at his mother's inventiveness. She had relaxed Thule's defenses, hoping to clear the way for Kahn.

At the same time, she had cleared the way for her son.

"Reah's in the city," Arthur said, his breath coming hard. After the sounds of a few minutes before, the antechamber seemed abnormally quiet. "She was in Thinner. Thinner was already dead . . ."

Kahn looked at Jeshua. "You knew, didn't you?"

"She is the *Shekhinah*," Jeshua said. "There is no deeper sin and error than in this city. She had to come here."

"God *damn* this mystic nonsense!" Kahn shook his hands in the air. "I need to know what lies on the other side of that!" He pointed in the direction of the amphitheater. "The ComNet doesn't tell us a damned thing."

"And I've located your chambers," Arthur said. "That is, the . . ."

"Where?"

"Archon," the homunculus on the terminal interrupted. It was cleaning its legs. "It is not recommended that you . . ."

The voice blurred, then became audible again, ". . . tour the city. I recommend you stay here. The primal Pontifex's chambers are not in order."

The image wavered. Kahn stepped closer. Another image replaced it for just a moment, a woman in long, flowing robes. Then the locust returned.

"What danger is there?" Kahn asked.

The locust's human-like face smiled at him, and the image vanished completely.

"Take me to the chambers," Kahn told Arthur. He led them back, retracing his steps. He didn't want to—what he had seen in the past few minutes was enough to derange him without repeats—but he knew he was marching down the trod, past all will, all hope. He had eaten the fruit, been given forbidden knowledge, and now he was part of the spirit game. Down the corridor, turning left instead of right, to the half-opened door.

"Here," he said.

Kahn stepped inside. The first room was small and dusty-smelling. The floor seemed to be covered with broken glass. The room beyond was larger, with broad tables covered with rolls of paper and notebooks. Here, too, the floor was littered with shards of crystal. Scattered amid the shards were bones and scraps of cloth. The furniture was pierced with needles of glass.

The only intact body was pinned to the opposite wall. Dark blood streamed down the wall, flaking with age. How long ago—nine centuries? Only bones were left, hanging in a white suit not very different from the one Kahn had unpacked and put on in Fraternity.

He stepped up to the pinned figure and examined it closely, clenching and unclenching his hands.

"There are four skulls on the floor, builder," Jeshua said.

Kahn reached carefully into the white suit's pocket and pulled out a jeweled personal computer. On the back he read an inscription: "Love in our third century". Next to the words was Danice's personal design, a rose with a star nestled in its petals.

It was just the sort of precious, tasteless thing Danice would have found for him—a jeweled tapas pad.

Kahn opened and closed his mouth, then looked up at the fleshless skull. The tapas beeped in his hands and he glanced down again. He had accidentally activated the small screen. A triangle appeared, its three corners marked with the symbol for Earth, "G.D.B.", and a lopsided figure eight—infinity.

He walked over the shards to the table and began to flip through the notebooks, pushing aside the rolls of city plans and bits of broken crystal. It took him several minutes to find the section he had hoped was there, in a notebook dated 2666/9/9. It seemed an afterthought: a scrawled chart showing solar maximums and minimums. The star was a Bollingen variable, something he had never heard of before. It had a period of six hundred years. "Now at minimum," the note said casually. "Climatic effects were severe at max., but not permanent. Coastlines altered with sea level rise, weather erratic."

Kahn figured in his head. If it had been at minimum nine hundred years ago, it was at maximum now. In a few years—or decades—it would decline. God-Does-Battle's residents had already suffered through a maximum and survived. They would very probably survive again.

They didn't need him. In a way, Matthew was right. His return, all things considered, was not crucial. But he could activate the Bifrost, complete what the original Kahn had tried to do . . . which was, as near as he could tell, to get everybody away from this foresaken teeter-totter world by walking them through the Bifrost.

One notebook was bound in a dull, frosty gold cover. He pulled it out of the debris and opened to the first page. There was an intricate diagram of a spherical object, surrounded by mathematics of a sort he wasn't familiar with, even though the writing was recognizably his own. Keeping hand-written notebooks was an affectation he had retained from his younger years, when he had imagined himself an equal to Leonardo.

Some of the numbers he could riddle: dimensions—the sphere was ten kilometers wide—and strength-of-materials analyses in one corner. Judging from the figures, the sphere obviously wasn't made of matter—it was practically indestructible—and its internal structure seemed amorphous, more like a gigantic circuit than a building, or even a vessel.

He turned the pages. The sphere's capacity was enormous, allegedly a trillion occupants. But in what form? Not in their bodies, that was certain. Other pages contained diagrams of different structures, one a much larger framework sphere within which the ten kilometer ball would nest. But only temporarily. There were facilities for the reception of travelers—or guests—or whatever they would be, but no docking terminals. Entrance was apparently gained through matter transmission systems.

Wonderful, he thought, the changes that could occur in four hundred years. What purpose did it all serve? Where would the ten-kilometer ball go when it exited the framework sphere? And how would it exit in the first place—no openings were provided, though it was shown pursuing some sort of complex path in higher geometries.

He looked back at the body on the wall, his vision blurring.

"She is here, Builder," Jeshua said. He turned.

Reah's image wavered in the middle of the room. Her voice was distorted, and things seemed to be flying around her, pushing her this way and that, but they could understand her words.

"Builder! You must hurry. The way is open. I have fought all my life, fought my own son when he stopped the children from coming to Resurrection. Now he is here, and you must hurry. You finished the bridge. Take my children across the bridge! Take them away from this place!" The image wavered violently and vanished.

"Matthew's here?" He tried to gather his thoughts, put everything in order through the fear and the compelling lassitude. *But he was already dead—what could he fear?*

"Let's go," Kahn said, picking up the notebooks and sticking them under his arm. If the Bifrost was working, he could get back to Earth, perhaps make deals the way his original had made deals—trading concession for concession. For the moment, there was nothing he could do on God-Does-Battle.

They left the primal Kahn's chambers and walked quickly down the ramps and stairs. Arthur tried to stay calm, but his hands were trembling. He didn't know how much more he could stand. In the same room—a man's corpse, and a duplicate of the man—

In the amphitheater, four shining framework pyramids stood between them and the steps to the stage. Two floated on either side of Matthew, who watched Kahn steadily, leaning on his jade-green staff.

"They're defense," Kahn said to Jeshua in a whisper. "They're the things that blew apart upstairs, made all the broken glass . . ."

"You're the builder," Jeshua said. "How can they kill you?"

"I don't know. But they did once."

"I'm being escorted out," Matthew said, his high-pitched

voice cracking. "Would you care to join me, before my mother loses her fight? If she loses, we're all dead."

"She said the way was open," Kahn said. "We have to go now." He held his hands out to the pyramids. "I am the builder. My word is—"

They advanced on him, humming like hornets, their crystal struts clattering.

"Thule doesn't want us," Matthew said to Arthur. "It only wants Kahn, and we can do quite well without him."

"I don't—" Arthur began.

"Your sun will burn you to a crisp!" Kahn lied. Then he knew his arrogance, saw it clearly.

"You made your mistakes," Matthew said. "If God wills it, we'll live. If not, we won't."

"I have to leave," Arthur said, his face contorted. Matthew walked toward them, pyramids following. Arthur ran across the grass to the old man, his stomach tied in knots. He couldn't control himself. He had to return to normality, to the run-down old farm or what was left of it, to familiar roads, away from the trod. Kahn's path was not for him and never had been.

Matthew took his upper arm and they walked quickly out of the amphitheater. At the gate, they were met by two more pyramids, and their escorts turned back to flank Kahn and Jeshua. "You don't want to go with them?" Kahn asked. "I think Reah's losing, wherever she is."

"I belong where you are going," Jeshua said. "There's nothing here for me."

"Then let's go." They walked toward the stage. The four pyramids drew in tighter, then backed away, humming. The closest to the stage broke formation and blocked their way. "Archon," it said. "You made the cities."

Kahn nodded, stiffening.

"You made the error. You are the demiurge, the false god who created the world with all its pain and evil. You stand between this world and the real God, who does not meddle."

"I'm no god." But he didn't try to deny responsibility. In

its own insane, distorted Gnostic way, Thule was right. "And after what you did to your citizens, who are you to accuse me of crimes?"

The humming grew higher in pitch.

"You murdered them, against all my laws," Kahn said. "You passed judgement on those who made you, just as you pass judgement on me. What a foul, ugly thing you are! I command you to follow your original programming."

One pyramid behind them shattered, throwing its crystal fragments across the grass and into the air. A mournful howl came from the walls rising in pitch. Bells seemed to be struck all around, and the amphitheater was filled with vague, distorted ghosts, like the flicker of a mirage—crowds rising from the seats in one section, then vanishing, the effect rippling around the central stage.

"She's still fighting," Jeshua said. He dotted five points on his forehead and drew two meshed triangles between them.

"So what are our chances now?" Kahn asked him. "Still going to gather the souls, fulfil your *Kaballah*?"

"The *Shekhinah* is with us," Jeshua said.

"Archon," the closest pyramid said pleasantly. "We must go through this again, each time you return, mustn't we?"

"I command you—"

The remaining three pyramids splintered into a cloud of shards and flew at Kahn.

"Don't look back," Matthew said. "Lot's wife, remember?"

But Arthur couldn't take his eyes away from Thule. Matthew darkened the glass to the rear of the aircraft.

Above Thule, the flier's silvery cube fused.

Thule withered under the sudden fireball, its spires blackening, falling away like the legs of a locust burned in a spyglass beam.

Arthur put his hands over his eyes.

"You'll go back to New Canaan," Matthew said, but Arthur hardly heard him. It seemed as if his heart had been torn away and his chest filled with pebbles.

* * *

Jeshua dragged the simulacrum up the steps, kicking away the fragments. Above, there was a roaring, and the darkness rippled like a pool of oil.

"Do it," Kahn said, quite clearly. He was still rational, calm, even though his body—filled with shards—could hardly move.

Jeshua picked him up and pushed him into the Bifrost, then stepped in behind, feeling heat at his back. The black tectangle wavered again, then melted away with the amphitheater and stage.

In Thule's city mind, the battle stopped. Reah stood free for a moment, her responsibilities ended. In her moment of calm, she felt a warm glow all around, then blinding light. Even now, a century dead, she tried to turn away.

But the glow surrounded, bathed. She could sense a giant molecule rising, addressing her.

Ready?

She had gotten Matthew out of Kahn's way, at the very least. She had not controlled the city perfectly; its strongest impulses had slipped past her. But even if she had failed, her part was done. She asked no questions, and dropped her scattered thoughts and fears.

Ready.

She joined.

Three points of a triangle—that had been the display on the tapas Danice had given him: Earth, God-Does-Battle, Infinity. Which point of the triangle was their destination?

Kahn was still alive in the darkness, still thinking. He could feel Jeshua's hand touching his.

He heard a voice. It was Danice. "Darling!" she said.

"I—" he started to answer, but he was forming. Jeshua stood beside him. "Darling!" the voice repeated. They were on a huge platform. Alone.

"You've finally come to us," the recording of Danice

continued. "Time is very short. Your people must follow instructions implicitly. I hope to be with you . . . in eternity!" Her symbol—a rose with an imbedded star—appeared in front of him.

He was weak, but not in pain. Jeshua supported him by the arm. The platform was open on one side to space, or so it seemed—an enormous transparent wall. Among the stars was the framework sphere he had seen in the notebook. He had dropped both notebooks when the pyramids exploded. Kahn's head slumped and Jeshua held him by the back of the skull so he could see. He was like a puppet in the mimic's arms.

"He wasn't taking everybody back to Earth," Kahn said.

"Who?" Jeshua asked softly.

"I . . . I wasn't. He was doing something else."

The Bifrosts, obviously, had been designed to bring all of God-Does-Battle's inhabitants to the platform. Squinting, he could see they were in a long hall of such platforms, gently curving, the end of the arc barely visible to either side through the transparent wall. Thousands of platforms. More than would be needed just for God-Does-Battle. This one staging area alone—hundreds of kilometers square—would have sufficed. The scale was overwhelming. "I built this . . ." It was half a question.

On the opposite side from the transparent wall were more gateways, their blackness as rich as the entrance in Thule.

A sign appeared in the air over their heads. Thousands of similar signs flashed across the platform. A gentle masculine voice repeated what was written on the sign. In the background, other voices read in other languages. He could imagine hundreds of millions of people filing from the Bifrost exits to the secondary gateways, being prepared by the messages for what they were about to experience.

You are about to join in the greatest adventure. You will lose only those things which have held you back . . . you will lose only pain, confusion, hatred. Your privacy will still exist. You will be one among billions, but all will be friends, all will work together. No one will command another, for the resources are vast. You sacrifice only your body, and not even that, for they will be stored in perfect condition, should the time come when you wish to use it again.

In the Golden Sphere, you will experience peace, a clarity of thought and purpose such as you have never known. The sphere will move from point to point in the universe, like a vast starship, but not subject to all the laws of nature as a starship is. Nothing in this universe can harm it. Should unforeseen damage occur, the network will automatically transfer all consciousness back to the bodies in their capsules, and you will go back through the staging areas to your various worlds. Other spheres wait to be activated if needed, and the journey will continue not long after . . .

It sounded like the prospectus for a long, grand vacation. Kahn felt a tug of unease. *He* had advocated *this*? It resembled the typical spiel of the cults and religions he had despised for centuries; the promises of the religions which, in their misapplication, had destroyed God-Does-Battle.

You will have access—by request and permission—to any memory in any other mind. On the journeys, which could conceivably take us from one end of the universe to the other, from the beginning of time to the end, you will experience what all living things have experienced. Mysteries will unfold, for in this joining you will be—along with the rest of humankind—far more capable of understanding, analyzing, feeling. Your senses will expand a millionfold. The Golden Sphere is that state desired by mystics and saints, artists and laborers, scientists and philosophers: the state of Freedom.

The state of change within near-perfection, of achievement within happiness.

Now it is time for you to pass through. Welcome.

We are now become as Gods.

"Take me down to the gate," Kahn said. Jeshua picked him up and they walked to the nearest rectangle of darkness. The original Kahn had designed something so incredible that his earlier self couldn't believe in it. And enough people had believed in the Golden Sphere that it had been built. But had it ever been used? Successfully? Or was it all some enormous boondoggle, and had Matthew been right to thwart him in trying to transport the people of God-Does-Battle?

The question was, simply put: did Kahn trust his later, seemingly more advanced self? He had failed on God-Does-Battle—

He was more than a little afraid. "Go through," he told Jeshua. The mimic obeyed.

They materialized on yet another platform, much smaller, surrounded by floating panels of instrumentation. A technician's eyrie, by the look of it. They were within the framework sphere. Within a few meters of the eyrie walls were glittering transparent cylinders, each containing a body, held in place by bronze-colored piping. They were ranked in layers for as far as he could see, millions, perhaps billions of them.

Capacity in the Golden Sphere, the notebook had said, was one trillion.

Male and female—and types he couldn't place—the bodies seemed alive, but the faces were quite blank.

"Go on," he ordered. Jeshua carried him into a smaller darkness at the opposite end of the eyrie. Why weren't they just deposited in the sphere, with all the other passengers? Why go from the platform to technical centers?

They came out in another eyrie, this one looking out across the middle of the framework sphere. There was a vast hollow. From the innermost surface, thin metal arms (thin! They must have been hundreds of meters wide) reached inward to grasp at nothing. Whatever they had once held—the Golden Sphere, apparently—was gone.

"We missed the boat," Kahn said.

"Is this where the regathering was to happen?" Jeshua asked solemnly. "Where all the souls would join, all the sparks come together?"

"In a manner of speaking," Kahn said weakly. He would have been the first in the staging area, if the plan had worked.

Danice had left a recording for him, and had gone on ahead. After centuries of marriage, she had still trusted him—and Danice had been a very level-headed woman. Perhaps it had worked.

What could he do if it hadn't?

"The vessel has received the drops of precious oil?"

"I don't know." As always. "I suppose it has."

"Then why have we been left behind?"

"We're fakes," Kahn said. "We don't deserve it."

"What about the people of God-Does-Battle?"

"They're out of the picture." Not entirely his fault, either. Their philosophies had been as much responsible for the disaster as he had been. "I guess none of us deserve to be hied off the God's waiting *sephiroth*."

"The next gate?" Jeshua asked. Kahn nodded. There was nothing here for them. They moved to the third point of the triangle.

Emerging from darkness into cloudy daylight, Kahn slumped to his knees, twitching, and Jeshua took hold of him again.

Kahn could feel the simulacrum failing, having endured as much as it was capable of enduring. It eased him gently, without pain.

"Where are we now?" Jeshua asked.

Kahn recognized the land the terminal rested on. Once it had been his. Forty acres lay between gentle hills on the African plains, surrounded by ancient Soleri cities. Even during daylight the cities had sparkled with lights and motion like giant termite mounds. Now they were still.

Empty.

"It's Earth." Kahn couldn't hold back the arrogance now, the final grand gesture. "If I'm so entitled, I give it to you. What the hell, take the whole planet." So be it. That was the way he was.

Perhaps the older Kahn had learned humility. But he didn't think so.

The simulacrum paled. The skin became waxy and the

limbs stiffened. Jeshua let the body down gently on the platform.

He camped beside an artificial lake, listening to frogs and insect chirrups. Earth's single moon was a scythe crescent, with a bright star hanging nearby—Sirius perhaps. He had set up a lean-to between two thick-trunked trees. The day before, he had carried two boxes down from the city on a mound a kilometer away. The boxes held books and tapes.

He had eaten fruits and nuts, abundant in the nearby jungle. He had looked at monkeys, and they had tamely played around his feet on the pathways. Briefly, he had seen a large animal, some kind of cat.

He subdued the pangs of loneliness. In time, perhaps, the people of God-Does-Battle would build spaceships and come to Earth—or perhaps skip that kind of travel entirely, and come by way of Bifrosts. Then he might have company again. But he would never have anyone like Thinner.

He felt very old, very out of place. Yet he was on Earth, and he had always been curious about Earth.

Perhaps the regathering wasn't complete yet. Obviously, not all the drops of precious oil had been collected. He could always hope.

Looking across the lake at the dark outline of the old city on the mound, his eyes were clear and his face was serene.

Arthur heard the chug of motor tricycles coming up the path. He remained seated in the chair, turning his head slowly, heavy-lidded eyes blinking.

Footsteps sounded on the front porch. He listened to the voices, then got up before the knocking began, swishing his tongue through his mouth to rid himself of the sour taste of his nap.

He opened the door on the second knock. A thin, dark-haired man dressed in black and sweating in the heat smiled at him, the smile flickering between ingratiation and embarrassment. "Arthur Sam Daniel?"

"Yes," he answered, looking over the man's shoulder at the three others.

"You told stories about city parts and Resurrection to the Founders, ten years ago, didn't you?"

"I did."

"Nobody believed you," the thin young man said.

"No."

"We found your story in the old files."

"So?"

"Can you come with us? There's a car waiting."

"I'm going someplace?"

"Yes, sir. We need your help, and so do the Expolitans in Ibreem. We're cooperating on this one, sir."

"I see." He looked across the fields at the Founder tractors and the lines of white tents covering the plants, coming almost up to his house. "Well, let me get what I need."

"I'll help, sir."

And he made the journey again, by car and truck and then by boat, across the flooded delta.

Resurrection rose from the waters like a drowned cathedral. The enclave had been evacuated a year before, when the ocean reclaimed the dry flats. He was taken from the boat to the top of the city wall in a metal basket. All the silicate spines had withdrawn.

Resurrection was dead.

"Why do you believe me now?" he asked as they led him through the corridors to the heat shaft.

"It's just as you described it," said a young woman carrying a black notebook. "It took us months to find the report, but the Founders keep everything on file."

"I know," he said ruefully. "I didn't see all that much here. What can I tell you?"

They took a makeshift elevator up the heat shaft, up the tallest tower, until they stood in a dead, brown forest. "We need an identification," the woman said.

His arms and legs ached with tension. He didn't want to show his fear, however, so he just stared at the unlit, scuffed path, his eyes wide. They took him to the cylindrical building with the 2 and the Omega on its side.

A half-circle door was open. Two older men carrying black cases came up behind them, one carrying a crude tape recorder. "Mr. Daniel, we'd like to make your statements permanent. If you'd just speak close to this . . ."

It took some persuading to get him to enter the chamber. "You seem to know so much about the old cities," the woman said. "We'd like to get it all down."

"I told you what was up here," Arthur said. "About the mimics—"

"In school, we were told they came from Fraternity," the woman said.

"Yes, well I imagine that's what he wanted you to think."

She flicked a switch on a portable floodlight and the dark chamber was almost bright as day. "We need to know who he is." She pointed at the chair in the middle of the chamber.

"Him," Arthur said after a moment. "That's what he wanted you to think, about Fraternity."

A skeleton was slumped in the chair. It wore white shorts and nothing else. A green cane lay nearby. "He was nothing without Reah, not really."

The woman looked at him quizzically.

"His name was Matthew," Arthur said. "He brought me back to New Canaan. After that, I don't know what happened." He made a shuddering sigh. "Now I have to get out of here."

"Yes, of course." They led him out and fed him lunch under a broad tent set up where grass had once grown. After lunch, he told them again what had happened, as much as he remembered, and they listened very closely. Then he slept.

When he awoke, night was upon them. They sat around a portable charcoal brazier, talking. He came out of the tent and looked up at the sky.

He pointed with a gnarled finger. "That's where it is, you know."

"What?"

"Earth. It goes around the pole star. So now all the Moslems know where Mecca is, and all the Christians and Jews know where Jerusalem is, and they can all point up there."

The people nodded and made their notes.

"Now if you don't mind, I'd like to go home," Arthur said. "I'm all done with this. Was all done a long time ago."

"Certainly."

And they took him home again.